# Natural

G000151273

# Exorcist

## Hadena James

Dedicated to everyone who sorta kinda hates their jobs.

# More By Hadena James

## Dreams & Reality Novels

Tortured Dreams
Elysium Dreams
Mercurial Dreams
Explosive Dreams
Cannibal Dreams
Butchered Dreams
Summoned Dreams
Battered Dreams
Belladonna Dreams
Mutilated Dreams
Fortified Dreams
Flawless Dreams
Demonic Dreams
Ritual Dreams

## The Brenna Strachan Series

Dark Cotillion
Dark Illumination
Dark Resurrections
Dark Legacies

## The Dysfunctional Chronicles

The Dysfunctional Affair
The Dysfunctional Valentine
The Dysfunctional Honeymoon
The Dysfunctional Proposal
The Dysfunctional Holiday
The Dysfunctional Wedding

## Nephilim Narratives

Natural Born Exorcist

## Short Story Collection

Tales to Read Before the End of the World

# Terrorific Tales

# Chapter 1

"Miss Burns?" A uniformed officer asked me. I didn't meet his eyes. I was busy watching someone destroy the food court of the shopping center we were all standing in. Or rather, it used to be someone, was my thought as he picked up a table that was bolted to the floor and hurled it and the chunk of concrete at its base into an Arby's. It took out the cash register and slammed into the shake machine before clattering noisily to the floor.

The police were ready to shoot him, not that it was going to do much good. He was already missing part of the flesh from his chest. I'd been told he'd died in a car accident five days earlier and that part of his face had been peeled off by a steel I-beam when he ran his SUV into the butt of a flatbed tractor trailer.

Zombies were strong and fierce and didn't feel physical pain. I'd dealt with them before, However, zombies are still people. Their soul is reintroduced to their dead body using magic and, after a short orientation period, they tend to be rather gentle. Unfortunately, this guy wasn't a traditional zombie. The spirit that inhabited him wasn't his, it wasn't even human.

1

Which meant the police were facing a twofold problem at this exact moment, the demon that had been pulled through the gateway and put into this poor guy's dead body by a black magic practitioner.

I was supposed to weaken the demon enough that it could be exorcized and sent back through the gateway. The local police had their own exorcist, a lovely woman who was a witch and had some psychic power.

Demons gain power from fear. The more chaos they create, the stronger they get. I was of angelic stock and my very presence was calming and gave everyone a warm fuzzy feeling. This feeling created by my very presence was interfering the demon's ability to create fear and chaos amongst those in the food court with us. Without fear feeding the demon, he'd eventually run out of steam and the demonic zombie would slump to the ground, unable to throw any more tables or chase after anyone.

Another reason for my continued presence was back-up, if she failed to send the demon back to the Stygian, I would do it. I often get asked why I don't just do it in the first place since I am generally stronger than then a witch when it came to the demonic and exorcisms, but I didn't really have an answer. I guessed it had something to do with the police department paying the witch large sums of money to deal with things like this.

Contrary to popular opinion the Stygian isn't Hell, it is a magical construct that like demons uses fear to power it. The more people who fear demons, demonic monsters, and the Stygian, the more capable it is of holding itself together. When it was explained to me when I was a child by my father, I was told it was the realm of nightmares. As an adult, I still thought of it that way. When one of my nieces a few years ago was suffering from night terrors, a common issue for children, even those with angle blood,

2

my father told her it was because the Stygian needed more energy. This seemed to help her, she became less afraid of the nightmares and they stopped just as suddenly as they had started. It hadn't helped me or my sister, we'd both had nightmares for about a month after hearing him tell her that. The power of suggestion I guessed.

As long as I didn't do the exorcism myself, they wouldn't have to pay us both exorbitant sums of money. In my case, I worked for the federal government, I would only see a small portion of the fee, with the majority going to them. Most police departments employed a witch or three, or at least had one as a consultant they could call as need be.

Which is why I worked for the federal government instead of a local law enforcement unit, I wasn't a witch and there was rarely a need for a nephilim to be present at a police station.

Watching the demonic zombie throw another table into yet a different food vendor, I understood why my sister worked in customer service. Even with me here, the happy happy joy joy feelings weren't strong enough and the demonic zombie wasn't weakening. I touched the officer closest to me and watched a relaxed look pass over his face. Slowly, I went down the line touching all of them.

It was incredibly difficult to stay afraid after literally being touched by an angel. Or half angel in my case. Feeling his power start to slip, the demonic zombie rushed towards us. Gunshots began to ring out. The zombie's head jerked to and fro as the bullets hit. Usually, shooting a zombie in the head releases the spirit trapped inside the body. But I had never met a zombie animated by a demon.

This zombie did not go down, regardless of it, missing a lot of his head. The body was still up and moving around. He was still trying to initiate fear in the police that encircled him. If he could get enough power, he could heal the dead body and make it serviceable to him again.

I had been in the mall when this all started, which is how I ended up being here to offer my help and services. I was shopping for a dress to wear to my sister and her husband's vow renewal ceremony, which was a ridiculous farce, in my opinion, that I didn't want to attend, but our mom and dad would not be happy with me if I missed it.

The older cops all stood their ground against the angry, demonic zombie. A few of the younger cops, though, their hands were starting to shake again. I considered calling my father and having him come down and help me keep everyone calm. He would have done it in a heartbeat, but afterwards, he'd probably lecture me about practicing with my power more and lecturing me on how if I had just tried, I could have done it without him. He was big on being independent and part of that was practicing my gifts, which I didn't do. Police officers were usually steady as a rock and able to bite back their fears easily with me around.

So, I didn't call him, instead, I walked back over to the officer I saw whose hands were still shaking a little. I put my hand on his shoulder and leaned in to whisper to him. I reassured him that this was probably the worst magic he'd ever see and that if he could control his fear today, in this very moment, he would have a long and successful career.

His hands stopped shaking and the witch began to do her thing. A spell left her lips and I felt magic begin to gather. The zombie fell into a kneeling position, the demon's magic not strong enough to continue to keep the dead muscles taut. The magic got stronger and I could see the wisps of it building in the witch's energy. When she let it go, it swirled around the zombie, entered it, trying to separate the body from the spirit that inhabited it. There was a struggle that I doubted most of the cops could see, her magic flaring here and there as it clashed with the demon's.

Then the zombie stood back up and the energy around it swelled to three times what it had been. Shit. I suddenly realized that she had never gone up against a demon and she had just lost, probably due to her fear and a mistake that I hadn't realized she had made.

"Get the demon's name!" I shouted to her. The brand on my arm was brightly lit, shining bright enough that it could be seen even through the sleeve of the shirt I had on, I had earned it when I passed the exorcist certification and it allowed me another source of magic. Somehow, I had missed that she hadn't gotten his name, probably because I had spent thirty minutes trying to get everyone calm enough that the demon could be exorcized by a simple spell.

Demons were maddeningly strong, sometimes even powerful witches couldn't exorcize them. It was worse if there was a source of fear nearby, because that fear was constantly refueling the magic, for every bit of magic it expended there was always more to replace it when terrified beings were near.

Instead of asking the demon for its name, she dropped to one knee and drew a piece of chalk from her pocket. A few heart beats later, she had a circle drawn around her, a circle she imagined the demon couldn't cross, because most magic couldn't. I didn't tell her any different.

She faced the demon and demanded his name, her voice small and squeaky. That's when I realized that she was too afraid to perform the magic needed to exorcize this demon. However, we needed more exorcists in the world and I didn't want to undermine her confidence. I debated with myself how long it would take for her to compose herself enough to do the deed and if was I willing to stand there and wait.

I didn't have much patience, not really. And dealing with demons made me cranky. I didn't tell people that the brand hurt when it was emitting light, it burned like hell fire, probably because that's what had made it. The archangel Uriel had given it to me after I had passed his course in exorcizing the demonic. While I technically worked for the government, as one of only twenty certified exorcists in the world, I was also allowed to freelance.

Everyone that worked with a police department was supposed to take courses with Uriel. Most would not become certified exorcists, but he taught witches, vampires, werewolves, mortals, and even nephilim how to deal with the demonic, even if they weren't certified exorcists by the end of it.

"Use a forceful voice and demand his name," I whispered to her. She tried again and was only slightly less squeaky than she had been. "He can't come near you as long as I am here." This wasn't exactly true. He could, but he wouldn't. Demons didn't like being forced to feel happy. Uriel believed it hurt them. Her voice was barely louder than a whisper as she demanded his name. He laughed at her. I shrugged.

"Watch me," I told her. "Demon, I command you to tell me your name!" I shouted at the thing animating the zombie.

"Go to hell, angel, you have no command over me."

"Demon, if you do not volunteer your name, I will take it by force," I told him. All demons had their names imprinted on them. If I walked over and touched him, he wouldn't have to say a word, and I'd still know his name.

"Dantalian," he croaked as I took a step towards him, Dantalian was a pain in the ass. It seemed like very other exorcism I dealt with anymore involved him. I looked at the witch, she was trying to gather her magic back together. When this was over, I was going to give her Uriel's card and remind her to take his courses in demonology. There were ways witches could force the name from demons too, I just didn't know how they did it because I wasn't a witch.

As the witch began her exorcism spell again, my cell phone rang. It was my boss. I sent it to voicemail with a text that read "dealing with demon, let me call you back." It was one of the standard responses I had programed into the phone since it seemed everyone on the planet felt the need to call when I was dealing with demons. Or, perhaps, I dealt with demons too often. I wasn't sure which.

A swirling red, oblong doorway appeared in front of the demonic zombie. The body it was possessing shuddered and then fell completely, the energy that moved around it disappearing. With a small popping noise, the demon was gone, returned to the Stygian.

Several of the cops thanked me as they started to take pictures of the damage. I turned to the witch. She was cute, but young, probably not old enough to drink alcohol legally in a bar yet.

I dug out Uriel's card and handed it to her. She flipped it over in her hands and stared at it. It had Uriel's cell number as well as the number of his school and the address of it.

"You need demon training," I told her. "Uriel has classes specifically tailored for witches."

"This was my second one," she told me, looking defiant.

"How'd you manage to get rid of the first?" I asked, and the look disappeared. "With a little training, you will be able to better control your fear around them, learn to be forceful, and learn how to get their name even when they are being uncooperative."

"But I got the information on the witch who called it, I was able to find and read their magic."

"That's good, but you still need training," I reiterated. "Dantalian is a lesser demon, not particularly strong. If it had been a stronger demon or more than one, he'd still be throwing tables around the food court."

In my head, I added, "Or worse, because even Dantalian could have killed someone, and then his magic would have been even stronger leaving her little circle unable to do much except trap her and her magic inside.

I redialed my boss's phone number. He answered on the first ring, meaning his cell phone was in his hand.

"Aren't you supposed to be off this weekend?" He asked instead of saying hello.

"I was shopping when a zombie entered the food court and began tearing things up." I replied.

"Your text said you were dealing with a demon," he countered.

"I was. A zombie animated by a demon."

"You don't see that very often." Azrael said to me. "Can I call you in off your vacation?"

"Considering the reason for my vacation, yes, please." I said.

"Good, because I think I need the strongest exorcist I have to accompany a Fugitive Recovery Team in Chicago."

"Okay, why?" I asked.

"Do you remember checking out a murderer named Don Rabbling?" He said after a moment.

"Yeah, killed his entire family, claimed a demon made him do it. He was not possessed." I answered.

"Maybe not at that moment, but this morning he bent the bars on his cell in Joliet and escaped taking out a few steel doors along the way. I think it's safe to say he's possessed now."

"Are we thinking he made a deal with demons after he was incarcerated?" I asked, dreading the response.

"Maybe, or maybe he was making a deal when he murdered his family, but since demons don't work in our time frame, they were slow about possessing him."

"That is not awesome." I said dryly.

'No, it's not. I'll call Raphael and explain."

"Thanks," I said and hung up.

# Chapter 2

In a week, I'll be forty years old and I had very little to show for it. I worked for the government. I owned a small house outside the city that sat on an acre lot in a subdivision surrounded by woods that most of my neighbors hunted in.

My last boyfriend had been eaten by a giant bear, that had been five years ago. I didn't really date, because once I told people what my job was, they tended to stop talking to me. I was an exorcist. I know everyone just said, "but wait, you said you worked for the government," and I do, I work as an exorcist. Mostly I work with murderers, to see if they are possessed by demons, and if so, can the demons be exorcized. I'm not a witch, if I was, I'd make more money. I am a nephilim, half human, half angel. I have the ability to see demonic forces, black magic, and other not so great things. And I can talk to souls that have been touched by the demonic.

Normally, this means souls that have been murdered by someone possessed, but once in a while, when a demon takes possession of a body, the soul gets forced out, misplaced. I can see these displaced souls.

It is nearly impossible for me to hide that I am of angelic stock. I don't have wings, thankfully, but even the most miserable people have trouble continuing to feel miserable in my presence. I volunteer at a care facility for people with terminal illnesses. Most days I sit in the common area and play games with the residents, or we'll just sit and watch a movie together, after which I always eat dinner with them. I've been told that my weekly visits have increased the overall satisfaction of the residents and that the effects last for several days.

But like everything, even good stuff has side effects. A person can get addicted to angelic influence and crave being around me and my kind as if we were a happy drug.

Interestingly, almost every other nephilim I've ever met is unhappy. So, while we can make others happy, we can't seem to make ourselves happy. My sister works a window at a municipal court where people pay fines. And while this is usually a place full of cranky customers yelling about the unfairness of it all, the one my sister works at gets great reviews from the fine payers.

But you can't look at either of us and guess we are nephilim. We don't have wings. We don't glow. We both have hair so black it has a bluish tint to it. I add to the effect by having my stylist introduce purple into the black once every two or three months.

The only physical clue that either of us are nephilim are our eyes. Mine are an ice blue with a darker blue edge around the iris. My sister's eyes are such a pale blue they look white, with the same darker edging that marks us as not completely human.

It was a Wednesday. I had two hours to get to the airport, and I was running late. My flight wouldn't leave without me, though, because I was hitching a ride with a US Marshals Fugitive Recovery Unit. They were hunting a fugitive had claimed to be possessed by a demonic spirit that had been lying in wait in the house they bought. I had already talked to him once, and his story had matched the plot of the Amityville Horror movie almost exactly, except that James Brolin's character had escaped before he killed his family.

At that time, he had not been possessed by a demon, however, three days ago, he had managed to bend the bars of his cell, then knock down several three-inch reinforced steel doors and just walk out of the prison where he was being held. Meaning it was possible that he was possessed now.

My presence would weaken the demon's strength, making it easier for the US Marshals FRU to slap silver handcuffs on him and take him back to prison, where I would perform an exorcism. That was, if he was possessed.

Most nephilim were like my sister. They went into jobs that were customer service oriented. I had spent one summer working in a store as a teenager and decided I had to find a different career path. nephilim see energies. The more good a person does, the more silver their energy. The more bad they did, the greener it looked. There was no way I was going to look at the energies of a thousand or more people a day and keep my sanity. I didn't even like to go to the store to shop because of it.

Thankfully, I didn't have to. I could order nearly everything online. This included groceries, clothes, necessities, everything. And then the only person I had to see the energy of was the delivery person. For instance, the guy that worked the UPS route my house was on was a very good person. His energy was so silver it was almost blinding. My postman was pretty average, a mostly silver energy with a few tendrils of green.

This was the way most people looked to me, mostly silver with little bits of green. When a person was possessed by something demonic, their energy turned yellow, and I didn't see them as people, they looked like demons; hulking bodies, horns on their heads, long tails, big leathery wings, but at that point I wasn't seeing the person or even the person's soul, I was seeing the true face of the demon and every demon looked a little different.

A perk of this job is it allowed me to travel, today it was Chicago, but next week it might be Los Angeles. I enjoyed working with law enforcement, it made me feel like I was making the world a better place.

I got to the airport seventeen minutes late, which might as well have been seventeen hours. I hated to be late. I'd rather just not show up than be even a minute late, but that wasn't always an option. I parked in a small parking lot within the fenced area of the airport, grabbed my suitcase off the passenger's seat, and headed towards the only small jet on the tarmac. There were three guys milling around outside the plane next to a staircase. All of them were dressed in dark suits that didn't quite hide the bulge created by their shoulder holsters. I had never worked with this Fugitive Recovery Unit, but their energies announced they were mostly good people.

"Miss Burns?" One of the men asked as I got closer.

"Yes, but please, call me Soleil or Asha." I smiled and instantly got smiles back from all of them.

"Your name is Soleil Burns?" He asked.

"My parents think they are incredibly funny," I told him. My sister had been just as blessed by their sense of humor as me, her first name was Helia. Of course, our parents had been nice enough to use our mother's maiden name for us instead of just applying the name Angel like most parents of nephilim. Or turning the angel's name into the last name.

Most angels think because they make people feel good, they must also be funny. I did not live under this delusion. My presence made people happy, but that didn't mean I would make a good comedian. I probably wouldn't have gotten booed off the stage, but my audience would have been there for the shiny, happy feeling I created, not the jokes.

My father, Raphael, had thankfully not decided to do standup comedy either, instead he was a motivational speaker, even archangels needed jobs these days. He traveled the world convincing people to be happy, which they were when they were in the auditorium with him. I didn't know if they remained that way after he left for the next city. My father did have wings, big feathery numbers that stopped him from needing to buy plane tickets.

"I'm commander Duke Hemingway." The leader of this FR unit extended his hand to me, I set down the small suitcase and shook his hand.

"I understand you're a supernatural, so I'll just warn you before we enter the plane, one of our team members is also a supernatural, a vampire, is that going to be a problem?" He asked, his face serious, the smile gone.

"No," I told him. I had worked with vampires before. They were not anymore dead than I was, or rather, undead than I was. Vampirism was a virus that kept them from creating some enzymes, they craved blood and extra rare steaks for the proteins that they had trouble making themselves. However, modern science had created an infusion cocktail that they could get about once a month and, as long as they didn't decide to give veganism or vegetarianism a shot, they were fine.

14

However, people still clung to the belief that vampires and angels could not co-exist in the same room. No one quite knew where the belief had come from, but it wasn't true. While most of my neighbors were lycanthropes interspersed with a few elves and a few witches, my next-door neighbor and her family were vampires.

We entered the jet. There were four other people inside it one, a woman in her late twenties with her hair pulled up into a severe bun, smiled at me. Her irises were a lovely shade of pink with the telltale darker ring around the iris, indicating she was more than just human, probably half human and half vampire since the darker ring wasn't double layered. Beings who were entirely supernatural had double iris rings, a darker color next to the iris and then an even darker exterior ring. My father had light blue eyes, with a medium blue ring around them and then an even darker blue ring that reminded me of the night sky. Not black, but blue so dark it almost looked black

I took the seat next to the vampire. She introduced herself as US Marshal Tabitha Whitlock and we shook hands. She didn't tell me she was a vampire and I didn't tell her I was a nephilim. Humans seemed to think this information important, but supernaturals did not. Like people, supernaturals just wanted to exist, live their lives, be happy, and maybe produce a couple of kids.

Despite being the daughter of an angel, I hate flying. I had loved it as a child, but that was mostly because my father had done the flying and airplanes crashed more than angels. I hadn't ever been in a plane crash, but there was a first time for everything.

# Chapter 3

Just like a commercial flight, those on board clapped when we landed in Chicago without the need for first responders. A burly man with a tattoo of an angel on his forearm grabbed my small suitcase from out of an area near the back, where it had disappeared to while I had found a seat on the small air craft.

I thanked him and wondered where he had come from. He hadn't been on the flight, there had only been ten people on the plane and he hadn't been one of them. His eyes did not have the ringed iris associated with the supernatural, meaning he was a human that had just sort of appeared on the plane, which was impossible. Tabitha seemed to notice my confusion and she pointed to the rear of the plane while explaining softly there was a door back there in a cargo storage area.

Within a moment or two, a few more guys came into the area where we were sitting, all carrying bags. The bags looked exactly the same, but they were being handed to specific people who took the bags with a thanks. Tabitha further explained that the luggage was stored by seat numbers and that all of them had assigned seats, except me, because I wasn't normally with the group.

All that made me feel a little better. I no longer worried that they were using a spell to read our minds and connect us to our luggage. Although, a charm might have done it instead of needing a full-blown spell.

We exited the small plane. The hair on the back of my neck stood up. It felt like the air was electrified. I looked down at the asphalt beneath my feet. It wasn't storming, which meant the electric sensation was coming from magic, strong magic, and lots of it. But I didn't see any magic, it hung in the air, as if a spell had just been cast close to me, but my eyes told me it hadn't. The feeling didn't go away as I stepped away from the plane. I looked at Tabitha, but she wasn't releasing any magic. I tried not to visibly scratch my head or begin gathering power myself. I felt like I was anticipating a fight, but I didn't know who with, I could just feel their magic. Was it one of the FBI agents, I turned and looked and saw nothing to indicate that it was them. The feeling was ominous and oppressive. My eyes kept darting around, looking for the source of the magic, even though my brain told me it wasn't nearby.

After we had gotten about 100 feet away, the jet began to power up again. The whine of the engines hurt my ears a little. Like most nephilim, I had sensitive hearing and could hear more frequencies than the average human. The oppressive feeling didn't go away, but it was less distracting for a short time.

The whine of the engines made me speed up my steps a little, trying to put as much distance between me and the plane as possible before it began to taxi to a hangar or wherever it was going.

Ten people, counting myself, seemed large for a fugitive recovery team. Usually there were only four or five people in an FRU. More than five was overly complicated, they hadn't used more than five to take down Tremaline the Insane back a handful of years ago. Tremaline had been a vampire that had decided to cross into the Stygian Plane. Most people said he had a few screws loose before he went. He came back with a lot more power and as a demonic host, and not host to a lesser demon, but one of the big bad, scary ones, a Hell Prince. Tremaline had knocked down a skyscraper in Los Angeles before a fugitive recovery unit accompanied by the archangel Uriel finally managed to get him in custody.

Since Tremaline's crossing, it had become illegal to enter the Stygian. The gateways had been sealed off using magic. This didn't make it impossible to cross over, but it did make it much harder, and there were gatekeepers who watched over them to help ensure people weren't jumping back and forth.

Demons were like party crashers. They drew power from death, destruction, chaos, and fear. So, when they did make it onto our plane, they attempted to do as much damage as possible. This usually meant causing black outs or trying to collapse bridges and whatnot. We tried to keep them out, but it was impossible to completely remove them from our existence, because there was always someone that wanted something more and demons could give it to them, for a price.

I wasn't sure if demons were evil or just unlucky. Demons were the only thing to draw power from death and destruction, all other supernatural beings drew it from life and nature, making it so that we had a beneficial relationship with Earth and people, unlike demons.

Five members peeled off from our group and headed to a different part of the airport. Commander Hemingway smiled at me, it was the side effect of being around a nephilim and wasn't actually aimed at me.

"They weren't smiling, I guess the power of the nephilim doesn't work on FBI agents," one of the other guys in our remaining group smirked as he spoke. I hadn't been introduced to him, but I was sure I would be soon enough.

"We hired a nephilim nurse when my grandmother got cancer really bad, and even though she was coughing up blood, she was still happy, meaning I think this proves that to be an FBI agent requires a personality-ectomy."

One of the other guys said, "I'm Walter Kemp," to me.

"Soleil Burns," I answered.,

"Your parents named you sun burn?" He laughed lightly.

"Me and my sister both, she got stuck with the name Helia," I nodded and felt myself smile in return.

"Can I be nosy and ask if your dad stuck around? I mean I've heard stories about nephilim who never meet their fathers, they just get stuck with his name."

"It does happen, usually a trait of the lesser choir of angels. My father is still in the picture." I told them all. Even Tabitha the vampire was listening intently. Not that this surprised me, there were hundreds of angels on the planet, but sterility was common among them, which meant most people, supernatural and mortal alike, could go a lifetime without ever meeting an angel or a nephilim.

"I only kind of remember the choirs from school," Walter told me, "it has something to do with power, right?"

"Yes, the higher the choir, the more powerful, and the longer the life. Not all angels are immortal. Archangels have the most power and even after thousands of years, most of the original ten are all still alive.

"What's your father?" Walter asked.

"If he becomes bothersome, just kick him," Tabitha told me, but I could tell even she was curious.

"My father is the archangel Raphael." I admitted.

"Wow, what was that like when you started dating?" Tabitha asked.

"Not all that unusual, except that my dad can read minds. Helia and I both would tell our dates to memorize stanzas of poems and recite them over and over in their heads when they met our father. Luckily, our mother is a good influence on our dad and reminds me that his mind isn't always as pure as freshly fallen snow."

"Did it work?" Walter asked.

"Not always, and by the time Helia went off to college he had gotten wise to it. He said it was weird that Helia and I only dated boys that constantly thought about poetry."

"Can you read minds?" Walter asked me.

"I can't, my powers lie more in the vanquishing of demons arena," I shrugged.

"What do you mean?" Walter continued to ask questions.

"Not all nephilim, not even all angels, can exorcize a demonic influence. The demonic all get uncomfortable around angels and nephilim, but not every angel can force their temporal spirit out of a host and back through the gateway to The Stygian. Which is great, because it turns out I suck at customer service. I seem to be able to make people feel good about being angry with me, but I can't make them feel good enough to keep them from shouting."

"Nephilim saturate the customer service departments of the world?" Walter raised an eyebrow.

"Many of them do, something to think about next time a debt collector calls you and you actually feel good about paying the bill." I offered. "My sister works the pay window in traffic fines, they have customers who admit they intentionally get parking tickets, so they can come in and feel good about paying them."

"Are you and your sister close?" Tabitha asked.

"We were as children, but not so much anymore." I told her.

"Why not?" She asked. "I have five sisters and we are all really close."

"Because she has a husband and kids, and I don't." I did not tell them that last time my sister and I talked she had screamed at me that I just didn't understand what it was like because I was single and selfish. I was willing to discuss a lot of things at a first meeting, but the dysfunction in my family, not so much.

Besides, telling them that my sister's husband was cheating on her with a woman from his office and she refused to divorce him because our father is an angel, would have been a conversation killer. Or that she had found out her husband was cheating two years ago, when he started acting weird at family Christmas and my dad poked around in his mind and found out and told my sister in front of me, because while our dad had good intentions with the announcement, he isn't always good at predicting how we will handle information. The announcement had caused an argument which ended when the Christmas tree caught fire and we had to rescue my nieces and flee the burning house.

Good times at the Burns' house.

"Do you do a lot of exorcisms?" Walter asked, and I was thankful for the subject change.

"Oddly, it depends on the weather. Really cold winters usually cause an increase in possession cases because when people are cooped up inside they fiddle with magical charms and spells without realizing it can have consequences." I paused for a moment. "And that's not just a human trait either, I find exorcisms increase for supernatural as well as humans during cold winters. The more time people must spend inside, the more exorcisms are required afterwards. For instance, when that big hurricane hit North Carolina last year and caused massive flooding, there was an uptick in demonic possessions."

"Then shouldn't you live in Alaska?" Walter asked.

"Alaskans seem better suited for being indoors for long periods of time with just each other or themselves for company. I have only been called there once."

"Maybe they just aren't finding the bodies," one of the other guys suggested.

"My job isn't just about murders, I can be called in by local law enforcement any time they think someone is demonically possessed. Before coming here, my last job was a little boy they thought was being physically abused by his father. Turned out, the boy was possessed and the bruises and cuts were inflicted by the demon, not the boy's father."

"Why'd they decide physical abuse was demonic possession?" Walter asked.

"Without getting into details, the father was arrested and held in jail, but the mother called to tell them that the boy had new bruises and cuts. The police went to investigate and as they were talking to him, his cheek split open. They swore he was sitting at the table eating a sandwich when it happened and no one touched him, so they called me."

"Can you tell us how he became possessed?" Walter asked.

"A classmate hexed him into being possessed because the boy stopped giving him his lunch money every day."

"What happened to the kid that put the hex on?" Tabitha asked, concern in her eyes.

"He was sent to the Periculo School. Where they will hopefully teach him to use his talents responsibly and not bully others." I answered.

"I have a son at Periculo," Walter said.

"Your wife must be the supernatural," I suggested noting that Walter was entirely human.

"She's fae." Walter told me.

"Are you guys local for Periculo?" I asked. It was a good thing I was nephilim and not a cat since I was naturally curious. Periculo was located outside St. Louis, Missouri. I had only been there a few times, mostly because the boys tended to get bored at night. However, Periculo had housing nearby that could be rented out by parents if they weren't local to the area. Some parents did, and it made the situation more tolerable for all involved. Periculo was like military school for supernaturals. It taught them discipline, how to use their magic, and kept them up to date on standard curriculum for all students. Most went for a year, sometimes two, and then returned to their regular schools. A few choose to stay beyond their sentence and the school had a great student success rate for both male and female supernatural troublemakers.

"Yeah," Walter shrugged, the smile still on his face, even though I could tell it bothered him to talk about it.

"You don't have to tell me anything," I told him, hoping he didn't feel obligated.

"Hell, I asked you a bunch of questions, seems only fair to share a little about myself and my family." Walter answered. "My son decided to spike the mashed potatoes in the school cafeteria with a love potion. The school had to be closed for the day because everyone that ate the mashed potatoes got so involved in making out with the person next to them that even a fire hose couldn't separate them."

"It could have been much worse," I tried to keep from smiling. It really wasn't funny, but at the same time.

"That's what I said," Walter smirked. "Which earned me a punch in the shoulder from my wife and our son having to go to court. We suggested Periculo in lieu of kiddie jail."

"Probably not a bad choice." Commander Hemingway stopped walking, so I did as well. We were in a parking lot full of people. Almost all of them wore suits and most had badges hanging from somewhere on their bodies.

# Chapter 4

We stood in the parking lot for nearly thirty minutes before a young girl with green skin and pointy ears came rushing up to us with keys in her hand. She smiled and apologized at least a dozen times, but the more apologies she uttered while standing near me, the less sincere they sounded. There was a good chance she really was sorry, but it was just hard to beat yourself up when you felt wonderful. The feeling that powerful magic was afoot hadn't diminished, I had just adjusted to its constant hum in my brain and was working to shut it out.

Commander Hemingway unlocked the doors to the SUV with government license plates and we all climbed in. After a moment of pushing and shoving, Hemingway looked into the back seat and just stared. Walter was practically sitting in my lap and Tabitha was smelling my hair from her spot in the third row behind me. The only other woman in the group, one I hadn't even been introduced to yet, was sitting on the other side of me, her head on my shoulder.

"Is it always like this?" He asked me.

"It can be at first," I admitted. "By tonight, the novelty of it will wear off some, and there will just be an overwhelming feeling of happiness and contentment within the group. But the first six to twelve hours of being around a nephilim, seems to be when the feeling is most annoying to others."

"And this is why people get addicted to you guys?"

"Yes, most people just feel good when they are around me after the first half dozen hours or so, some always feel this way, and some feel it even more intensely, it feels similar to a natural high. Those are the ones that get addicted."

"You should sit up front," Commander Hemingway said to me. "And I think we will get some lunch and check in with the Chicago police department before we go after our fugitive."

"Probably a good plan." I pushed out from between the two US Marshals, dragging my hair away from Tabitha as I did so, and moved into the passenger's seat of the SUV. Maybe after everyone had eaten and been around me for a little bit, they'd be able to focus on their jobs better.

"This happens to you a lot?" He asked as he pulled the car out of the parking spot.

"Not this exactly, most people just smile a lot when I'm around. However, within law enforcement, it isn't uncommon. It's the stress of the job. The more stressed out a person feels, the better they feel around me, which can lead to some very strange behavior."

"So, even being happily married doesn't combat the feeling?" He asked me.

"Not really, because even a happy marriage has stress. Look at Walter. I get the impression he is just as in love with his wife today as he was the day he asked her to marry him, if not more so. But his son acted out, and that is always stressful to parents and leaks into the portion of their lives that are husband and wife. You can let go of your concerns that being happy in my presence is a sign that your marriage is in trouble."

"My marriage was in trouble before we even went to get the license, we've been divorced five years now."

"I'm sorry to hear that," I told him.

"I'm not. I regret marrying her, I don't regret it ending."

"That sounds a bit cynical and bitter," I commented.

"Maybe it is." He answered as the GPS told him to take a left in a quarter mile.

"Where are we headed?" I asked.

"We're in Chicago, so we are going for Chicago Deep Dish pizza at the best deep-dish place in town."

"And you know the best deep-dish place in Chicago but still need GPS to get there?"

"I grew up here. After graduating college, I joined the army. I never had a reason to call Chicago home again. My dad passed away while I was serving overseas, my mom moved to New Jersey to be closer to my sister and her family, so when I was discharged, I moved to New Jersey."

"Now you run a marshal team out of St. Louis?" I asked.

"Kansas City, actually," he corrected me. "But you were in St. Louis and Walter and his wife moved closer when Fred got sentenced to Periculo, so we stopped there to pick you both up on the way to Chicago."

"Are you sure the pizza place is still there?" I asked as he made another left.

"Yeah, my cousin met her husband there, his family owns the place."

"That was fortuitous," I smiled weakly.

"Nah, she was a waitress there while in high school. His grandfather owned the place and he worked there when he was home from college."

"From waitress to store owner, not bad," I said and then grimaced. I had meant for it to be funny, but even to me, it sounded snarky. I started to apologize, but Commander Hemingway cut me off with a wave of his hand. I kept my mouth shut for the rest of the ride to the pizza place. I wasn't sure if Chicago pizza restaurants could be called pizzerias as east coast Italians could be persnickety about these sorts of things and I was sure a Chicago deep dish was tantamount to blasphemy in certain circles.

To say the restaurant was crowded, was akin to saying the ocean had water in it. The collective energies lit the place more brilliantly than any electric lights could have. There was a line that stretched out the door, however, once we got in line, everyone began shuffling their feet, the sound of conversation died down to a more mellow murmur and smiles slowly spread across the faces of those who waited. By the time we left, everyone in the restaurant would be having a great day, except me.

The abundance of people in line was maddening and highlighted why I didn't want to work in customer service, no one should be forced to see that many auras all lined up in front of them. It felt like an endless tide of the good, the bad, and the worst. I always wanted to hit those that had mostly green energy and tell them to figure it out.

Because, doing good didn't require much effort; opening the door for someone, letting someone cut in line at the grocery store because you have an entire cart packed with stuff and they only have six items in their tiny basket, dropping a dollar into the cup of a homeless person without passing judgment upon them as you did it.

These little, good things nullified the not so great things we all did, like swearing at the driver in front of you because they aren't going as fast as you'd like, or complaining about your food because you were cranky and your bacon didn't seem crispy enough.

The little things slowly added up, keeping energy silver or turning it completely green. And it was constantly changing. Even as I watched, someone a few people in front of me had a streak of green suddenly shoot out from them, swirl through the silver, and leave something that looked like a tear in the silver energy.

Then there were people like the guy nearly at the door. His energy was mostly green, a sickly green, that let nearly no silver quiver through it. If my dad was here, he would have been able to give someone an inventory of every bad thing the man had done to turn his energy into a throbbing whirlpool of negativity. Perhaps he had killed someone. Perhaps he'd been in a fist fight the night before. I couldn't tell why he wasn't silver, so I said nothing. I stood and watched and hoped our table wasn't close to his.

Nearly an hour later, we were seated, and the entire atmosphere of the restaurant was changing. Our waitress was a cute, bubbly girl that looked like she was still in high school. After taking our drink orders, she came back to our table more and more frequently, her bubbly personality spilling over into pure joy.

"To create the happiness, do you have to do anything?" Samuel Majors asked me, as he sipped an iced tea.

"No." I answered.

"Can it influence bad people to do good things?" Tabitha asked me.

"I don't think so. I've never thought about it before, so I haven't watched for it."

"So, that angry guy in the corner with the girlfriend nearly half his age, isn't going to leave an extra-large tip just because you're here?"

"Probably not," I shrugged, realizing for the first time that perhaps vampires could see energies too, because she was talking about the same guy I had noticed while waiting in line. Their pie had already arrived, and the girlfriend had a single slice on her plate and was slowly picking at it with a fork.

We ordered three large pizzas, one vegetarian, two with lots of meat. I didn't know if the vegetarian was because someone at the table really liked veggies or if it was because of me, lots of people just assumed angels and nephilim were vegetarians. I was definitely a carnivore, though. I liked veggies and I would probably grab a slice of the vegetarian, but I would couple it with a slice of the pepperoni and sausage and a slice of a max topping, which had everything from hot peppers to bacon on it.

"This guy's file said you did the initial possession assessment and declared him not possessed," Commander Hemingway said after a moment.

"He wasn't," I said. "It's possible that he killed his family as an offering, but demons rarely want sacrifices. Killing people is scary, sure, but it doesn't last. Whereas, living people are a veritable buffet of fear," I frowned and aside from Mr. Jerkoff, was probably the one on doing so. "He wasn't exactly a shining beacon of good deeds when I evaluated him, his energy was sick and dark, and I felt it went beyond just that single act of murder. I felt like he had been working up to it for a long time. Unfortunately, I can't read minds or intent or deeds just based on energies. Sometimes when someone is very corrupt, I can feel that it is not a temporary bad deed, but that isn't always the case."

"Like the guy with his girlfriend," Tabitha said.

"Exactly, for all I know, he might have woken up cranky and slowly as the day has worn on, he's been a jerk as a result and it's changed his energy field from what I normally see to something darker."

"Meh," Tabitha said. "I don't think he's just having a bad day, for me to see dark energy it has to be cumulative and I can see his, so he's probably a jerk most of the time."

The pizza arrived. The smell was heavenly. I kept expecting my parents to call me and yell at me for being in Chicago and threatening to come get me for tomorrow's vow renewal ceremony. I had zero desire to celebrate my sister's cheating husband's recommitment to her. I didn't believe he'd changed, even with my father reading it in his mind, and six months from now he'd probably have yet another girlfriend. I didn't buy the whole once a cheat always a cheat theory, I believed people could change. I just didn't see my brother-in-law being one of them.

"May I ask where the last name Burns came from?" Walter asked after everyone had gotten pizza. I was surprised he grabbed multiple slices of the vegetarian, but I didn't say anything about it.

"My mother's maiden name," I told him. "Since my father doesn't have a last name, she kept her own when they were married."

"How long have your parents been together?" Walter asked.

"Five hundred years," I replied.

"I thought she was mortal," Tabitha answered.

"She is, she is ageless because of my father."

"But there is only you and your sister?" Walter asked.

"They've had a few other kids, but nephilim aren't immortal. We might not age, but we can be killed." I paused and thought for a moment. "My sister is only two years older than me, but we would have a brother, if he hadn't died nearly five hundred years ago. After he was

31

killed, my parents decided not to have more children until very recently."

"So how old are you?" Walter asked.

"Forty," I answered. "Unlike most nephilim, my parents have kept track of birthdays and ages."

"You look maybe 25," Tabitha said.

"I know and in forty more years, I'll still look this age."

"So, I have heard of mortals gaining immortality from supernaturals, but I don't quite understand how it works for angels."

"True love," I responded. "Vampires share their vampirism, same with lycans, but fae, angels, and the like can keep a mortal from dying by falling in love with them. The trick is it has to be true love. In the five hundred years or so that my parents have been together, they have had some impressive fights, some of them I have seen, and they always say things like this is nothing, you should have seen the one we had in 1759 or whatever, but they always stay together. Once, they separated when I was a kid, but after a few weeks of roses being delivered to my mom every day at work, and then a mariachi band showing up at our house to tell my mom that she was the only woman my dad would ever love, they got back together."

"That is true love." Tabitha said.

"Yeah, and as long as she loves dad and dad loves her, she doesn't age. My mom looks like she's in her 30s but she was born in the 1500s, go figure, people ask if she's my sister when she and I go out together. Sometimes I worry about it, but then I realize my parents are more affectionate than most high schoolers with their first love and realize that they will probably be together in five hundred more years."

"I stopped aging a few years ago," Walter offered. "However, it wasn't instantaneous, even though I think it was love at first sight with my wife."

"Love may happen at first sight, but true love requires familiarity with each other," I nodded.

"I also heal faster now than I ever have." Walter said.

"A benefit of immortality," I took a huge bite of pizza, enjoying the sauce on top and the cheese and toppings inside, under it. I was going to have to make note of this place so I could come back next time I was in Chicago.

"Huh, I just realized that means your mom is older than indoor plumbing," Walter chuckled.

I nodded in agreement, my mouth too full to offer a verbal reply. We sat and ate and talked and they asked me more and more questions. When we finished, I felt like I had eaten enough food for a month. It was a miracle my clothes still fit. Thankfully, I have a super-fast metabolism, so by tonight, I'd have used up most of the calories provided by the pizza. We stood and I felt the need to rectify a situation. I walked over to the jerk and his girlfriend. She was still nibbling on that first slice of pizza she'd taken.

"Are you actually happy with him?" I asked her, putting my hand on hers. "I've been watching, I ate five slices of pizza while you picked at just that one. You are a beautiful young lady and a good person, I see the energy that surrounds you. Leave him, he's a jerk. He probably berates you for being fat, which is why you are starving yourself, and you and I both know he's going to complain about something involved with this meal to justify him not tipping the server." I paused, not removing my hand from hers. "You can tell a lot about a person by how they treat servers and I think you know he's a jerk and just aren't sure what to do about it. If you want to leave him and are just afraid, I can help you," I dug around in my wallet and pulled out a card. It was for the Nephilim Network, a group of homes for abused and battered women run by nephilim with some big, bad trolls on staff to discourage jerks from hanging around the place. They had safe houses in basically every major city.

"Thank you," she stammered. The guy stood up, I put my hand on his chest and pushed a small amount of energy into him, forcing him to sit back down.

"The biggest thanks you could give me is to walk out of here with me and my US Marshal friends," I told her. Her eyes flicked to Tabitha, Samuel, Hemingway, and Walter. "Okay." She said after a moment and stood up from the chair. She lifted her chin for the first time since I had seen her. "Why are you doing this?" She asked me.

"Because helping others makes me feel good," I told her. "Besides, life is too short to be treated like a broken-down sofa."

"I don't have anywhere to go, or anything." She gave a small sob as we exited the place. The jerk didn't follow, he was probably still coping with the small amount of magic I had sent into him. People describe it in different ways, some say it feels like being shocked, others like being punched, and one person once told me it was like getting really bad heartburn. I hoped it had felt like all three to him.

"But I have somewhere you can go," I said as Hemingway hailed a taxi. I handed her the card for the Nephilim Network and all the cash I had on me, because people just feel better when they have at least a little money on them that's theirs.

"No, I can't," she stammered.

34

"Meh, it's just money," I told her. "Take this and go start a new life and be happy." I forced the wad of bills into her hands. It was maybe a hundred bucks. I really liked the digital age and debit cards, I only carried cash because my father was still a touch old school about it.

A taxi pulled up and Hemingway helped her into the car and off she went. I hadn't even asked her name, how rude of me.

"That was," Hemingway blinked at me. "I don't think I have ever seen someone do that. It's the kind of thing my mother would tell me that she read about on social media."

"Most people just need someone to take their hand and tell them it's okay to leave, when something like that exists," I told Hemingway while we all headed to the parking garage and got the SUV.

We arrived at a small police station in a section of town that looked like it needed to be seriously renovated. Across the street was a store that had lots of naughty things in the window display. Someone had tagged the building with a huge, blue penis. The words deliver us from evil were spray painted underneath it in red. The red paint had run, I wasn't sure if the runny paint had been deliberate, but it gave the words more emphasis. Chicago, like most big cities, had slums, and those slums were filled with poor people and people who were hiding from regular society, usually because they practiced more black magic than white.

Oddly, the only magic that was illegal was death magic; magic that either required a human sacrifice or magic that resulted in the death of someone. I wondered why the words were written on the wall. It was true that Chicago had seen a significant crime increase lately, but it seemed like normal crimes; shootings, muggings, it wasn't rampaging demons or even black magic practitioners casting death spells.

Besides, Chicago was big enough to have a division of magic, an investigative unit that dealt only with magical crimes. St. Louis didn't have one, but that wasn't because of its size, it was because Azrael and Uriel had lobbied to have the Bureau of Exorcism placed there. With their consultant witch and the Bureau of Exorcism in the city, they didn't see a need to have an entire investigative force for it. Politics played a huge role in what sort of investigative units a city had, not just size. In St. Louis, the mayor was convinced that supernaturals just didn't commit crimes. She was delusional, of course, but it didn't matter how much proof was given to her, she still refused to allow budgeting for more than a consultant witch.

As we walked into the police station two things happened simultaneously, I nearly passed out, and the Fugitive Recovery Commander, Hemingway, brushed his hand against mine. The brand on my arm burned with the light of a sun, making my entire arm ache. The brand burned brightly enough that my jacket was letting off little puffs of smoke. I took it off before it could catch fire. My shirt sleeve was trashed, the brand had already burned through it. I had never felt it this intensely before.

There were five people sitting on benches near the entrance, all of them had a sickly yellow energy around them that I associated with demonic possession. As did the cop at the counter in front of us. Was it possible the entire building was filled with demonically possessed beings? I would have said no until a few moments ago. Now, I wasn't so sure.

From beside me, there was a loud screeching noise that wasn't even remotely human. The sound had emanated from the throat of one of the women on the bench in the short, narrow hallway. She clamored to get on top of the bench, so there was no way I could touch her, even accidentally.

Angels aren't divine, just like demons weren't exactly from hell, but because an angel's natural power removed the power source of demons, demons feared anything angelic, even nephilim.

"This is not a place we should be," Tabitha said from behind me.

"I agree," I said without turning to look at her.

"What is it?" Commander Hemingway asked, starting to take a step forward. I caught him with my hand and pulled him backwards.

"They are all possessed," I whispered to him. He looked at my arm. "It's possible the entire building is filled with possessed."

We walked backwards out of the police station, slowly and carefully. I stood a few feet from the door considering what I had just seen and the graffiti across the road made more sense.

"What is this place?" I asked.

"The Division of Magical Investigation," Commander Hemingway said to me.

"That's a problem," I answered. "I don't think they know they are possessed. I bet they come to work every day and goof off because they can't figure out why they feel a need to be here, just that they do."

"What about the people inside?" He asked.

"The ones in the hall were possessed, as was the desk sergeant." I frowned.

"How could they all be possessed between yesterday and today?" He asked me.

"They couldn't be, this was gradual." I commented. "The thing about being possessed is that, most of the time, the demon is fine with letting the human soul stay inside and drive the host. As a result, the people act mostly normal, until something interests the demon, then the demon takes control of the body and does something to gain power. Because ultimately, the goal of any demonic possession is to destroy the soul, letting the demon gain a body to use since their true forms can't come through the gateways between the Stygian and here. Plus, by allowing the soul to stay in control most of the time, the demon learns the habits of the person, which makes it harder to figure out there is something wrong with the person once the soul is destroyed and the demon has taken over." I told all of them.

"So, demons are parasites," Walter said.

"Yes." I agreed, trying to figure out the best way to perform a mass exorcism. I wasn't even sure Uriel and Azrael would know what to do and they literally wrote the books on demons and exorcism.

"What should we do?" Commander Hemingway asked me.

"I think we start by asking the people that work in that shop how long the words have been on the wall." I hooked a thumb over my shoulder. Everyone turned to stare where I was pointing.

"Why?" Hemingway asked me.

"Because whoever wrote it knew," I said.

"Maybe the shop is the evil place, it is a sex store and the world is full of prudes," Hemingway answered.

"That was my thought when I first saw it too, but the only way the desk sergeant gets possessed without anyone in the Division of Magic sending up red flags is if they are all possessed. So, I'm guessing whoever wrote that was a supernatural and knew the cops here were possessed."

"I thought only angels and nephilim could see when people were possessed," Walter commented.

"Angels and nephilim are the only ones that can see demons, but all supernaturals can sense when a person is possessed." Tabitha told him.

We walked across the street and entered the sex shop. There were six or seven guys milling around, looking at merchandise. There was a guy and girl behind the counter, the girl was probably a lycanthrope, but I didn't know what kind, I could just feel her magic flare a little. She had lovely amber eyes with dark brown rings around them. The guy looked like he needed a shower with lots and lots of shampoo. For some reason, men who worked in sex shops always seemed smarmy, while the women appeared more even keeled.

I was a few steps behind Hemingway.

"Dudes, really? You're going to scare off my customers," he whined and then abruptly stopped. The customers that had looked rather furtive at our arrival went back to quietly shopping, smiles on their faces. "The angel can stay, but the rest of you have to go."

"Nephilim," the woman next to him said. "No wings."

"What is a nephilim doing in here?" He tried to frown at her and couldn't seem to remember how.

"The graffiti outside, when did it show up?" Hemingway snipped at him, sounding angry.

"It's been there for a long time, a few years," he said.

"Not the penis, the words," I corrected.

"Oh, that's been there for two months or so. I had someone remove it, and a few days later, it had been redone. The original was in black spray paint, which is how I know the cleaners didn't just fail in their removal."

"Have you noticed any changes in the police that come and go from there?" Hemingway asked.

"Yeah, they don't come and go," the guy said. "They have their own parking lot in the back. They used to constantly be leaving and coming back, now they almost never leave, and when they do, they don't use their sirens and lights."

"What about people, not cops, coming in?" I asked.

"They don't. People in this neighborhood used to just walk in to report crimes, usually a few a day, now they walk up to the door and then leave, without ever going in. I've heard people in the neighborhood whisper that they are all ghosts."

"Well, they aren't," Hemingway said. "Thank you." The last bit seemed to cause Hemingway pain, I smiled at him, but he frowned in response. Considering he had just brushed my hand a few minutes ago, I didn't know what the frown was about. He turned, so we all turned and followed him back outside.

"Why hasn't anyone noticed that have all been possessed for two months?" Hemingway asked me.

"Because people are sensitive to demonic influence just like supernaturals are. They may not see it, but they can feel it. I imagine most people walk up to the door and feel uneasy about going in." I said. "But today it was turned way down, like they didn't want anyone to notice it."

"They can do that?" Hemingway asked.

"Yes," I answered. I was positive that he had taken a class in demons since he was law enforcement, but he seemed to have forgotten most of it. I found it annoyed me.

"Do we go in and start exorcizing everyone?" Tabitha asked me.

40

"I'm not that good," I told her. "Now, we call the Bureau of Exorcism and I try to get more exorcists to help me, and then we ask the Chicago police department how they managed to lose an entire division to demons without raising the alarm." I tried not to stomp my feet as I walked back to the SUV. I was pulling out my cell phone and just expected that everyone would follow me as we had done with Hemingway a few moments earlier. I was a leader more than a follower.

# Chapter 5

Azrael answered on the first ring. I was positive the archangel had surgically attached his cell phone to his hand.

"Find him already?" He asked. "That's a new record even for you."

"No, I found a police department full of the possessed."

"Well, it's not uncommon for criminals to make deals with demons for power."

"Cops, Azrael, not criminals." I corrected.

"What?"

"The Division of Magic within the Chicago PD seems to be made up of the demonically possessed. The demons don't feel like they have been there for an exceptionally long time, but they didn't join the ranks today." I told him. "According to some graffiti, it's been going on for about two months."

"It would be hard to possess cops that worked in a division of magic, because they watch out for that stuff."

"Yep, that's why I called you. I admit, it kind of spooked me. I think I'm going to need more exorcists."

"How many of them are there?"

"I don't know, my brand caused my shirt sleeve to burn off, so I'm going with a lot."

"It shouldn't get that hot."

"It never has in the past," I told him. "It always burns a little and glows when I'm around the possessed, but today was something special, and not in a good way." I considered telling him about the feeling of oppressive magic and decided not to, simply because I wasn't sure I could describe it.

"I can probably send you six exorcists, but we need to leave some in the bullpen in case they are needed elsewhere."

"What if you left most of the exorcists in the bull pen and you and Uriel came here to help me?" Azrael had been in the office for a very long time, but he had been the one to show me the ropes two decades ago.

He'd shown me the law enforcement and investigative side, while Uriel taught me to do exorcisms and protect myself from demons. They were both very good at it. Better than any exorcist on staff. But part of that was because Azrael, Uriel, and myself were the only angels in the Bureau of Exorcism, the rest were witches with a few vampires and werewolves thrown in for good measure. Every supernatural had the skill and could exorcize a demon, if they wanted to learn, but angels were born with the skill, it just needed to be honed. Of course, the majority of nephilim, wanted nothing to do with demons, preferring to work regular jobs.

And the same was true of angels, which was unfortunate. But I could understand. This wasn't a job that brought lots of warm, fuzzy feelings.

"How many people work in the Division of Magic?" Azrael asked me after a moment.

43

"No idea," I answered. "We are getting ready to go to Chicago PD headquarters and ask about it, but Chicago is a big town, so there could be quite a few."

"Call me back when you get the number."

"Sure," I said, but Azrael had already hung up.

"Is your boss coming?" Hemingway asked.

"Maybe," I shrugged. "Azrael can be difficult at times and this appears to be one of those times." I considered calling Uriel directly and put my phone away instead. Uriel would give me a bunch of zen nonsense about how if I wanted to exorcize all of them, I could, I just needed to decide to do it. Uriel often spoke in ridiculous circles that made it unclear what he was actually saying. He might be very good at dealing with demons, but he wasn't as good at dealing with his students. And since I was going to have to call Azrael back anyway, I decided Azrael could tell Uriel I needed help.

The car was silent as Hemingway weaved his way through Chicago traffic heading towards Lake Shore Drive. After a few blocks, Hemingway turned and suddenly Lake Michigan was visible on the left side of the car. He hadn't turned on the GPS, but he was angry, which I understood. Demons were not supposed to be able to take over an entire police station full of supernaturals without anyone noticing. Then there was the very real possibility that they had noticed and just hadn't done anything about it, which was frightening.

It took us more than 20 minutes to get to our destination. It was a newer building, at least ten stories tall, with Chicago Police Department in large letters about half way up the building wall. It was a glass and steel monstrosity, but it sat across from a pretty park, with a picnic area near the road and some new growth forest at the back of it.

Even vampires drew magic from life and nothing was more alive than a forest. As a result, they were being planted in urban areas everywhere. The irony wasn't lost on me.

People were still breeding faster than supernaturals, even though vampirism and lycanthropy were caused by incurable viruses. It's because supernaturals tended to breed slowly. My sister had been married for 20 years and her oldest child was now 10. Also, immortality just meant supernaturals didn't die of old age, we could all be killed with the right research and effort.

Hemingway seemed immune to my happiness discharge. He was frowning and angry. While I believed the others in the group weren't exactly happy about the situation, none of them were frothing at the mouth with rage, they had to work to keep themselves from smiling. It made me wonder. I had never met anyone except another nephilim or an angel that wasn't automatically happy in my presence. Even my jerk brother-in-law, who had little nephilim children and a beautiful nephilim wife, was happier in my presence.

Hemingway flashed a badge at someone who was standing next to a metal detector, and then began to empty his pockets into a little grey tub. Everyone else did the same, I brought up the rear.

I didn't have near the stuff they did. I took off my amulet, a small necklace imbued with magic to help keep me from taking a bullet to the head, which would hurt a great deal, and cause me to lay in a hospital bed for several weeks while my brain tried to repair itself. The only other item I put in the tub was my wallet, a man's trifold wallet that could adequately carry everything I needed.

As my sister had added children to her life, her purse had slowly gotten much larger. I was sure it could hold a family meal from Taco Bell in it at this point, and it seemed every year both children spent in school, the bigger the bag grew. By the time my oldest niece graduated high school, my sister would need to carry a carpet bag, like Mary Poppins.

Like us, my sister's girls were only two years apart in age; however, unlike us, my sister had named the girls after fairy tale princesses. The oldest was Ariel, the youngest was Aurora. It beat Soleil and Helia, or worse, Asha and Spring, which were our childhood nicknames that neither of us could remember how we had gotten, although both of us had been inventive children with plenty of imagination, and our parents swore they only started calling us this after we started calling each other by the names.

"For someone who makes everyone else smile, you don't seem to smile much yourself," Tabitha pointed out as she got through the metal detector. She was beaming at the policemen working the metal detector. Both were smiling from ear to ear, as if they had just won the lottery.

"Like most nephilim, I am not particularly happy," I said.

"So, it affects everyone but you, and as a result, you aren't happy?" She said.

"Maybe," I shrugged and stepped through the metal detector.

"Later, Whitlock," Hemingway snapped at her. Which was good, because I had never quite figured out how to answer the why aren't you happy question. Someone I had known as a child, had suggested that nephilim were unhappy because we didn't feel we deserved happiness since we weren't pure angels and we weren't divine but were treated as such. I wasn't sure if I believed this or not, but it sounded as plausible as anything else I'd ever heard about why nephilim aren't a particularly happy

46

lot. I didn't feel like I was unhappy, I just didn't feel like I was happy.

I had been once, I had even been engaged to a nice young wizard who was exceptionally tall, because I liked tall men, and very nice, he had been incredibly sweet. Unfortunately, he had trained as an exorcist too, and in a rare case of Alaskans getting bored, he and I were sent to a very remote Alaskan village to check out the fact that they seemed to have a rather large population of demonically possessed after a brutal winter. Now, the village only had about 10 residents that stayed during the winter, so there were only 10 people possessed, they found them when the rest of the village returned in the spring and swelled the total population to 70.

Unfortunately, he was eaten by a starving polar bear. The possessed do not require food, and the bear had gotten stuck in the village supply store over the winter. It had hibernated and eaten everything inside the store, and given birth to two very pretty bear cubs, and then my fiancé Steve had gone into the village store to get heavier boots and been eaten. The store owner hadn't returned with the rest of the villagers, he had stayed behind in Anchorage for a few extra days, which saved any villagers from being eaten. No one was sure how the polar bear got in the store since animals avoid the possessed.

Hemingway was talking to one of the cops while another was on his walkie-talkie telling someone on the other end that a Fugitive Recovery Team with two supernaturals was in the lobby and very unhappy about something.

A few minutes later a detective came down. He was dressed in a dark grey suit that was nearly the same color as his hair, and he wore a bright purple tie with grey stripes through it. The overall ensemble was very fetching on him. As he got closer, I realized the dress shirt under the suit jacket was the palest shade of purple I had ever seen. He was one of those very good people whose energy was such a bright silver that it hurt the magical receptors that saw such energy. I didn't see it with my eyes exactly, so I couldn't say it hurt my eyes, but it hurt something in my brain that was similar to blinding light shining directly in my eyes.

"What can I do for you?" He asked Hemingway without introducing himself.

"We were just at the Division of Magic and the desk sergeant is possessed as were several people that were just sitting in the hallway and our exorcist says she felt like there were lots of possessed people in the building, so I'm wondering why no one here at headquarters noticed that the Division of Magic wasn't really doing their jobs?" Hemingway snipped at him.

"Well, they are overseen by Captain Wellesley, you'd need to talk to him." The man said, looking disturbed, despite my happy influence.

"Can you take me to see him?" Hemingway snarled.

"Sure, come this way," the man said, still not having introduced himself. I was wondering why he had come down if someone else was in charge.

"Why were you sent to get us, if you aren't the captain?" I decided to poke at it, because he would respond better to me interrogating him than Hemingway.

"Wellesley just returned to active duty yesterday, he still isn't at full strength." The man replied.

"What happened to him?" I asked.

"He came down with a nasty case of pneumonia, nearly killed him," the man replied. "Spent six weeks in the hospital."

"Then who has been running the Division of Magic while he's been sick?" I asked.

"Lieutenant James Albright," the man said. "But he's out today, his wife thinks he might have pneumonia now."

"Pneumonia in June?" I asked skeptically.

"I know, right? It's been going around the entire department." He answered. "We've had entire precincts come down with it, and several of us got sick in the Special Investigations Division a few weeks ago."

"How many is several and where did it start? Has the Cook County Health Department investigated?" I asked.

"They said thirty cases didn't warrant an epidemic and didn't send anyone. They just told us to start disinfecting everything."

"It's June." I repeated. Bacterial infections as well as viruses were more likely to hit during cold weather, just like possession and for many of the same reasons.

"That's why we called the Cook County Health Department, but they said it wasn't unheard of for pneumonia outbreaks to happen in June. Most of us went home and stayed home for a week or so, took antibiotics, and felt better after five or six days. It's bad enough that if the doctor pronounces us as having symptoms, we get sent home until we have finished an entire round of antibiotics, plus three days, to make sure it is fully gone before we can return. Wellesley wasn't the only one that ended up in the hospital because of it, his just lasted longer than anyone else's."

"Interesting," I whispered to myself, already considering calling Azrael to tell him about the pneumonia outbreak. Most people didn't know that possessed people were exceptionally good carriers for diseases, including

49

pneumonia. Since possessed people didn't show symptoms of being sick, they could have it for as long as they were possessed and pass it to everyone that came in contact with them and no one would be the wiser. "When did it start?" I asked.

"Late April, I guess." He shrugged. Late April and it was June, that was two months ago. Someone had infected the Division of Magic with pneumonia and managed to cause possession amongst them at roughly the same time and everyone that had come in contact with them since was sick.

I kept trying to think about how to possess an entire building full of cops with demons and all I could come up with was to open a portal and just leave it open. But portals were monitored and tricky to keep hidden, so how was it a portal if it hadn't been found.

For a demon to possess a person, normally the person must request it and make a deal with the demon. On rare occasions, a witch could curse someone into being possessed, which was a form of black magic, or they could open a portal and just let out a certain number of demons, but again, people tended to notice portals.

Captain Wellesley looked like he should still be in the hospital. His face was sallow, his eyes looked sunken with bags under them dark enough that I had to look twice to make sure he wasn't sporting two black eyes. His lips were pinched together in concentration and nearly bloodless. I couldn't identify any one thing that made me think he was still sick, but that was my first thought upon entering his office. I couldn't have guessed his age, even with a clue from someone.

# Chapter 6

I excused myself and went to call the Cook County Health Department. I was transferred twice before a woman came on the line and said she couldn't release pneumonia rates in the Chicago area.

I reiterated who I was and that I was calling because I was worried there was an infestation of demons in Chicago and that I wasn't asking for confidential patient information, all I wanted was a breakdown of the number of pneumonia cases currently in Chicago by area, including any that reported working as civil servants, like cops, EMTs, firemen, etc.

It took her another few minutes, but her tone was much more pleasant as she told me she'd need to look up the information. I asked her to expand it to other communicable diseases that didn't normally occur in Chicago such as measles, mumps, and the like, and influenza since it was rare for outbreaks of it to occur in June. I expected to be put on hold but could soon hear the clicking of computer keys and humming. As much as hold music sucked, it didn't normally include melodies that were hummed.

I heard the keystrokes stop and took a breath.

"Miss Burns, I have that information for you," she said pleasantly.

"Great, I'm ready," I told her.

"Do you want me to email or fax it to you instead, so you can see the numbers by geographic area?"

"You can do that?" I asked.

"Of course we can, what's your email." I spelled it for her slowly, Soleil was not a common word, let alone name, and the word exorcist wasn't the easiest to understand over the phone. "All done, thank you for calling, it really brightened up my day."

"Mine too. One last thing, how often does communicable disease information get reported to the health department?"

"The two biggest hospitals report once a week, the smaller ones every 10 days or so." She told me.

"When are they due to report again?"

"Any day now," she said.

"Great, I will call back tomorrow before you close."

"Miss Burns, would you like me to put out a health notice and get the information reported to us faster?"

"You can do that?" I asked.

"Yes, we can."

"That would be amazing," I told her.

"Great, here is my direct line. I will issue the notice now and we should have some information first thing in the morning. I get in at 9."

"Thank you so much," I said and hung up. I felt a little bad about it, but I also knew that in areas with a high number of possessions, communicable diseases rose as well, and if I could make someone feel good while helping me over the phone, then I felt duty bound to use my talents to help them help me, and when I'd hung up, nothing illegal had happened and everybody was happy, even me, and I was rarely happy.

I opened the email on my phone. She had attached six months of disease log files. The first couple of months were winter months and the number of pneumonia and flu cases were higher than what one might expect, but it was still basically normal for a hard, cold winter. I flipped over to May and instantly saw a spike in three geographic areas of flu, pneumonia, and surprisingly, or not surprisingly, chicken pox. I took the information into Wellesley's office. The man looked like warmed over death, and as I stood there not thinking about the communicable disease logs, I realized he wasn't giving off any energy. None.

Even trees gave off energy. I stared at Wellesley a little longer. Tabitha snapped her fingers lightly behind her back and judging by her dilated pupils she knew there was something very wrong with Wellesley too.

"Sir, do you feel okay?" I asked him, moving closer to the desk.

"I was just fine until you assholes busted into my office whining about a few cops that are over worked." He snarled at us with enough rage that a dry white foam flew from one of his lips. It landed on his desk, thankfully. I tugged lightly on Commander Hemingway's shirt and took a step backwards again, tugging just a little harder. Tabitha stepped backwards with me, and seeing her do it, made the other guys do it, and then Hemingway relented to my gentle tugs and finally took a step backwards as well.

"Sir, we are sorry, we will get out of your hair." I exited the office, continuing to pull Hemingway with me.

"What?!" The commander snapped once we were outside.

"Wellesley is dead," I told him.

"That's impossible," Hemingway glared at me.

"No, sir, he's dead," Tabitha backed me on it. "I tried to get your attention to tell you, but it's hard to convince a normal that the person talking to them is dead."

"Just because he looks bad doesn't mean he's dead." Hemingway protested without much feeling.

"Right?" I smiled at him. "He does look really bad, because he's freaking dead." People in the office turned and stared at me, a few had raised eyebrows. Others looked shocked.

"If he was dead, someone would have noticed." Hemingway looked around the cubicles stacked practically on top of each other.

"Yeah, because mortals are really excellent at being able to tell if someone is alive alive or alive because they are being manipulated via magic."

"Necromancy?" Hemingway asked.

"If he had been brought back to life by a witch via necromancy, he should at least have the witch's energy swirling around him, but he doesn't, so I don't think so." I shrugged. "I think he's being animated by a soul, just not a human soul or a demonic soul."

"What?!" Hemingway shouted and I wasn't sure if he was shouting at me or about the situation.

"Exactly," Tabitha's voice was low and fearful.

"Don't be cagey," he stepped in very close to me and he smelled like cinnamon and cloves. I held my breath so I wouldn't have to smell him. I had cinnamon and cloves in my wax warmer at home, it was one of my favorites.

"I'm not being cagey, I'm just not entirely sure the best way to explain it." I told him. "Nearly all supernaturals can raise the dead for a short time, some witches can work necromancy, which returns the dead soul to the body, and with the help of the witch's magic, the body and soul can walk around. But that leaves a mark, so to speak, some of the witch's magic gets trapped along with the body's soul to keep them tethered together. I could go into a cemetery right now and raise a recently deceased person, but it wouldn't do much. The soul is what gives it the power to move beyond its own grave. So, if I were to pluck a spirit that didn't belong to that person and shove it in the reanimated corpse, a few things are going to happen. Mostly the person isn't going to remember anything from its former life in the beginning. After a day or two, it will gain access to the memories of that person, but it still won't be that person, does that make sense?"

"Nope, doesn't make sense. If he's dead, but he's up and moving, doesn't that mean his soul is back?"

"Nope, it just means a soul is there, not necessarily his soul, and the incompatible soul goes a little mad."

"Why do it?" Hemingway asked.

"Why not?" I gave as the answer. "Yesterday, I watched as a witch attempted to exorcize a demon from a zombie. There isn't much of a reason to put a demon in a dead human body. They can't do anything with it and as the body rots, the demon loses its ability to recharge its power source until, poof, the body decays to the point that the demon can't stay, and no exorcist would be needed to send it back to the Stygian."

"What do you think is in Wellesley?" He asked.

"Beats me, not a demon, but I'm positive it isn't human."

"If it isn't a demon and it isn't a human, that doesn't leave many options."

"Sure, it does, dogs, cats, rats, hippos, alligators, and the list goes on and on." I told him.

"Animals don't have souls," he told me.

"Says who?" I countered.

"They aren't self-aware," Commander Hemingway told me.

"But they are, they feel things, even if they are primal and instinctual; hunger, pain, fear, tiredness, happiness, lust, all of those things I would say require some degree of self-awareness." I resisted the urge to do something childish like stick my thumb to my nose and wiggle my fingers at him.

"You are kind of stubborn and argumentative."

"Pot, meet kettle," I didn't smile, but it took effort. However, Hemingway didn't cover his smile quite as easily, and for the briefest moment, I saw it.

Nobody was even trying to hide the fact that they were staring at us and eavesdropping on our argument. I imagined most of them thought I was out of my mind, which was possible. I refused to rule anything out. Life was meant to be a journey of self-discovery according to my guruesque father.

Wellesley suddenly lurched out his office door. His steps were jerky and uneven, one foot dragging the floor as he attempted to move it, then he fell onto the floor and lay there for a moment, trying to right himself. He rolled from one side to the other.

"Maybe turtle?" I offered.

"Do something," Hemingway snapped at me.

"Like what?" I asked. "I can help him to his feet, probably, but anything else is beyond my capabilities, I exorcize demons not turtles."

"We need a witch," Tabitha said.

"Yes, we do. Unfortunately, I'm positive the ones that work for the police are currently possessed by demons."

"There must be a witch in the city that doesn't work for the police department, and therefore, isn't possessed," Walter said.

"There is, but we've had problems with witches in Chicago lately." Someone finally spoke up that worked with Wellesley.

Wellesley began to make a clicking sound deep in his throat. It was loud in the room, even with the whispers that surrounded our current situation.

"Is anyone related to a witch, no matter how low his or her power might be?" I asked.

"My wife is part witch, but she's never done necromancy," someone offered.

"She doesn't need to be a necromancer." I told him. "Can you get her here?"

"Maybe, what are you going to do?" He asked.

"I'm going to try to avoid having Chicago's finest shoot one of their own in the head." I told him.

"Oh, yeah, let me call her."

"Why would we have to shoot him?" Someone else asked.

"Because he's dead," Tabitha told them. "He's dead, but there is something animating his body. We either have to remove that spirit via magic or we have to remove the head so that it can free itself."

"Are you sure he's dead? I feel like his wife would have said something about it." The guy next to the guy calling his wife asked.

"She may not know," Tabitha offered as I knelt next to Wellesley dialing Azrael's cell phone. As normal, my angelic boss picked up on the first ring.

There was some disagreement between Tabitha and the people in the room about whether Wellesley's wife would have noticed he was dead and now a zombie.

"How bad is it?" Azrael asked instead of making small talk.

"I am looking at a zombie, he was in charge of the Division of Magic, but I'd bet a donut it isn't his soul that was put back into his dead body, and it wasn't a demon either, so I am helpless to do anything about it."

"Get a witch to remove the foreign soul," Azrael told me.

"See notes on first phone call."

"Ah, yes, I see."

"We have a guy calling his wife, she is a low powered witch who has never dealt with necromancy before."

"And you don't have a clue what to tell her to do."

"Correct." I told my boss.

"Uriel is already on his way there."

"By his own power or commercial flight?" I asked.

"Like Uriel is going to fly in a plane," Azrael scoffed and hung up on me. Uriel had spent centuries collecting all kinds of knowledge about immortals, including witches. He might know the spell she would need off the top of his head. All I was going to be able to do was hold her hand and make her feel better about it while they shot Wellesley in the head. Knowing Uriel was on the way, made me feel better.

Angels are fast, they can break the sound barrier when they really want to, as long as they aren't carrying anything, like a suitcase or a book, or a person. He'd probably beat the witch to my location. I didn't tell Hemingway that Uriel was on the way, there is no way to prepare to meet an archangel.

They are big and intimidating. They look like winged thugs. Uriel was not the tallest, but he was close at 7 feet tall and had an impressive wing span of twenty-two

59

feet and four inches. I knew because he bragged about it at the holidays when he had one glass of wine too many. Archangels can't handle liquor.

Three New Year's ago, Samael wet the bed in our spare room because he bet my sister he could out drink her on whiskey shots. He lost. My sister handles her alcohol just fine.

Uriel walked into the room with both cops from downstairs holding their guns on him. He appeared to not realize they were there. He hadn't put away his wings and they hung from his back like boneless arms. And he was freaking glowing, because Uriel likes to make an entrance.

"I don't see a witch," Uriel announced to the room, disappointment in his voice.

"She's on her way, sir," someone said in a loud whisper. Archangels made you feel happy and terrified at the same time. I had to admit, even growing up around them, they were impressive. Unfortunately for Uriel, I was used to him.

"Stop glowing," I snapped at him.

"Soleil." He said the syllables of my name slowly, like it was the first time he had ever heard the word.

"Room full of good guys and a zombie," I also spoke slowly, enunciating the syllables. Of all the archangels, Uriel was my least favorite. He might have been a bottomless pit of knowledge, but he was a narcissist. I wanted to add for him to stop showing off, but even I wasn't quite that rude. Chances were good that no one in the room had ever seen an archangel anywhere but TV, so it was possible they thought archangels glowed all the time, which wasn't the case.

"There is a deer inside that man," Uriel suddenly blurted out.

"Precisely why we sent for a witch." I didn't say anything else, because I wanted to really lay into him. "But she doesn't know any necromancy or reverse necromancy, so she'll need help pulling the soul out of him, and since it isn't demonic, I can't help."

"Poor little nephilim, out of her depth." Uriel purred the words. Killing an angel required you to burn their wings using hell fire, also known as Stygian Flame. It was a sulfur mix, not unlike brimstone. There were times I had considered using it on Uriel. His children were angels because his wife was also an angel and he threw that fact into the faces of my nephilim kin every chance he could.

"Are you going to help or are you going to be an asshole?" I asked Uriel.

"I wouldn't have flown all this way if I wasn't going to help." Uriel answered. I walked over to him, putting mere inches between us.

"By the way, Uriel, you can deride me all you want, but you can't pull that deer out of that zombie either, so being an angel isn't any more helpful than being half angel in this situation. Furthermore, at least my father's impure children grew up to have lives, they aren't living off his money unable to get jobs because their brain power is running on empty." I whispered. "If all angels were as worthless as your children, the race would die out in just a few generations, and everyone would be just fine with it."

"You are a cruel child." Uriel whispered back.

"Not usually," I answered. "But I am sick of putting up with your shit. You can look down on us, but at least the nephilim, are smart enough to figure out how to get the next generation of children."

Uriel and his angelic wife had fourteen children, all of them centuries old, and not a single grandchild from the entire brood. If he hadn't been a jerk all the time, I might have felt sorry for him.

Uriel didn't respond, but he stopped glowing and just stood there, looking at the man on the floor.

"Azrael said an entire division of magic had become possessed." He finally said after several moments of silence.

"Yes," I rubbed a hand down my face, literally wiping some of the tension from my it.

"What does this have to do with that?" Uriel asked.

"We don't know yet," I told him. "This man, Captain Wellesley, is head of the Division of Magic. It can't be a coincidence that his team gets possessed and he dies of pneumonia, but someone manages to raise him from the dead before anyone notices he's dead and inserts a soul into his body that isn't his and isn't demonic.

"Beyond this event, do you want my help with the investigation and exorcisms?" Uriel asked politely. Hemingway took a step forward.

"I'm Commander Hemingway of the Fugitive Recovery Team. We are in town to capture an escaped murderer that is suspected of having become possessed while serving his sentence in Joliet Federal Prison. It can't all be coincidence."

"Agreed," Uriel held out his hand to Commander Hemingway and the two men shook. Afterwards, I noticed Hemingway wiped his hand on his jeans.

"This was supposed to be a simple fugitive recovery and has turned into a giant mess," Uriel stated. That summed up the day well enough, although I would have classified it as a giant fuck waffle as opposed to a mess, but one did not say things like fuck waffle in front of family.

"What can I do to assist beyond the exorcism that needs to happen to this poor man?" Uriel asked.

"I don't know yet, I haven't had time to completely figure out the situation either. We arrived around lunch time, had pizza so everyone could get used to being around a nephilim, headed to the Division of Magic to check in, and walked into a room where my brand nearly caught fire due to the demonic energy in the place. The desk sergeant and the civilians that were waiting were all possessed. I didn't stick around to check on anyone else."

"Then how do you know they were possessed?" Someone asked me.

"Because an entire division of supernaturals are going to notice that their desk sergeant has been possessed by a demon," Uriel offered. "Unless, of course, they are also possessed."

I nodded my agreement. I could have said the same thing but coming from a guy with a twenty feet wing span just made it sound more impressive. "It is getting late."

I checked my watch and confirmed it was nearly five in the afternoon. Only three and a half hours until dark and I didn't know if the Division of Magic worked on shifts like patrol units or stayed until the work was done, like detectives.

Exorcisms could be done after dark, but it wasn't recommended, people were just more afraid of things after dark, even things they weren't afraid of during the day, they were afraid of after the sun went down.

The dark made normal shadows terrifying monsters. I was constantly scaring the crap out of myself, mostly because of my vampire neighbor and her desire to practice decorating tips from Better Homes and Gardens. Last year, she had put a trellis near our shared fence so that her climbing roses could fill the trellis and cover the fence. It's good in theory, but at night, that trellis looks like a person standing in her backyard about to jump the fence. On more than one occasion, I have forgotten what it was, and it has made my heart race. Lyzette says she forgets about it too, and it occasionally scares her as well.

Which is why exorcisms after dark were kind of a no-no. It was better to restrain the possessed until mid-morning, demons were weakest around 8 am, after everyone was awake and moving around, the terrors of the dark a forgotten memory, and the possibility of a great day lay before them.

Uriel leaned in very close to me, "You have magic surrounding you, but it doesn't appear to be yours. Can you feel it?" He whispered the words only an inch from my ear.

"Yes, but I don't know where it came from," I told him just as quietly and told him I had felt it when I stepped off the plane at the airport. Uriel gave a swift nod.

"Is this homicide then?" Uriel asked, loudly meaning it wasn't directed to me.

"No, that's on the fourth four, this is the captain's division." The man in purple and grey told us.

"You are a captain?" I asked. He dressed more like model.

"No, I'm a watch commander for homicide." He told me.

"Then why aren't you with homicide?" Uriel asked him.

"No room," someone commented. "This is also the overflow area for homicide."

"How terribly complicated," Uriel said. In my head, I agreed. However, it wasn't the first time I had seen police forces in large cities spread out well beyond precincts. My guess was that they had built this new fancy building that had extra space and restructured it to fill the expected extra space, and then the restructuring had only worked in theory, so the careful planning had gone out the window.

The problem with metropolitan policing was that space was at a premium, you couldn't really expand outwards, so you had to expand upwards. I had seen a few precincts that were five or six stories tall to combat the lack of ground space. This was fine until the elevators broke down. Then you had overweight captains and limping lieutenants trying to huff it up six flights of stairs, because almost no one picked desk jockey as a career.

"How long before Mrs. Detective gets here?" Uriel asked. He didn't sound as smug as he had when he first arrived. Uriel was the oldest of the archangels and sometimes he needed to be reminded that oldest didn't mean best or most powerful, it was just a birth order.

"With traffic, maybe another thirty minutes or so." The witch's husband answered.

"Great." Uriel looked at me. "Is there anything we can do to fill the time?"

"I've talked to Cook County Health Department and gotten their communicable disease logs for the last six months, they show the infestation started nine weeks ago."

"Easter?" Uriel asked.

"Uh huh, there is a sudden spike in all communicable diseases in April and we found some graffiti near the Division of Magic that they say appeared in late April. They cleaned it off, but a few days later, it was back."

"Shall we find out about weird murders, then?" Uriel asked. "Because to possess an entire police division would require a ritual."

"Nothing comes to mind, sir," the watch commander in grey and purple said. "We don't get a lot of weird deaths here, everything is fairly mundane."

"Everyone has weird murders," Uriel commented.

"Not us, we haven't had a homicide go cold in more than three years and they are all run of the mill, gang shootings, bar fights that escalate into stabbings, muggings gone wrong, life insurance murders, home invasions, that stuff. Five or so years ago, there were some murders in a cemetery, but those turned out to be stupid kids who, despite all the education offered to them, still thought they had to use human sacrifice to become vampires." Tabitha made a scoffing noise behind me. I had almost forgot the marshals were there.

"You two investigate this, we'll go catch our fugitive and call you if we need you."

"I don't think that's wise," Uriel said.

"Why?" Hemingway asked.

"Because, in theory, your fugitive is also possessed. I don't believe in coincidences. I don't know why you think he came to Chicago, but if he's here, it wasn't just a random choice, he came here because he figured he could hide among the other possessed." Uriel said.

"Demons have their own psychic network that they talk through." I told Hemingway. "Which means if Mr. Rabbling is possessed, he came here because he knew the Division of Magic was also possessed. Hell, some of the possessed might be hiding Rabbling."

"You said the demon allowed the soul to stay so they could learn the mannerisms of the person they were taking over." Hemingway reminded me. "Police officers aren't going to hide a fugitive."

"You forget there were possessed civilians in the foyer at the Division of Magic, they could be hiding him." I commented.

"And I know where to start looking on that end." I held up my phone, which was less impressive than if I had the logs printed and been able to hold them up. "But that would be a tomorrow search."

"We can't wait until tomorrow," one of the detectives said.

"We don't have much of a choice," I commented. "We need a few things we don't have right now."

"Like what?" The man asked.

"More exorcists," Uriel said. "I'm good, Soleil is good, we could probably do ten exorcisms a day, each, but there were at least six possessed visible from the doorway of the Division of Magic and removing the possessed from certain supernaturals is even harder than from a person."

"That's bullshit," the guy said. "They have families they are going to go home to and infect."

"Possession isn't communicable like influenza," Uriel said. "And they have been living with the possessed for this long, another night isn't going to kill them. Besides, we need to learn about those that work in the Division of Magic, because it is easier to exorcize demons from good people than from the ones that kick puppies."

"You're a fucking archangel!" the guy spat.

"For example, if you became possessed, I think it would take several exorcists a couple of days to remove the demon, because according to your energy, you seem to kick a lot of puppies." Uriel had just as much venom in his words and drew the revelation out with a long pause afterwards. "Whereas, the tall guy in the grey suit with purple accents wouldn't take much effort at all, if he could even be possessed, because he's such a good person saints would weep for him. Besides, as Soleil was kind enough to remind me, archangel or not, I can still only do so much. Exorcising demons takes a lot of energy and magic, which means we will both need to pace ourselves, to ensure that we do not become so weak one of the demons we pull out can insert itself into us."

I hadn't seen that happen, but I had heard about it. The last possessed nephilim cut out their own heart and ate it. A sure-fire way to kill one of my kind. I had no interest in committing suicide at the hands of a demon.

A woman suddenly appeared in the doorway. She stared at Uriel, who still had his wings hanging behind him. Archangels can fold their wings up, making them very tiny little nodules on their backs. Uriel claimed it hurt to do this, so he always let them hang down. My father claimed that letting them hang hurt. I didn't know which one was correct, and most of the time, I didn't care, since I didn't have wings. I was happy about this, wings seemed inconvenient appendages, like the appendix and tails.

# Chapter 7

Uriel walked Christina Lindsey through the spells to exorcize the deer soul from poor Captain Wellesley. The room was silent as he tutored her and gave her a charm to protect herself from any backlash the magic might kick out. We didn't need for her to accidentally separate her own soul from its body because she was new at this.

I stood close to her as she drew her circle on the floor. It would also help protect her from the magic. Uriel might be smart enough to walk a witch through spells, but his people skills mostly sucked, which negated his innate power to make people feel good. If she screwed up, he'd no doubt yell at her, because he was like that. He always expected perfection from every being he met, an impossible standard to be sure.

I hoped my presence would reassure her enough that she wouldn't make a mistake simply because she was nervous. Magic was brutally unforgiving about mistakes. She nodded to me, ignoring the archangel directly across from her. I motioned for Uriel to give her some space, and to my surprise, he did. He walked out of her line of sight, and after she took a deep breath, she began to pull energy together.

Her husband had been right, she was a low-level witch. I was guessing she mostly made charms and potions with her magic. As she gathered it together, I began to worry there wouldn't be enough to exorcize the deer soul.

"This is going to kill him," someone said.

"He's already dead," Uriel answered.

"His wife should be here," the person answered.

"We do not have time for such things," Uriel answered. "Besides, he isn't newly dead, he's been that way for a while, I imagine once she learns of the situation, she will be grateful she wasn't here for it."

I felt a falter in the magic gathering and said a few reassuring things to Christina. As cold as it sounded, Uriel was right, Wellesley was dead and had been for a while, animated not by his soul but by the soul of a deer. This was why necromancy was mostly illegal. People didn't like to say goodbye to loved ones a second time and Wellesley's wife would only complicate things and might result in Christina being called some nasty names, like murderer, which she wasn't.

The little magic nimbus around Christina stopped growing and she looked down at Wellesley's body. Exorcisms are not fun, they aren't pretty. And while people think of them as only happening with demons, when the wrong soul was in a body, it was still a form of exorcism to remove it. There was a moment of absolute silence, like even time was holding its breathe.

The words trickled from Christina's lips forcefully, just like Uriel had told her to do and the magic crashed into the thrashing body of Wellesley. Suddenly, a spectral deer sprung into being over Wellesley. The thrashing and clicking stopped as the deer looked around, every bit as confused as a spectral deer should be when it suddenly finds itself in a room full of people who were staring at it in surprise and fear.

Then it took off like a sprinter at the sound of a starter's pistol. It took ten steps and then disappeared into a wall, gone. Everyone let out a breath, even me. It is easier to remove a soul than put one in, thankfully, or we'd have reanimated corpses everywhere. Christina's legs wobbled, and I caught her on the way down, her magic circle shocking me like I had just touched a live wire.

"Are you okay?" Her husband was asking.

"Get her something with caffeine in it and some pretzels." Uriel told him. "Magic like this is very draining. The caffeine will give her a boost of energy and salty foods help stabilize her blood pressure, which tends to drop after doing these types of spells."

Christina sat on the floor, eyes closed, leaning against me, while someone went to get her something to eat and drink. I kept telling her she did great, and she'd now have a story to tell her coven at the next full moon, after all, it wasn't everyday a witch got to pull a deer soul from a zombie.

She smiled weakly at me and told me she didn't know why, but she felt safe around me. I explained I was a nephilim and that I just generally made people feel good as a result. She told me that wasn't it. Considering what she had just done, I didn't argue, even though I was sure that was it. It may not have looked impressive or like it was a big spell, but it had been both.

Especially for Christina, who was just a notch or two above mortal on the magical power hierarchy. I went to let go of Christina to stop the electric shock the circle was sending into me and instead she broke the circle.

"I'm sorry, I know it's weird, but would you mind just sitting here with me for a while longer and letting me touch you?" She asked weakly. I nodded. It wasn't all that weird. She had just performed a reversal of necromantic magic. Necromancy was considered black magic because most people weren't willing to wait for a corpse, and reversing it was not a fun thing. "It was so cold and sad." She told me. I nodded at her. I'd heard that before. Almost everyone who had to touch a necromantic spell complained it was cold and sad magic, the very anthesis of the magic they used, and it left the person reversing it feeling cold and sad.

I held her hand and focused on my own internal magic, the one that made people feel warm and fuzzy, turning it up a little, so that it could pour life and warmth and happiness back into Christina. She'd still feel like crap for a day or two and I'd recommend she had a coven member or two over for a few days to just help her out and give her someone to talk to about this experience, because her husband wasn't going to have a clue what she was going through no matter how many people explained it to him.

Behind me I heard a woman's voice shout, "What do you mean he's dead?!" I didn't turn to look at Wellesley's wife. Instead I looked at Uriel, the archangel could surely handle a hysterical woman whose husband was now dead, dead. Necromancy only worked once per corpse. No one else would be able to shove a soul, any soul, into Captain Wellesley's body. Uriel took the hint and stood up, disappearing from my view. Uriel and Hemingway would surely ask if Wellesley had been acting strange and for how long.

"She looks angry," Christina whispered to me.

"I bet, she sent her husband to work today after he got over pneumonia and expected him to come home tired, not to show up at the police department and learn that at some point he died while having pneumonia and that we just pulled a deer soul out of his body and so now he's well and truly dead, unless she decides to have a seance and try to talk to his spirit that way."

"Mathilda doesn't believe in the supernatural."

"Well, that's not at all bizarre. Did she grow up in this world or sprout into being fully developed from a seed pod?" I asked. My parents had told me that until the 20th century, vampires and things had kept to the shadows because people liked to burn them at the stake, which is why when archangels decided to stop living in the shadows everything else followed their lead; it hadn't gone real well at first. The history lesson had been meant to educate my sister and I about things like why some people believed angels, especially archangels, were divine. On the flip side, the nephilim were seen as aberrations and mistakes. And vampires were still feared for the most part, as were lycanthropes, both of which was ridiculous because, from what I understood, humans didn't taste very good. My lycanthrope neighbors preferred to hunt deer and furry things over humans. The weretiger male half of one of the younger couples who lived next to me was still debating if he even had it in him to bite her bad enough to give her the virus to extend their lives together. So far, he was still waffling on the subject and kept asking me if I thought it would be weird if he had his mother do the infecting, to which I had said yes, putting me in agreement with his mortal wife. I believed that this was something that needed to be figured out before they started having kids, because their kids would be mortal at this moment in time since mom was a mortal, and they didn't want to outlive their kids or have to bite them.

Because so far, science had not perfected how to pass the virus on in laboratories. The virus was fragile enough that it didn't survive outside it's host. This meant no accidental infections, which was good, but it also meant turning people the old-fashioned way, a little wine and candle light, and a huge bite that drew lots of blood and forced the virus to start healing the body so it would reproduce within the body of the non-host and infect them.

There was something special about the saliva to blood contact that allowed for the transfer of the virus and then it had to be activated, usually by healing the bite wound.

I felt Christina's grip tighten on my hand and could guess that Wellesley's wife was coming towards her.

"Murderous whore," she shouted. By the time I turned around, she was gone. Not just not behind me anymore but gone from the room. I squeezed Christina's hand.

"You are neither of those things," I gently told her. "You didn't kill him, you removed an inhuman spirit from his already dead body and I'm sure he would be grateful for it. Souls don't rest very peacefully when they know their bodies are wandering around without them." I told her. "It might be good to have a coven member or two with you for a few days, they can help you talk through how you feel about it."

"Okay," she nodded, but I wasn't sure she believed me. If I could have conjured spirits I would have conjured Wellesley's to tell her she had done the right thing, regardless of what Mathilda the Terrible thought.

Christina's husband returned with a soda and a bag of potato chips. Christina accepted them and chewed like she was trying to force herself to eat them, and maybe she was. He had missed the fireworks, but one of the other cops in the room was explaining what had happened. Although the entire event had taken less than five minutes, by his telling, it would be at least an hour long. After she got a few potato chips down and had a drink of the soda, Christina looked better and the potato chips seemed easier to eat. I stood up and went to Hemingway, Uriel, and the rest of the fugitive recovery team. They were standing a little way from the police officers in their suits.

I hoped Uriel returned to St. Louis tonight, but I said nothing. Mostly because I was sure two angels in one hotel broke some kind of quota law. Several of the officers in the room shouted at us as we left, convinced we were condemning the families of those that were possessed, but as long as everyone pretended they hadn't noticed, they wouldn't be a liability and life would go on. Uriel told them as much in his departure speech.

Once outside, Hemingway and Uriel made plans to meet the following morning at eight am to begin the exorcisms and Uriel promised to bring back up. Which meant the hotel wouldn't spontaneously combust because Uriel and I were both staying there. It was a win.

# Chapter 8

At the hotel, Hemingway handed each of us a thumb drive. We were to go through personnel files tonight and give him our impressions in the morning. Then we said our good nights.

I was comfortable and waiting on room service to deliver a bacon cheeseburger with all the fixings when my phone rang. My father's name flashed up on the screen. I sent it to voicemail with a preprogramed text him a response. He texted back, telling me he'd see me in the morning. I glared at my phone, willing it to explode, maybe if I didn't know he was coming, he wouldn't show up. Ah, if only. I reminded myself that my father was an archangel quite capable of exorcising demons and I should welcome his help.

Except that my father hadn't done an exorcism in two millennia, possibly longer. In his own words, he'd gone out of the exorcism business around the time of Christ, because there wasn't any money in it.

My phone didn't explode. Instead I got a different text message, this one from my mother telling me to keep my father safe tomorrow. I didn't respond to that one either. I loved my parents, but they were borderline insane. And while I was sure every child felt that way about their parents, making my feelings rather mundane and expected, it didn't change the fact that I was sure that time was wearing on their minds and bringing out some sort of madness that I only hoped wasn't hereditary.

I opened the first personnel file and just stared at the computer screen. This was a colossal waste of time. A report wasn't going to tell me if they were a good person, I needed to see their energy for that. Everyone has bad days and sometimes people lied. So even if a cop had an excessive force slip in their file, it didn't mean they were a bad person, it just meant that someone had filed a complaint against them, and the person filing it may have done it with bad intentions. Plus, I'd had another thought. I stared at the face of a lovely young female cop that was reportedly a witch. Her first name was Marcy. What had Christina said? Mathilda Wellesley didn't believe in the supernatural.

Ok, I got that some people just refused to believe in angels and demons and vampires. To each their own. But her husband was the captain of the supernatural division of police officers for the entire city of Chicago.

Cop wives chattered with other cop wives. And once in a while, cops got together with other cops for barbecues and things. How had Mathilda Wellesley staunchly maintained that supernaturals were a bunch of bah humbug while drinking a glass of wine with a vampire? That took some willful ignorance.

To me it was odd that she could maintain that stance when her husband obviously didn't. Had Wellesley been supernatural himself? Most people in charge of magical divisions were. That was a headscratcher. Supernaturals didn't die of pneumonia, not even witches. Their bodies repaired the damage too quickly. What the hell had Wellesley died of then?

I rubbed my hand down my face again. Maybe I was wrong, maybe he was mortal and had indeed died of pneumonia in June in a city not known for pneumonia outbreaks during the summer. And the entire fuck waffle flipped over once again. Because the reason there was a pneumonia outbreak was because there were possessed people running around Chicago. Now, I was back at the beginning, chasing my own tail again.

How many possessed people does it take to cause an outbreak? I asked myself. Six? Twelve? Fifty? In May, Cook County Health Department had three hundred cases of pneumonia reported to them, an astounding amount for June in Illinois.

But three hundred cases didn't constitute an epidemic, meaning no investigation and undoubtedly some of those three hundred had gotten infected from people who weren't possessed. Finding the starting point was a Herculean feat to be sure. One person infects six, which infects forty, which becomes seven hundred in just a few days. I had too many hosts to track each case back to a single point of exposure. Especially in a limited window of less than twelve hours to figure it out.

There was a quick knock on my door. I got up and answered it. There was a woman wearing the hotel uniform at the door and she had a tray in her hands. It smelled like handheld heaven. That's when I realized she was a little pale and her eyes were practically bugging out of her head. There was a noise from down the hallway that sounded a lot like a gunshot. I pulled her into the room and shut the door as a second one sounded.

"Are you okay? Do you know what's going on?" I asked her.

"I think so," she stuttered after a few seconds.

"You're safe now," I told her, sitting her down in the chair I had vacated. She set the tray down in front of her.

"I was coming up with three room service orders, I delivered the first two fine, but when I got to your door to knock, I heard someone come over the radio," she pointed at it to make sure I saw it on her hip. "And he said there was a man in the lobby and he'd just started eating another man. Then I knocked and there was a growl from the elevator I had just exited, one of the doors opened across from the elevator and a guy with guns stepped out from the hotel room."

The room immediately across from the elevators was being occupied by Walter Kemp. I stood up, told her to stay in my room, and exited. I heard the lock on the door click behind me and hoped she was in the condition to let me back in later.

I could hear voices coming from the elevator. Both male. I gingerly stepped forward and poked my head around the corner. The elevators were slightly recessed into the walls, just like the doors to the rooms. Hemingway and Kemp stood in the elevator, a body between them on the floor. Blood was pooling around their shoes, but it was too dark to be living blood.

"You two okay?" I asked.

"Maybe," Hemingway answered and poked the dead body.

"Everyone else?" I asked.

"Everyone else went to the hotel restaurant." Hemingway told me.

"I don't think he was alone," I told Hemingway.

"Probably not." Hemingway agreed, pushing on the corpse with his foot. He and Walter managed to push it out of the elevator without touching it with their hands.

"I really hate zombies," I told them.

"How do you know it was a zombie?" Walter asked.

"The room service waitress said someone was eating someone else in the lobby." I answered.

"That's how I knew to open the door and take a look," Walter announced, obviously proud of his initiative.

"She had just left my room when it happened." Hemingway told me.

"Now that we all have alibis, let's check out the lobby." I told them.

"We should take the stairs." I followed them, because I didn't have a gun on me, but it was something I considered getting, sometimes people were determined to hang onto their demonic parasite.

At each floor I listened at the door, waiting to hear screams. When none came to my ear, I motioned to the next floor down. When we got to the first floor or lobby level, I didn't have to put my ear to the door to hear the screaming.

"And behind door number one, we probably have more zombies." Walter said. "Can you do anything against zombies?"

"Yes," I answered, my brand starting to feel a little warm. I didn't think zombies were the biggest problem, even though they ate people under the right circumstances.

Walter and Hemingway both ejected the clip on their guns and checked their ammo limits. I had only heard two shots and I wondered if they had used bullets at some other point and just hadn't restocked. That seemed like bad form, but I wasn't a cop, so I could be wrong.

"Ready?" Hemingway asked. I nodded. I was probably readier than them.

"Do not get bit," I told them. Zombies were like Komodo dragons, their saliva was full of bacteria and most of it was antibiotic resistant, making even a love bite from a zombie fatal.

They both nodded solemnly. I heard a gunshot and was thankful that at least someone was alive that had a gun. Duke, Tabitha, and Walter were the only ones that had spoken to me directly, but the other Marshals had lots of silver energy coming off them. And some people were afraid of nephilim, even while they were happy.

Hemingway pulled open the door. There was a body, very dead, about three feet into the lobby area. The elevator doors were open and there was an alarm going off. Another person covered in blood was lying between the doors of one elevator. In the corner of the second elevator was the zombie that they had already killed. I didn't remind them to go for head shots, surely they knew that.

The lobby of this hotel had been neat, clean, and nicely decorated when we first arrived. There were two cops standing outside the doors of the hotel. They were looking in, but not coming in. The reason police departments had magical divisions was to keep every guy in a uniform from being psychologically scarred from going up against things like zombies.

The restaurant doors were pulled closed, and there was a crowd of diners behind them, their faces barely visible over the security door that had gone into place.

Tabitha popped out of a room marked authorized personnel only. She had blood on her, but I didn't think it was hers. There were seven zombies in the lobby. All of them leaking sickly yellow energy that I associated with demons.

"Chicago PD is trying containment," Tabitha shouted.

"Figures," I grumbled. Zombies animated by human souls were smarter than zombies animated by other things. Demons weren't all that good at the mechanics of doing simple tasks like opening doors.

"I got everyone in a back office that has a security door," Tabitha said. "A few were bitten."

"That's not good," Hemingway said.

"Um, I need to talk to one first, because these aren't human zombies, even though they look like it."

"Deer again?" Hemingway asked.

"Demons," I countered.

"We can't risk you getting bit," Hemingway said.

"If I get bit, I get a cold," I told him.

"Fine, kill all but one."

"Won't work, they have to be exorcized or the demons will just put them back together again, if they are powerful enough."

"Damn." Walter said.

"Stupid demons," I offered. "How do you do an exorcism on a dead body?"

I didn't respond, instead, I stalked towards the closest zombie. It snarled and bared its teeth at me revealing fangs. It had been a vampire when it was alive, that was interesting. Using a supernatural as a zombie took more magic. I snarled back, showing him my teeth. I didn't have fangs, but he shrank away from me anyway, my magic carried toward him in the air I had exhaled with the snarl.

I grabbed him tightly by the front of his shirt, pulling him closer to me. The body flailed and jerked, and the shirt ripped. My fingers slipped through the material and against the skin. The demonic zombie began to give a strangled scream. The other zombies turned to look.

Demons, like angels, have sigils, a symbol that represents their name. Some people spend a lifetime memorizing every sigil. I just hear the name when I see it.

I pushed and the zombie pinwheeled its arms, trying to keep itself upright as I shoved it backwards. There was a gunshot behind me. The marshals could keep the zombies at bay while I interrogated this one.

"Grigorii, I command thee to speak to me. I demand you tell me who brought thee through the Stygian to inhabit this body," I shouted at it. It snarled again, flinging foam onto my arm. My instinct was to wipe it away, but I'd have to loosen my grip.

A moment later, the zombie was falling backwards, taking me with him. I landed on top with a thunk and the air was forced out of my lungs, but I didn't loosen my grip. I had no intention of trying to grab him a second time. It wouldn't be as effective since the element of surprise was over.

"The witch brought me forth." His voice sounded like bees buzzing, even as it formed words. It hurt to listen to it.

"What witch?" I asked.

"The Coven of Seven and the witch that leads them." His voice got stronger as he spoke. And while I understood the words, they didn't make sense. He laughed, and it hurt to hear the inhuman sound. "You will die nephilim."

"Everyone dies," I responded. "Even demons."

"I am eternal, you cannot kill me." He laughed again, and I realized Grigorii didn't really know what he was talking about.

I stuck the palm of my hand against his chest, my body across his thighs keeping it pinned to the ground. I stuck the other hand at his head and I began to draw in magic. I could see the magical energy flowing into my hands, turning them from the usual silver color to gold. The demon inhabited body began to scream as a sizzling sound emanated from under my hands. I could smell burning rotting meat and was glad I hadn't eaten my cheeseburger before coming down. The screaming got louder. A demon had once told me it hurt to be exorcized. Demons lie all the time, but I was pretty sure it hadn't been lying simply because when I grabbed a demon it screamed a lot.

Flames erupted from under my hands and I stood up, jerking the demonic spirit from the body when I did. Grigorii was a very small demon. His small spirit kicked and screamed in my hands reminding me of a toddler having a tantrum. Size mattered in the demon world, the smaller the demon, the less powerful, and Grigorii was among the smallest I had ever seen. It was unlikely he had the power to possess a living human host.

His spirit had the form of a demon. Horns, tail, muscled body, all of it visible, but translucent. As I held him, his spirit began to turn gold just like my hands and the smell of sulfur filled the air. I readied myself for the blast of magic that was about to happen. Grigorii screamed louder, his voice still sounding of bees, he had to have been sired by Beelzebub. Most demons don't sound like bees.

His spirit began to shake in my hands, I tightened my grip and forced more magic into it. I pictured it exploding in my head, the spirit released to go to whatever after life demons went to. And even as I pictured it, it happened.

There was a blast of magic that blew my hair back from my face and my hands lost the warmth that had spread through them. Grigorii wasn't there any longer, and the buzzing I'd heard in my head went away.

"Why don't you kill every demon that crosses the Stygian," Hemingway asked, and I realized I was staring at the ceiling. I didn't remember falling down, but that just meant I didn't remember it. The escape of magic when a demon dies is powerful, and it wasn't the first time I had fallen after doing it.

"She isn't powerful enough," a different demon spoke, and I recognized the voice.

"Are you fucking kidding me?" I pushed myself to a standing position. The zombie was maybe seven feet from me. Its voice sounded like silk dipped in honey; sweet, smooth, and sexy. Tabitha took a step back from it, and I didn't blame her. I finished pushing myself up and stared at the zombie.

"That witch wasn't all that powerful, you should have done it yourself, nephilim." Demons considered the word an insult. And maybe to some it was, but I wasn't filled with self-loathing simply because I was half angel.

"Dantalian, I command ye to tell me who brought you forth," I shouted.

"No, nephilim," it told me. "That might work with Grigorii, but not me." I hated Dantalian, and he was becoming an old foe. I had exorcized him at least a dozen times in the last two years. He kept coming back. Mostly because his father, his sire, couldn't cross over. Dantalian was correct, he was not as weak as Grigorii and I wasn't sure even Uriel was powerful enough to rip apart Dantalian's spirit form.

"You love to brag, maybe you should rub it in my face that you were kicked off this plane yesterday and already back today," I didn't mention it might be some kind of record. Most demons who were exorcized took weeks or months before they were able to cross back, even with the help of a necromancer.

"No, nephilim," he responded. "You will not bait me into revealing my return." I shrugged.

"Fine, I'll just send you back," I took a step towards him. He took a step backwards and like this we crossed half the lobby, him trying to stay out of my reach and me trying to get close. He actually didn't want me to touch him, but for me, I was just biding my time, trying to pull in magic as we walked, I wanted this to be done with this quickly. Dantalian had some nasty powers, just like his sire, Astaroth. "Go stand by the restaurant and make sure no one tears open the security screen when I do this," A statement I aimed at everyone in my group. Dantalian laughed and it was even more appealing than his voice. Dantalian was an incubus, and Astaroth was the father of all the cambion on Earth at this exact moment.

Thankfully, I wasn't dealing with Astaroth. I lunged forward catching Dantalian by the shirt.

"I know you want me, there are easier ways to have me," he purred at me and it felt like fur in my brain, soothing the feeling Grigori's voice had left.

There was truth in Dantalian's words, I did want him; I wasn't immune to the charms of the incubus. But I was strong enough to fight the desire that rose in me the moment I touched him. And it would be his undoing, because I could use it to fuel some of my own magic.

My hands instantly burst into flames as I touched Dantalian's human host. They were glowing gold and getting brighter by the heartbeat. Dantalian let out a strangled scream.

"She might not have had the power to send you all the way back to the Stygian, but I do," I whispered to him, leaning in close and letting him feel my desire was not tinged with fear, although that is typically the response an incubus gets. Dantalian's eyes grew bigger as I shoved the body backwards, ripping his spirit out as I did so. The corpse crumbled to the ground.

"I'm going to make you a deal Dantalian, since I know that's the kind of thing demons really like." I told him. "I'm going to hurt you, a lot, before I send you back to the Stygian, unless you give me something less nonsensical than Grigorii."

"I like pain." Dantalian told me.

"Not this kind," I smiled at him. His spirit was taller than me. It didn't have visible horns and it looked mostly human. It was very tall with chiseled features and a sinewy body that spoke of strong muscles, perfect for carrying a woman across thresholds and things.

My hands began to burn Dantalian's spirit. He screamed, and it sounded wonderful. I had never seen Astaroth in any form, but if Dantalian looked like him, I could understand why women went to him. Dantalian's voice was practically orgasmic.

The screaming got louder and changed in pitch and quality. I continued to burn him, not forcing any magic to send him back to the Stygian too fast. After all, he'd told me he liked pain. There were gunshots, and I remembered the other zombies in the room. I turned my head and saw them shuffling towards us, probably trying to stop me from torturing the demon in my hands. I threw his spirit to the ground. He was too wounded to cross back without my help and too weak to take another host. The demon tried to stand and his steps faltered, he opted for crawling a few feet away from me. His eyes were angry.

I grabbed the closest zombie and found another demon like Grigorii, weak and new to the whole possession thing. As I grabbed him, I could see this was his first time. I tried to search his memory for who had called him from the Stygian, but it was blank, one minute he had been doing demon things and the next he was here, inhabiting a dead body and listening to Dantalian bark orders.

The demon was afraid of me. I ripped it from the corpse and watched the corpse collapse. I didn't kill it like I had Grigorii. But I pushed magic into him, picturing the Stygian Plane. There was a pop as his spirit disappeared.

Every part of my body ached already. I had a massive headache and felt like I hadn't eaten in years. My stomach growled loud enough for everyone to hear as I grabbed the next zombie. Another foot soldier without any weapons. Whoever had conjured these demons had expected Dantalian and the fear they created to be enough to power them. I forced him back into the Stygian. As I did, a zombie bit me. I didn't cry out, I grabbed the zombie by the throat and felt the flare of magic and a name flashed through my mind, a second demon like Dantalian, Zepar.

Demons were classified by their power and by their sire. Zepar growled at me and I felt his magic slide over my skin like a million marching ants, all biting as they moved. The sensation moved up my arm. I had only faced Zepar once before. I stared at the zombie and then pushed with my magic. Zepar didn't fight me to retain his dead host. He slipped from it easily, easier than any of the others. His spirit laughed in my face.

"Gotcha," he smiled at me and then his spirit clamped down on my arm and I felt the biting insect sensation increase. It made it hard to concentrate on gathering my power and picturing Zepar crossing back into the Stygian Plane. I wanted a shower more than anything else on the planet, to remove the invisible insects from my flesh. I told myself it was an illusion. No different than Dantalian's sweet sounding voice. But I had more experience with Dantalian, I was used to his tricks and fighting the sensation of pain that Zepar was causing was more difficult than fighting the lust that Dantalian inspired.

As my fear grew, so did the pain. I heard Dantalian laugh, that honeyed smooth sound, and my brain snapped to attention, squashing the fear I had felt. I pushed back on Zepar's magic. I turned my panic into magic, gathering it in my hands until I heard Zepar cry out in pain, a sound that broke the spell, the sensation of biting ants disappeared. I shoved all my magic into Zepar and felt him go back into the Stygian. Then I collapsed, still holding a demonic zombie.

"Poor Soleil is all used up," Dantalian said in a sing song voice.

He was right. Hemingway said the name Uriel and I smiled at Dantalian and then fear washed over me in a tidal wave, the demon was no longer translucent. His skin was nearly the same color as mine, a dark olive complexion that would hold a tan nicely. His hair was light brown and if his eyes hadn't held red irises, he could have passed for human.

# Chapter 9

After exorcising Zepar, I didn't have enough energy to get off the ground. I sat on the floor of the hotel lobby and waited. Hemingway had shouted to me that he was calling Christina Lindsey back and Uriel. Tabitha was currently searching for chalk for me. I could do some physical magic even if my body was exhausted. Two demons of higher ranking were scary. Usually when a person called forth multiple demons they were all the size of Grigorii, they weren't dukes of the Stygian. Tabitha found chalk in the restaurant.

Hemingway went to the door and brought the two uniformed police officers inside to help calm down the crowd that had taken shelter in the restaurant as well as keeping people in their rooms upstairs, and if they found a powerful witch with experience in exorcism, so much the better.

The chalk sucked at drawing on the carpet, but I got a pentagram drawn and the five points of the star labeled with the magic I wanted. The lines instantly turned gold and the smell of burnt carpet wafted up to my nose. They would probably charge me for the carpet damage while ignoring that I had saved their guests from demonic zombies, because people were like that.

Tabitha knelt beside me, helping me stand up. My knees felt rubbery and weak. Dantalian was in full form now, his spirit version replaced by his true form. The restaurant and hotel were probably a giant lightening rod of fear at this point. Which I hadn't considered when I had plucked Dantalian from the zombie and thrown him onto the ground. But even that had been exhausting and I had needed to do something about the other zombies before exorcising the duke. Bad luck there had been a second duke.

If one of the two remaining zombies contained a third duke, it was game over. Even the pentagram funneling magic into me wouldn't be enough help. Hemingway and Walter were keeping Dantalian from Tabitha and myself with bullets, shooting him in the head when he got close. I didn't stop them because Dantalian was using energy to heal himself with every hit.

Like the zombies they were aiming for his head, and I was impressed by their aim. I hadn't asked Tabitha where the two other marshals were. I figured if she wanted to talk about it, she would have volunteered the information.

I could feel the magic the pentagram was channeling moving up and into my legs. Magical symbols such as pentagrams and sigils drew magic from places that normally weren't accessible by supernaturals. I needed food, a hot shower, and some good sleep to recharge my batteries. I wouldn't get the sleep, Dantalian would haunt my dreams tonight from the Stygian, enjoying that I had let him loose and hadn't had the energy to control him afterwards.

Tabitha grabbed one of the zombies, the one that was the most decayed. Bones were visible through tears in the shirt where his skin was just completely gone. I took him from her, feeling the energy from my pentagram flow

91

down my arms and into the zombie. There was a shriek and I let go, staring at the zombie. Lashkar laughed at me, and I realized I was the one that had screamed. Lashkar was a count, not a duke, but he was almost as powerful as Dantalian and Zepar. He stepped into me, taking hold of my hand, forcing the burning magic in my hands back up my arms. I desperately needed Uriel or Azrael or my father or any of the archangels. I wasn't even sure a trained exorcist witch would be strong enough to get rid of Dantalian and Lashkar.

I screamed again as the power burned me, flowing down my arms and residing in my womb. Lashkar was the demon of pregnant women and stillborn babes. If I had been pregnant when Lashkar touched me, it would have died right then and there. I screamed and fought back against the reversal of magic, drawing more of it from the pentagram, forcing my own control back into place, using sheer will to control the power. I was stronger than Lashkar damn it. It was time I acted like it.

I grabbed the zombie that Lashkar inhabited by the back of the head and forced his mouth down to me. It stunk of rotting flesh, but I put my lips on its lips anyway, releasing magic into it, forcing it down. The burning stopped, and Lashkar stepped back, screaming as golden magic poked holes in the zombie's rotting flesh, causing it to bleed golden light. Lashkar cursed at me as his spirit stepped from the zombie's husk, forced to move out of it. I stuck a hand on his chest and smiled as his spirit turned golden like the magic. I forced myself to think of the Stygian plane. There was a swell in the magic and Lashkar screamed louder, wordlessly, and then he was gone.

"Well done, nephilim," Dantalian clapped slowly. "Every time I think you're beaten you come up with something new. But there's still one left, and so far, you've found two dukes and a count, which makes me wonder what the last one is."

Lots of insults roiled through my brain, but Dantalian was a demon, an incubus at that, so he wouldn't find any of them all that insulting.

"Your spirit form is hotter than your true form," I finally said and watched his smile falter for a moment. "Furthermore, it's kind of pathetic that as a duke you don't have horns. Did you inherit that from your daddy? Is the great Astaroth also a hornless demon?"

"Before this ends, I'll have my fun."

"Me too," I answered as Tabitha grabbed the last zombie. I almost didn't reach for him, afraid of what I'd find animating him. Lashkar, Dantalian, Zepar, these were powerful demons that couldn't be summoned by just anybody. And if a coven could summon these three, who else could they have brought forth?

My fingers brushed the zombie and I jerked them back. My first duchess of the Stygian. Someone else was going to have to deal with Lumia. She was Dantalian's twin, a succubus that was capable of seducing both men and women. I pointed at the zombie and Hemingway shot it in the head. I pushed it away.

"Was there an ETA on Uriel?" I asked him.

"Soon," was the response I got. Soon didn't help much. The front doors opened, and I expected Uriel to be smug about his arrival, maybe do some glowing, sermonize about going up against multiple demons in a single night. But it wasn't Uriel and it wasn't Azrael, it was my father.

My father jokes he does motivational speaking because it pays better than exorcising demons. It did indeed pay better, but happy people were harder to possess than unhappy people, so in a way, my father was still fighting demons even though he was a motivational speaker. He looked at the floor where I stood smoldering a hole in the carpet and at the zombie missing part of its head a few feet from me. Then his eyes found Dantalian and I saw the demon avert his gaze.

I did not point out that he had made Dantalian blink first in the contest of wills, but only because I was exhausted.

"Asha are you okay?" Raphael asked me

"Yes, just tired." I told him. "This is Lumia and you know Dantalian," I nodded at the zombie and demon respectively. Dantalian slunk back towards a wall.

"It has been a long time, Dantalian," my father glowered at the demon and the demon pressed himself firmly against the wall. My father tells me we should feel sympathy for demons because the Stygian doesn't have a sun like Earth. At the moment, he didn't seem to feel all that sorry for them. "I will deal with your sister first, Dantalian." My father swept his eyes across the room. "Do you have the power to pull her from the zombie?"

"Maybe," I told him.

"I promise it's the last thing you have to do tonight, Soleil." My father almost never used my real name. He had called me Asha for most of my life. Tabitha grabbed the zombie with Lumia in it and dragged it over to me, kicking and screaming, literally. Lumia jerked and clawed at me, trying not to let me touch her. She struggled with Tabitha, but Tabitha was vampire and vampires are strong. I felt Lumia try to turn up her seduction level, she seemed to forget she was in a rotting corpse. I got a hand on her and pulled her forward until her feet touched the pentagram. It blazed to life, sending even more magic up into me and into the feet of the zombie. Lumia was issuing a long, wordless shriek of terror even before my hands touched the bare skin of her host. I pushed the magic and felt Lumia's spirit separate from her host. I grabbed hold of it and the corpse fell to the ground, well and truly dead this time. Lumia's spirit continued her ear-piercing shrieks as I tossed the spirit onto the ground near my father, letting magic carry her part of the way.

Tabitha caught me as my knees buckled. Raphael took hold of the duchess and I closed my eyes, letting myself lean back and rest against Tabitha, grateful for the vampire. I could hear Lumia pleading with Raphael not to kill her, but I blocked it out. I could also feel her fear. Demons, even ones about to be exorcized are rarely scared enough to release fear magic. That was a more human trait, because even mortals had a little magic in them.

There was a gasp from behind me and I looked up in time to see little bits of Lumia go everywhere. She was in her true form and unlike Dantalian I didn't think it had been her gathering fear magic that caused it. I blinked at my father. Anger swirled around him, deep scarlet. He stalked towards Dantalian and I saw a big, wet, silvery tear slide down the demon's face. My father grabbed him and the moment his hands touched Dantalian, Dantalian was gone. He hadn't exploded like Lumia; his true form and his spirit had been exorcized. Tabitha moved behind me and I looked up to see my father holding out one hand to me and the other to Tabitha.

"The pentagram was smart," he pulled me in for a hug. "Uriel was going to come, but I know how much time you like to spend with him, and Azrael is busy tonight with a different demon problem." He paused squeezing me tight. "Besides, I owed Lumia, so it worked out."

"You killed her." I said after a moment.

"Yes," Raphael answered. "Vengeance is mine, sayeth Raphael." He gave a short chuckle and even though

95

I had just watched him kill a Duke of the Stygian plane, I stayed against him, hugging him back.

Besides, I had killed a demon tonight, too, so glass houses and stones and what not. My father was thanking Tabitha for helping me, at least physically, when Hemingway and Walter came over to us.

"Sir, I'm Commander Hemingway, I want to thank you for coming out tonight to help." Duke Hemingway held out his hand and my father shook it. Hemingway was smiling. A really big there's an angelic presence here smile. I studied it. It was not unlike the smile Walter and Tabitha and the rest of the group had displayed upon meeting me for the first time.

Paramedics suddenly began to rush into the hotel along with several cops.

"Better late than never," I whispered to Tabitha.

"Or something," Tabitha whispered back. I could feel her magic as she exhaled close enough to my ear that it moved a few errant strands of hair. I was tall for a woman at five feet, nine inches, but Tabitha was still an inch or two taller than me. She was thinner than I was, but not in a bad way. Neither of us would have passed for heroin chic, in other words. But she looked like a gymnast or runner and I was lucky enough to have a fast metabolism to go with my love of cheeseburgers, and even half angels didn't have to worry about cholesterol.

Ten minutes later, my father was packing all my stuff into my little suitcase and informing me that I was not staying at a hotel with such poor security, which was odd because they had security doors and a restaurant, and it was something the government would pay for.

This was the problem with dads, they came in and just randomly took everything into their own hands when their daughters were involved, even if the daughter was an adult. I didn't text my mom to tell her it was wrong of her to let dad come to Chicago because I knew my mom would take my dad's side. Oh wait, she already had when she told me to take care of him tomorrow, which meant my father had probably been on his way at that exact moment of electronic communication.

"I like your dad," Tabitha said to me as I met her in the hallway. I was still exhausted beyond reason and I basically just wanted to go to bed. The room service waitress had still been in my room when I returned. She had eaten my bacon cheeseburger and cried herself to sleep on the bed. I understood, zombies were tiring enough, demonic zombies were worse.

The other marshals were at the hospital Tabitha told me as we waited for Hemingway and Walter. They'd been injured in the crush to get out of the restaurant when a zombie had ambled in there. The restaurant's chef had cut off its head with a cleaver. Which was probably a good way to deal with zombies. There had been a flash of light and the smell of sulfur and the zombie had dropped. That was when Tabitha had started firing on it, even though she was pretty sure the flash of light had meant it was dead. The wait staff and cooks had dragged the body outside into the alley while she had taken everyone into the back offices after realizing there were more zombies in the lobby.

"Everybody likes my dad," I told her. Everyone liked my parents in general. I occasionally wondered if my past romantic relationships had gone beyond their expiration dates simply because no one wanted to give up spending time with my parents.

Raphael left a twenty beside the sleeping waitress and another twenty on the TV stand for the maids with a note. Then he brought out my suitcase. Everyone was in the hallway when Raphael entered it, and we followed him downstairs. Hemingway was pointing out we were exceeding our allowed expenditures for hotel stays for the night by changing hotels and my father waved it away while digging out his platinum card.

Angels are hoarders. But it means every so often when they have to clean out their treasure chests, they make a whole lot of money. My father's hadn't been cleaned out in a very long time. Instead, he and my mother were living off gold bars that he had stockpiled when they lived in Central America before the conquistadors came searching for the city of gold.

When one takes gold to the bank to be turned in to cash, it is amazing what kind of special treatment the bank gives you, including credit cards with no limits. I had no clue what my parents paid in taxes, but I bet it was a lot and my father continued to work.

My mom did too, when she was bored. Right now, she was working as a freelance artist for a publishing firm that specialized in hard core bondage erotica. But my mom had been around a long time and sex was part of life. Without it, you didn't get offspring.

In the lobby, my father pointed to a limo and said that was our car. I stared at it. How had dad gotten a limo so fast? I raised my eyebrows and wandered towards it as Raphael explained to Hemingway that someone else would bring the rented SUV to the hotel and that it was just too dangerous to continue to discuss it and that the limo was bulletproof and warded against magic spells. And suddenly, I knew the reason I had to call Azrael back before he sent Uriel to help me with the deer was because he had called my father to make arrangements for Raphael to come out of retirement for at least one last massive exorcism. I couldn't yell at Azrael for this, no matter how much I wanted to, because Azrael had been looking out for me or at least, that was the excuse he'd use. I was sure he'd been trying to get Raphael to go to work for him at the Bureau of Exorcism for a while and here was his chance, handed to him on a silver platter with deer soul garnish.

The limo pulled up in front of a large old hotel on Lake Shore Drive that probably cost more than my weekly pay. There were valets and doormen standing outside the entrance of the building, and when we got out, they rushed forward to get all our bags, calling my father by his name. As my father explained what had happened at our previous hotel a large man with gold eyes walked out of the hotel in uniform. The gold was rimmed by a darker yellow, almost a goldenrod.

Nearly half the staff were supernaturals. My father introduced us to several of them and then we were whisked into the lobby. Hemingway wrapped his arm around my waist as one of my shoes seemed to catch on the marble tiled floor.

"Food," I smelled food and my stomach growled again.

"The best room service in Chicago," my father told me and as he checked us in, he ordered a bacon cheeseburger with spring vegetables on the side be delivered to my room. When he realized none of us had eaten supper, he made sure to get orders from all of us. I swiped at my room key and my father handed it to Hemingway. Then my father amended the room number the cheeseburger was to go to.

"Tenth floor," Hemingway said to the elevator attendant. I left my dad with Walter and Tabitha to sort out the rooms and luggage and things.

"Tenth?" I looked at the envelope around the key card and saw a pentagram on it, along with my room number 1006.

The doors slid shut and the elevator lurched into motion. I tried not to slide to the floor. Everything hurt, even my eyes. I hoped my food arrived quickly. I sniffed and smelled something that smelled yummy.

"I have beef jerky, Miss Burns," the elevator attendant held the bag out to me.

"You are a prince among princes," I said to him as I took a huge chunk of jerky and started to tear at it.

"How'd you know I needed beef jerky?" I asked after I had swallowed that piece.

"I could tell when you got out of the car," he answered, and I noticed his eyes had the tricolored irises of a full-blooded supernatural. "You worked a lot of magic tonight, I hope someone has food ordered for you."

"Yes, my father is here," I told him.

"Ah yes, Raphael is a favorite among the staff. We always enjoy it when he and his family visits."

"Like you didn't know," I smiled at him and he smiled back, and it wasn't because I was giving off happy vibes. It was a smile exchanged by two people in the know.

"Tenth floor, I'll have your luggage delivered soon."

"I have a single bag," I told him.

"Then I'll have that delivered soon," he said and helped Hemingway get me out of the elevator.

"You know him?" Hemingway asked as he put my key card into the door.

"Not personally," I answered. "But everyone knows and loves Raphael."

"I see," if something else was going to follow that it died on his lips. He was looking around the room. "You're rich," Hemingway said after a moment.

"My parents are rich. My dad is older than most civilizations." I responded. "I make about the same amount as a uniformed police." I told him.

"I make more than that." Hemingway said.

"I would hope so." I commented dragging my feet as I walked to the table. There were four chairs around it, a small sofa sat in front of the TV. The decor was expensive, for instance the little four-seater table was solid wood. The small sofa would fold out into a bed, that would probably have a touch button air mattress on it. I was sure if I called down to the front desk, someone would come push the button and put clean sheets, pillows, and blankets on it, because even though it was technically a junior suite, that was the sort of service my father would get.

# Chapter 10

I put my head on the table and closed my eyes, waiting for the telltale knock on my hotel room door. Once I ate, I'd strip down to a camisole and underwear and crawl, possibly literally, into the bed between the comforter and sheets and not wake until I was forced to do so in the morning.

I didn't have to wait long. The knock came before I passed out at the table. Hemingway went to the door. The man who had my food was young, maybe just old enough to drink, and completely mortal. He asked about the resident in 1008 who had ordered a grinder. Hemingway tried to take possession of the food, but the waiter brought it into the room and laid out the little table with napkins, silverware, condiments, and an extra plate and told us to call down or leave it outside in the hallway when we were done.

I dug a rumpled ten-dollar bill out of my pocket and handed it to the waiter as he left. Hemingway removed the cover from his plate as I did the same with my two plates. The second plate had a huge pile of onion rings, more than I could eat alone. Especially since my father had ordered the spring medley vegetable mix to go with my bacon cheeseburger. I lifted the top bun and began to add mayonnaise. He had also added sautéed mushrooms to my burger. One thing about it, despite his attempts to get me to eat healthier with the vegetable medley, he also understood that burgers should come with as many toppings as possible.

"Onion ring?" I asked Hemingway.

"This is quite the spread," he responded. He had a massive pile of fries to go with his grinder which appeared to be a sandwich at least 10 inches long and layered with meat and cheese.

"My family believes food shouldn't just be about necessity." I told him. "It is something to savor, plus eating together gives people a chance to talk."

"My family doesn't even eat together at holidays. Men eat in the living room, women eat in the dining room with the kids."

"Every family is dysfunctional in their own unique way, according to Tolstoy," I told him.

"I do have a serious question for you," Hemingway said as he took a few onion rings.

"Other than how are we going to eat all this food?" I asked.

"Well, I was wondering about that as well, but yeah, this one has to do with the demons," he bit into the sandwich. "Zipper seemed to actually hate you, a great deal, but Dandelion didn't, he acted like you were old friends giving each other a hard time."

"Dandelion and Zipper?" I smiled at the butchered demon names. "Dandelion was my first," I commented, preferring the name Hemingway had given him.

"Okay," he said it very slowly, emphasizing it.

"Not like that," I realized what I said. "He was my first exorcism after I became a certified exorcist, and I have exorcized him more than once. I've never tried to kill him like I did with Grigorii tonight, partly because I'm not sure I can, and partly because of all the dukes of the Stygian." I paused. "Dantalian's main skill is letting loose someone's sexuality. I figure that is far less harmful than if he were blowing things up like other demons do."

"Let's loose people's sexuality?" Hemingway asked.

"I know it sounds bad," I shrugged. "People have sexual desires they don't act on all the time. Dantalian, when he possesses someone, taps into those repressed desires and lowers inhibitions. The last person he possessed was sad when I released her, until I told her it was okay for her to like men and women as a non-possessed person."

"What if the person is secretly a pedophile?" Hemingway asked.

"I'm not sure, I've never run into that," I commented. "However, I've never seen Dantalian possess anyone he found morally repugnant, and I know because he's told me about it a time or two."

"A demon with standards," Hemingway scoffed.

"Sort of. I think its inability more than standards. It's hard to possess someone that is truly a good person at heart and we all have deviant bones in our bodies, denying that deviant behavior is part of what makes us a good person."

"Like I don't kill scum bags in my custody," Hemingway said.

"Yes." I answered. "Unless you get hexed into demon possession, even powerful demons have to work to get into a living host. It's why there aren't more hell princes jumping the Stygian bridge."

"Hell princes?"

"Demons like Astaroth, Dantalian's sire. In my nearly 20 years as an exorcist, I have never encountered a prince. They are powerful, I don't know that I could exorcize one. I think it would almost certainly require the attention of an archangel, and I don't know what sorts of powers they would even have over their host, but I'd be willing to go with not good ones."

"Why is it harder for hell princes if they are so powerful?"

"Because the Stygian Divide actually works against them, to keep them there."

"Since I'm right next door, I'm going to have a room like this, too, aren't I?" Hemingway asked as I finished my cheeseburger and took a few more onion rings.

"I imagine the entire group does." I told him. "And tomorrow, when Murphy and Jones come back, if they get to come back tomorrow, they will have them to."

"That seems like an awful lot for your father to do for us."

"Do not try to pay him back or argue with him about it. You will lose."

"This is too much," Hemingway said. "When he ordered our dinners, he told the front desk manager to make sure that it all got charged to his room."

"Sounds correct." I chewed on an onion ring. "My father likes to spend money on people, even people he doesn't know all that well. He can read minds, and this is his version of penance for the invasion of privacy. By the time he goes home tomorrow, the group is liable to have presents waiting for them in their rooms and he will insist we stay here until we are done with the apprehension. He will insist we continue to charge meals instead of paying for them. That's the way he is, even though he knows it can be off putting to people. At some point, he'll make up an excuse as to why you need to stay here and continue to charge things to his account even after he's gone home."

"He's already done that."

"Then expect him to be even more insistent tomorrow." I told Hemingway. "I always tell people to accept his generosity, he truly wants to do it, so swallow some pride and let him, it makes him happy, and since he makes everyone else happy by existing, we should give him this," I shrugged and pushed three bites of onion ring away as well as most of the vegetable medley. I love veggies, but I wasn't crazy about the liquid smoke on these.

"Do you need anything?" Hemingway asked me, standing up.

"Not unless you're willing to give me a piggyback to the bedroom," I told him.

"Let me set these trays out, everything is negotiable," Hemingway smiled at me. I tried not to giggle, surprised by the flirtiness of his response. Then I wondered why not? Sure, I was probably a couple years older than him, but I wasn't a hideous fucking chud, as they had said in *Clerks II*. Besides, chances were good that I'd never work with him again; I rarely worked with the fugitive recovery teams. It had happened twice in five years. There were about fifty exorcists in my department, and we weren't needed by the US Marshals service very often, really just a few times a year. I'd work with the Chicago Police Department long before I worked with Hemingway's FRT again just because Chicago was going to need me faster than they would.

And Hemingway was both attractive and taller than me, something I greatly appreciated. He was a good six inches taller than me, and in good physical condition, like most Marshals. Then I had a moment of doubt. My father had put him and the rest of the team in their own suites and probably bought him a forty-dollar grinder. Was he flirting because of my father's generosity? Did he feel like he somehow owed me because my father liked to spend money on people? That would be a letdown.

Hemingway set the trays outside and held his hand out to me when he came back into the room. I looked at him, eyes narrowed.

"Come on," he said. "I won't give you a piggyback, you aren't six, but I will help you, since it seemed to drain you to exorcize those demons.'

"It was killing Grigorii," I told him. "That was a mistake. It takes nearly ten times the energy to destroy a demonic spirit than just send it back to the Stygian."

"Then why do it?" He asked.

"Because I expected all of them to be minor demons and I didn't kill him, not really, I killed this form of him. He'll be reincarnated in a handful of years, possibly as someone more powerful. Lesser demons like Grigorii get picked on by more powerful demons like Dantalian, so I might have done him a favor," I shrugged and let him pull me to my feet.

"Demons are bullies?"

"Yep." I nodded once and then leaned against Hemingway. He wrapped an arm around my waist and swung my body up off its feet. He was strong enough to carry me to the bedroom, but he dumped me unceremoniously on the soft comforter.

"Since you're weak, I won't take advantage of you tonight."

"Does that mean you intend to try it another night?"

"Yes," he whispered.

"Well, thank you for the assistance to my bed."

"You're welcome." He smiled and shut the door on his way out. I lay there in bed for a moment. I was willing to bet this was not just because my father had been nice to him and his team. I shimmied out of my clothes, crawled under the blanket, and was instantly asleep.

I was sleeping well when Dantalian ruined it. My dreamless sleep was suddenly interrupted by a naked Dantalian on a platform full of strippers. I got the gist of the dream as I jolted awake in the dark. My phone was in the other room on the table where I had left it. The hotel clock displayed the time as 3:10 am. I rolled over and got up. My stomach growled again and the phantom magic that I had been trying to ignore since arriving in Chicago seemed heavier now.

The problem with staying in a hotel is that it can be hard to get a midnight snack. But my stomach refused to listen to logic on the matter. I got dressed and began the search for a vending machine.

There wasn't one on my floor. I pushed the elevator button and the doors opened after a moment, there was still an attendant. I nodded and got in.

"Which floor miss?" He asked.

"The one with the nearest vending machine."

"Lobby then," he answered. Awesome. A hotel without a vending machine in this day and age. He instructed me to go to the front desk.

The vampire working the front desk blinked at me a couple of times, surprised that a hotel guest was wandering the hotel at this hour.

"I am looking for a snack." I told him.

"What would you like?"

"Protein; nuts, cheese cubes, beef jerky, whatever." I told him.

"Our kitchen is still open if you'd prefer something from there."

"Knowing my daughter, she wants bacon." I heard a voice say behind me and looked to find my father sitting on one of the couches in the lobby.

"Ah, Miss Burns," the front desk guy slid a menu over to me. I eyed it suspiciously. I didn't think I wanted a full meal at three in the morning.

"Beef jerky and some peanuts if you got them," I told the desk clerk.

"Of course, miss," he replied and disappeared through a door.

"Dantalian?" My father asked. I nodded. "We are having a Dantalian sucks party in my room."

"Who's we?" I asked.

"You, me, the Marshals."

"Is everyone awake then?" I asked, and my father nodded.

"Tabitha was already down here when I came down at around two-thirty."

"If he can find a way, he'll be back by tomorrow night." I told my father.

"It is his nature." My father told me.

"Think we have enough power between us to deal with the Division of Magic?"

"Yes," my father nodded as the front desk attendant came back with beef jerky and peanuts. I took both bags and followed my father back to the elevator.

My father had the biggest suite available from the looks of it. Three bedrooms, a large miniature kitchen, a large living room, a nice bathroom with walk-in shower, and a jetted garden tub. He had opened a bottle of wine, probably to help him sleep and now it would help everyone else sleep through Dantalian's dream wanderings. Walter was already passed out in one of the spare rooms. Tabitha and Hemingway were having an earnest, but slurry, conversation about whether she could be trained in exorcism by morning.

Shortly after my arrival, Raphael and I began to give Tabitha the basics of exorcisms. She was not a weak vampire, and with some training, she would be formidable. More importantly, she took to it, even after several glasses of wine, like a fish takes to water.

I had fun. After I finished my beef jerky and peanuts I went and crashed in one of the other rooms in my father's suite.

# Chapter 11

"I hate zombies," I woke up and told my father, wondering where it had come from. Obviously something I had dreamed, but I couldn't remember the details, however at least zombies weren't Dantalian related.

There were maybe three cups of coffee left when I got out of bed. It wasn't what I was used to, meaning it was obviously my father's current preferred blend of coffee. He poured me a cup in a real bone china cup, which I was sure was taboo, especially considering how I was going to brutalize the coffee before I drank it. He also passed me a small carton of milk and a sugar bowl overflowing with cubes. By the time I got sugar and milk in my coffee, it was almost white.

"I should have given you instant coffee," Raphael smiled at me from behind an island that separated the kitchen from the living room. I nodded in agreement. I drank a breakfast blend. My father drank coffee that had enough body it didn't need a cup to hold a shape. He drank it black.

I wasn't the only one with nearly white coffee. Walter's coffee was a light tan in the cup. He looked a little hungover, but I didn't say anything about it. Demons stalking you in dreams sucked. He'd played nice in my dream, but that didn't mean he had everyone's.

"Did you sleep well enough?" Hemingway asked. I nodded once. No killing of minor demons today, not even for the purpose of intimidation. I'd have Raphael and Uriel with me, that would help, and it was possible that Tabitha could help as well. She wasn't a full-blown exorcist yet, but everyone had to start somewhere.

Uriel met us in the lobby. No grand entrance. No glowing skin. My father hugged him and we all loaded into the SUV and another car that my father had rented. It was a Cadillac with lots of room, I was sure the extra room made it easier for those with wings to sit in. I rode in the SUV. I did not want to be trapped with Uriel and Raphael in a car.

From the outside, the Division of Magic looked normal. During the time we'd been gone, someone had added onto the "Deliver us from evil" graffiti making it read "Deliver us from evil dear angels." I love my father and he's a great guy, but anyone who referred to angels as dear didn't spend any time with them. Uriel's pride and vanity were not an isolated event. My sister had the same traits and she wasn't even full angel.

"How do you want to handle it?" Raphael asked. Uriel launched into a long speech and my father let him ramble for a good two minutes and then said, "I was talking to Hemingway and my daughter." If looks could have killed archangels, Uriel's glare would have turned my father to ash where he stood.

"I'd like for the marshals to go in with Soleil first, we will try to bring the possessed outside to deal with them." My father nodded, impressed that Hemingway had been listening to him, despite the wine in the wee hours of the morning.

The smell was rancid. My brand burned exactly like hell fire. There were different civilians on the benches in the hallway leading to the desk sergeant. They all looked terrified and none of them were possessed. The demons were thinking, which was never a good sign.

It was the exact same desk sergeant, however, and he was still very much possessed and starting to lose the battle to his demon. I could tell because he smelled of infection. Oozing sores were not uncommon among those possessed long term. The pus smells of decay and brimstone. Phones were ringing like crazy behind the closed door to the right of the desk sergeant, but I didn't hear anyone talking on them.

"Go," I told the civilians. They looked at me and for the first time I noticed they were handcuffed to the benches. Awesome.

I began to gather magic. The desk sergeant wasn't just going to let us waltz into the restricted areas without a fight and I decided to land the first blow. Once the magic had gathered, I shouted, "Begone!" The magic shot from my hands and hit the desk sergeant square in the chest. The words were unnecessary, but I had seen the movie The Exorcist a lot, and it always looked cool when they did their forceful commanding of the demon. It probably looked ridiculous when I did it, but no one had told me that, so once in a while, I still broke it out. There was a screaming noise and the three Marshals began to uncuff the civilians.

And the demon began to chant. If it had been a minor demon or even a lesser demon, the blast would have separated the body and demonic spirit. But of course, it didn't, because where's the fun if it isn't a challenge.

The demon used Latin to focus and release his magic. It flew from the fingertips of the desk sergeant and

113

I knocked Hemingway off his feet. The magic slammed into the wall where he'd been standing.

Tabitha had brought out pieces of chalk and was already drawing pentagrams and sigils on the floor for us. Tabitha suddenly broke the chalk and handed a piece to Walter and the other to Hemingway, they followed her led and drew a pentagram near where they stood. Even mortals had the ability to use minor amounts of magic, they just couldn't produce it themselves. I wouldn't step on it until we were hightailing it out the door, I didn't need a boost yet, but I might as we retreated.

Tabitha moved faster than my eye could follow as she moved forward and hit button to open the door for us, even faster than the demon could follow. The door buzzed and opened. The noise from the inner chamber grew louder and there was a lot of confusion on the other side.

"What do you think you're doing?" A tall man in a suit stepped out. His eyes were a beautiful shade of grey with the triple irises, getting a darker grey as the iris moved towards the white of his eye.

Tabitha grabbed him and tossed him into the corridor. I stood next to where he landed.

"Don't get up, demon, save your energy." I told him, and he snarled at me. If demons ever decided to truly organize themselves, we were all in trouble, but they wouldn't because demons didn't want a chain of command or to listen to directions, they most only listened to their sires. I grabbed him and jerked the spirit from the body. The body shuddered, then its knees buckled and it sat down hard on the bench.

The spirit I held was a lesser demon and it was too scared to tell me anything. I pictured it crossing the black and rainbow Stygian Divide, and the demon was gone from my hands.

Tabitha said something snarky about how I made it look easy. I smiled, and she forced magic into a second being that was lying on the ground, convulsing under her touch. I could feel her magic force its way into the body, overpowering the demon's magic and the spirit was suddenly standing beside the body. Hemingway helped up the newly exorcized police officer and sat him on the bench next to the first. Tabitha commented on how tiring it was to do it and I nodded at her. I knew she would push herself as much as she could, but we still needed her skills as a vampire. I couldn't think of a way to tell her this without sounding condescending, so I kept my mouth shut and stepped into the cubicle area where the Division of Magic officers worked on cases.

There were twenty or so officers left, all wearing suits of one sort or another. One wore a cloak and a pointy Halloween witch hat. Who says demons don't have a sense of humor? If the female cop turned out to be a vampire, I was going to be disappointed. I grabbed the nearest officer, a man who was mid-twenties or so. His hair was already turning grey and he had jaded eyes with the triple iris pattern that denoted a supernatural with two supernatural parents.

I pictured the demon coming out at the ends of my fingers as I pulled it away from him and then I jerked my hands back from his chest and head. The demon came with them. It struggled and swore and spat at me. More magic went whizzing past me, diverted by a protective circle that Tabitha had put into place.

The spirit in my hands was not a lesser demon, Abydzou kicked and screamed at me, my hands golden and burning him. I could see the golden magic spreading from where my hands held him. Abydzou was stronger than a lesser demon, but not as strong as Zepar or Dantalian. He clawed at my arm and the magic in one hand began to fade slightly. I threw him down to the ground, his body falling half in and half out of the circle of magic. He screamed, and half his spirit body went rigid and started to turn gold.

I knelt next to him and whispered my own Latin spell. Within moments, the gold had spread through his entire body. There was an audible pop when his spirit disappeared. I felt something akin to an earthquake beneath my feet and I struggled to stand up on the trembling ground.

"Should that happen?" Hemingway asked.

I didn't answer, instead shoving him towards the door we'd come in. Tabitha exorcized another demon and sweat beaded up on her face. I shoved Walter through the door and went for Tabitha.

"Exhausting," she whispered weakly. I nodded and picked her up, casting a spell as I did so. I felt warm light on my back as I took Tabitha through the open door. The hell fire on my arm didn't burn as badly and the light from it was fading.

Hemingway pushed open the door to the police station and we hurried outside, propping the door open as we did so. They would no doubt understand how to open the door anyway.

Having touched Abydzou right off the bat made me sure that this ragtag assortment of possessed cops was going to be like the zombies, there were going to be more dukes and counts than lesser demons, which is why I was heading outside. The archangels needed room to maneuver and they wouldn't get it in the crowded cube farm inside the station house.

My feet stopped moving and my eyes took in the sight outside. In the hazy morning light, we had attracted a crowd. Fifty or so people stood in a semicircle around

Raphael and Uriel and the Division of Magic. None of them had the yellowed energy of the possessed. One boy, a teen, but not old enough to drive a car yet, judging by his baby face, held a spray paint can of black paint. As I watched, he wrote the word nephilim in all capital letters and crossed out the blue penis written on the side of the building and then he moved to a new clean spot and began to write in Latin.

Was I wrong, were they possessed, and I didn't know it? I opened my magical senses wider. I do not like to use this because it doesn't show energy, it shows the soul. And a person's soul should be private. Looking at him now, he was practically featureless. There was no warring spirit fighting for control with his soul, but he wasn't a mere mortal either. His soul was dressed in the traditional garb of a witch, cloak, hat, mask. No one knew why souls of witches wore masks, but it was agreed they all did. Archangels weren't much better. I scanned the crowd, trying to keep my eyes from landing on Uriel or Raphael. I had seen their souls in the past and didn't need to see them again, ever. And because I was trying to avoid them, my eyes landed on Raphael. His soul was not featureless like the wizarding boy. His soul was blinding gold light that had streamers of silver weaving in and out of it. The gold was his magic, the silver were his deeds. It hurt to look at him. However, for some reason angel souls have fangs and scary faces, even my fathers.

Souls are where magic comes from, the more you have, the brighter the soul. A few beacons of light showed among the crowd, witches, wizards, vampires, lycanthropes; one of whom surprised me by being a bird, a shifter species I had only heard of, never seen, an elf, and a big man that I was sure was a very powerful leprechaun.

None of them had streaks of evil in their magical signatures. And in that moment, I realized these were residents of the area that knew the Division of Magic had been taken over. Many of them wore talismans and amulets. The boy with the spray paint began to cross the street, moving towards me. Using his tagging paint, he drew a pentagram on the concrete road a few feet away from me. Then he slipped a leather cord over his head and hung it from the end of his fingers and let it dangle where I could take it if I wanted. I didn't take the boys amulet, it was probably full of protection wards and I felt they would serve him better than me, especially if we failed. I took his hand, curling his fingers around the leather cord and let some magic flow into him from me.

"I got more," he told me, taking another one off his neck. "They keep demons from being able to possess you."

"That's strong magic," I told him, taking the second one he had pulled from his pocket. "I need three."

"It's what I'm best at," he told me, and his hand went into his pocket and he pulled out another one. I did the same, sticking my hand in my pockets, glad the first hotel had had an ATM machine in the lobby and I'd been smart enough to use it. I pulled out money and shoved all of it into his hands. I took the three amulets, each a silver angelic sigil. I didn't smile even though one was the name Raphael. Instead, I handed them to Tabitha, Walter, and Hemingway. It wouldn't do for the Marshals to become possessed.

I could feel the magic coursing through them. He was a natural born exorcist. Uriel needed to talk to him, because the silver pendant could have been a tulip and the magic would have been just as strong. The boy walked away counting the money I had given him. I didn't know how much was there, I guessed it was probably more than his going rate, but still not nearly enough, since I was positive the amulets would work.

The possessed followed us out of the Division of Magic, as I had expected. Their human captives attempting to get to assistance, while their demonic inhabitants saw the opportunity to embarrass a nephilim, or more accurately, an exorcist.

Outside, I could still smell their oozing wounds, but it wasn't as overwhelming in the fresh air. The possessed looked around at that semicircle and at Raphael and Uriel. Hemingway and Walter were standing with their backs to the doors, guns ready.

It was our intention not shoot any of the possessed, but non-lethal injuries might be necessary if they became aggressive. A possessed cop swiped at Tabitha as she put on the necklace. Tabitha bared fangs at it, hissing as only vampires can.

Then she grabbed and tossed one into the road. Normally when a crowd gathers around demonic entities, the fear makes them stronger. This crowd wasn't afraid. For whatever reason they were all calm and collected, watching. I didn't think it was just a matter of Raphael and Uriel being there.

As I thought their names, Raphael grabbed one of the possessed and pulled him into the fold of his large, long arms. He covered the man with his wings and for a moment, my memory latched onto the image from the movie *Beastmaster* where the batesque creature digested the guy running past it in the fold of its wings, dropping goo and bones out the bottom.

My father didn't digest the cop, thankfully. Gold magic flowed through the wings for several seconds and then my father opened his wings and dropped the cop, who's energy was no longer yellow.

Uriel pulled a demon spirit from one of the other cops using magic. And I thought maybe my father couldn't physically remove the demons, maybe he could only smother them in happiness. Maybe that was why he had told me last night to remove Lumia even though I had been near collapse with exhaustion.

The exorcism itself was what wore me out, I could pull demons out all day long. Forcing them back into the Stygian was exhausting after a while. I grabbed a cop, placing my hand on her head and felt the demon recoil at my touch. I shoved the physical body of the cop away and tightened my hands into the ethereal magic that made up the demon's spirit. The cop fell to the ground and the demon stayed in my hands. It spat at me, a thick ectoplasmic goo that wasn't really saliva. I frowned at him and handed him to my father. The demon shrieked, and I turned from it.

Everything was going well, until I ran into someone like the next cop I grabbed. The demon was another duke and he laughed at me, it was the host's soul that shrank away. It didn't want me to exorcise the demon. Most hosts wanted the demon exorcized, but every so often I found one that liked what the demon offered or liked being able to have the excuse that they were possessed. I could still force the demon out, but it made the host aggressive because they knew I knew that they hadn't wanted it done. I tossed the cop away from me, letting its head hit the ground, hard. Considering it was a supernatural, it seemed to me that this was probably the reason the entire Division of Magic was possessed.

"Soleil!" Uriel scolded me by just saying my name. I shook my head, deciding Uriel could deal with that one, he'd fight to not have the demon removed. Hemingway didn't walk over and render aid, something in his instincts telling him if I didn't want to do the exorcism there was a reason and he was trusting of me. I nodded, and Walter suddenly drew out his cell phone, bringing the realization that I hadn't, we need paramedics for most of the exorcized. They would be malnourished, dehydrated, psychologically scarred, and at least a few were going to be covered in lesions.

I grabbed another cop and felt the demon try to hide behind the soul of the host and then I screamed. The demon's magic touched my arm and it felt like flaming acid. Another duke. Good grief. Gusion assisted his father with the creation of monsters. He lured mortals and supernaturals alike into the Stygian to be transformed into beasts like gorgons, minotaurs, and nagas. The magic that burned like acid allowed him to twist those unfortunate souls to make the transformation easier.

"Come forth, Gusion," I called, commanding him forward where the soul of the host couldn't be harmed any more than it already was. Gusion did as I commanded, and I jerked him from the body, leaving the host screaming as he fell to the ground. Gusion's magic ran down my arm, melting my skin as it did so. Blood dripped from the wounds. Tabitha took a step towards me, and I shook my head for her to stay there. My arm erupted into flame, but the pain from the melting acid eased. I didn't wipe at the flames, refusing to let it spread to my other arm and hand. Raphael looked at me for a moment then he took two steps, closing the distance between us. Raphael grabbed Gusion and the demon screamed like the acidic fire was being poured on him. His face swelled. His hands and feet lost their definition and he began to glow with golden light.

Parts of Gusion went everywhere. His former host was curled into the fetal position, unashamedly weeping.

"How many?" I asked already healing the damage caused by Gusion to my arm. My purifying fire removing the remnants of acid.

"Eight," Raphael answered. I didn't say is that all, but I thought it.

"Let me help?" The boy with the amulets shouted from across the street.

"How old are you?" My father asked him.

"Thirteen." He answered.

"The wizard has the gift," Uriel said his head cocked to one side.

I wanted to scream at Uriel. He was only thirteen, not old enough to fight dukes and knights of the Stygian, no matter how great his gift was, or how good his amulets worked.

"Buy all the amulets," I told my father. He gave me a look but didn't argue. He crossed the street in five steps. My father has long legs. The boy tried to give all his amulets to my father, but Raphael insisted on paying for them.

"These are incredible," I heard my father say. I nodded in agreement having felt their power earlier when I had bought the three for the Marshals. Uriel stood and talked to the teen and I vowed that if Uriel brought him over to exorcize any of these demons, I was going to kick his archangel ass.

Raphael came back and began to hang the amulets around the necks of both the remaining possessed and those that had been exorcized. The possessed began to scream. It didn't take long for the lesser demons to jump out of their hosts all on their own. Once free, my father, Tabitha, myself, and several witches from across the street began to cast spells that sent them back across the Stygian Divide.

# Chapter 12

The amulets left us only seven possessed police officers. Seven that were strong enough that while the amulets glowed, the demons didn't exit their hosts voluntarily, including the host that didn't want his demon exorcized. I went to grab another of the possessed, and pain crawled up my leg; I sorely missed Dantalian, duke or not, he rarely tried to cause me pain. The demonic host holding my leg began to open its mouth and I heard bees. Damn. More of Beelzebub's brood.

I jerked my leg from its grasp, if it was going to hurt me with magic, it was going to have to work for it. Distance magic required more energy than touch magic. The host grabbed for my leg a second time and I moved out of the way. Its fingers flailed where my leg had been. I got the impression the host didn't want to hurt me but was no longer strong enough to fight.

Focalar's host stood up, swiping to grab me again and failing. I grabbed the police officer and stared into his eyes for a moment, letting Focalar's magic prick at my skin. Soon blood was running down my arms. I ignored it, leaning in close.

"You don't have to fight, I'll do it for you," I told the soul of the police officer. The sound of bees got louder.

I moved him, forcing the body to walk, until I was standing over the spray-painted pentagram. My blood fell on it, and it started to glow. Focalar screamed wordlessly. The demon suddenly began to swear at me, the sound of bees getting louder. I grabbed the demon's spirit and jerked it free of the cop's body. There was a sigh from the host as he stumbled before falling to the ground and crawling away from us.

Even with the pentagram, I didn't have enough magic to kill Focalar, but I could hurt him and make him dread crossing the Stygian again anytime soon. I shook the demonic spirit and began a spell in my head. The demon lost some of its translucency. I wasn't weak and winded like I had been yesterday, and I was angry. Angry that this had happened to a bunch of cops and angry that a whole neighborhood had been mostly powerless to do anything about it. I filled the spell with my anger and felt Focalar solidify in my hands.

Once his true form was completely put together, I slammed an exorcism spell into him, trying to rip his spirit from the body. I filled it with more magic and hit him again with it. Focalar began to bleed, yellow blood oozing from his ears, nose, and mouth. I forced more magic into him, continuing my exorcism assault. The magic of exorcism was not meant to be used this way and I expected it to lash back on me. But it didn't, it just let me keep pouring it into the demon's true form. He sobbed, and I stopped, dropping his body to the concrete sidewalk, right on top of the pentagram. A massive red swirling portal popped up in front of him and Focalar's true form crawled through it.

As soon as he was gone, I felt guilty. It wasn't exactly Focalar's fault he was a demon, he'd been born that way, just as I had been born a nephilim. I felt tears fall from my eyes and run down my cheeks. Raphael came up to me, wrapping me in his arms. I felt stupid, a grown woman bawling on my daddy's shoulder, but I couldn't help it. I had gotten angry with demons before, but most of this group had come here because they had been called, meaning they hadn't had a choice.

My anger had been misplaced. Sure, I was mad about the pain, but pain ended and wounds healed. And as far as I could tell, the demons here weren't doing anything terrible. They weren't shooting people in the streets, they weren't blowing up buildings, they were a distraction. Whoever had summoned them wanted them to keep the Division of Magic from interfering with their plans. That was not exactly the fault of the demons. They could have summoned gorgons or water sprites or nymphs. Demons were just the easier of that list to summon. The beings I was really mad at were the ones that had done the summoning. Oh, and possibly the jerk that didn't want to be exorcized. That was annoying like a freaking pebble in a shoe.

"Did you do this?" I heard Uriel ask and turned to see him facing the cop that hadn't wanted to let go of his demon.

"No," the cop answered, and unfortunately, I believed him. The semicircle was letting a half dozen ambulances through, and wouldn't you know it, the cops were finally arriving. There was a chance I was also angry at them for letting the entire division get possessed without doing anything about it or even saying anything to anyone. They could have called the Bureau of Exorcism when they figured it out, but instead, they had pretended they hadn't noticed because it was easier and most of them probably hadn't understood what the Division of Magic did anyway.

126

I pushed off from Raphael and walked a little way away, still drying tears. The young wizard ran up to me. "Are you okay?" He asked.

"Have you ever just realized that you were mean to someone when they didn't really deserve it?" I asked him.

"Yeah," he nodded, and he gave me a weak smile.

"Me too," I told him. "I feel like a jerk for turning into a bully."

"But he was a demon." The boy told me.

"He has about as much choice in being a demon as you have in being a powerful wizard."

"I'm not powerful, I'm just good at a few spells." He mumbled.

"With the right training, you could be one of the most powerful wizards I've ever met."

"You think?" He asked.

"No, I know." I told him. "Do you study under anyone right now?"

"My mom can't afford it."

"Oh, is she here?" I asked. He pointed to a lovely woman that looked almost nothing like him. Her skin was nearly a light bronze while his was the color of good milk chocolate. Her eyes had single irises but were still a lovely shade of green. The boy's bicolored with brown and green. "Can I meet her? I'd like to thank her for allowing your assistance in this matter"

"Of course," he grabbed my hand and I let him pull me across the street. I caught my father's eye and he watched us intently.

"Hi, I'm Soleil Burns, professional exorcist, your son has amazing talents."

"Valerie Dusain," she answered. She looked tired.

"Let me guess, his father was a wizard?" I said to her.

"Yes, he died when Jerome was only a year old."

"Now you work two jobs just to pay bills?" I pressed, and while this would have been offensive from anyone else, she smiled since it came from me. I just had that effect on people.

"Yes," she nodded.

"Is it Mrs. Dussain?" I asked. She nodded, and I pressed forward. "I'd like to help. I'd like to sponsor Jerome to train at the School of Witchcraft. It wouldn't be charity of course, I would like him to keep me stocked up on those amazing amulets, I would require about thirty a month."

"I guess that's between you and Jerome," she said. "But the School of Witchcraft, those amulets aren't worth that much, not even thirty of them."

"Considering they just made a handful of lesser demons exorcize themselves, I'd say they are worth every bit of that. Plus, if Jerome can master his powers, he could eventually make a great exorcist and there are so few of them."

"So, you aren't just talking about this year, are you?"

"No, I'm talking long term. If he can pass the entrance exam to the School of Witchcraft, and I'm positive he can with no problems, he can eventually get into Uriel's Exorcism school and become certified."

"I have to be able to keep my job," Jerome told me.

"What job is that?" I asked him.

"I run deliveries for the corner market four afternoons a week." He told me. "Mr. Chen likes me because people don't mess with me. And the extra money helps my mom."

"Hey Jerome, is the Chinese place any good?" I pointed to a small little Chinese takeout place that looked like it should be condemned.

"Nah, you want Dim Sum's, if you want Chinese."

"Where's that?" I asked, trying to steer him away from his mom so she and my father could talk. I could afford Jerome's tuition, but not extra money to help his mom with bills or moving into a better neighborhood where the police didn't get possessed and Jerome wouldn't have to see dildos or risk running into perverts on his way to work every day. No, that would require my father's help.

"Can you run an errand for me?" I asked him.

"Sure, why?"

"When you make your amulets, do you get tired and hungry?"

"Yes."

"Me too, when I exorcize demons, and I am craving Chinese," I walked him towards the marshals. "Jerome is going to run and get us all Chinese food from a place called Dim Sum's. He says it's the best Chinese in the neighborhood. So, place your orders, because I'm famished, and I'm sure Tabitha, Uriel, and Raphael are too." I placed orders for me and my dad and gave Jerome far more money than he was going to need and told him to get himself and his mom some food too.

"What's going on?" Hemingway asked after Jerome had turned the corner.

"Raphael and Soleil help the needy." Uriel snipped.

"Shut up." I glared at him.

"Okay," Hemingway looked at him doubtfully.

"Those amulets are the most powerful I've seen, so it isn't like it isn't worth it, but he's all raw talent and no focus." Uriel told me.

"Not for long," I answered and explained to Hemingway, Tabitha, and Walter about Jerome's skills, his living situation, and how my dad and I could help. I didn't add that Uriel could help too, if he hadn't been paying for three coked out angels already. But I sure thought it really hard.

After a moment, Hemingway asked me how much the School of Witchcraft would cost a year. I told him, and he let out a whistle. I nodded and then I told him those amulets were basically worth their weight in gold, and they were. Tabitha agreed and said she wanted some for her five kids, because you just never knew when a kid's idea of a prank was going to result in demonic possession. Which was true. I needed a few for my nieces. I'd be sure to see how many more Jerome had to sell when he got back and how much he actually charged for them.

By the time Jerome returned, I was sitting on the steps that led up to the Division of Magic, and my stomach was growling loudly. Tabitha explained magic required a lot of energy when her stomach had growled as well. Walter nodded in agreement, having experienced it with his half a dozen fae children and wife. Jerome handed me change and I looked at him.

"I'm not a thief, and you overpaid for the amulets earlier." He told me.

"Funny, I don't feel like I overpaid you for the amulets earlier and I told you to get you and your mom something if you wanted and to keep some of the money for running to get food for us." I responded. "Also, do you have more amulets because we just realized we need some for members of our families."

"Is that your dad talking to my mom?" He asked.

"My father?" I feigned innocence.

130

"Yeah, the tall guy with the massive wings, you are a nephilim. Plus, you have the same facial structure."

"Good eye. He is making arrangements with her regarding sending you to the School of Witchcraft in exchange for making these amulets for the Bureau of Exorcism."

"I think I have ten or so left," Jerome answered. "People have been buying them like crazy the last two months." His eyes slid to the Division of Magic building and I don't think anyone needed him to say more on the subject.

"May we buy all ten?" I asked.

"You already paid for them a dozen times over." He told me. "They are only ten dollars."

"We need to work on your pricing," I told him. "These things are worth way more than that."

"Only when there are demons in town. It's a matter of supply and demand. I made a bunch when there was no demand and didn't feel right upping the price because the demand suddenly went up."

"Regardless, they are worth at least fifty a charm. Besides, how much did those angel sigils cost you?"

"I got a guy who made me a hundred of them for ten dollars and then I buy the cord cheap at the craft store when I get a coupon. Last time I got a hundred feet for three dollars. So, I might have a dollar in each one."

"Plus, your time and magic." I told him.

"That was counting time and magic," he answered. "I do all the pendants and the cord at one time. Then I just have to cut the cords and put them together."

"You can put that much magic into each pendant and the cord in a single spell?" I blinked at him.

"Yeah." He nodded once and gave me a strange look.

"When you graduate from the School of Witchcraft, I need an apprentice. Normally, I only take nephilim apprentices, but for you, I'd make an exception, if you still want to be an exorcist after you've been tortured by Uriel."

"Cool," was all he said to that. I tried not to look as astonished as I felt. I had never even heard of a wizard that could bespell charms in bulk. Possibly because one had never existed, and I wanted to the be exorcist whose apprentice eclipsed them. If in seven years, Jerome still wanted to be an exorcist.

"Amulets?" I asked after a moment. He smiled sheepishly and ran off down the road. He turned to enter an apartment building that had seen much better days, like before it was built.

I gave Valerie my card and told her if she ever needed anything, anything at all, to call me, no matter how silly she thought the request was. It wasn't just that Jerome was incredibly powerful, it was that he was incredibly powerful and living in an area of great poverty. Wizards who grew up that way tended to end up resentful, and I didn't want to face Jerome in fifteen years, after he had brought Lucifer across the Stygian.

Jerome brought us his last ten amulets and I forced him to increase his price due to demand increases, at least for us, and I gave him fifty dollars an amulet for the ten new ones. He smiled and immediately handed the money to his mother.

"You keep it, Jerome." She smiled and kissed his forehead. He looked at her not comprehending that he had just landed his mother on easy street for the rest of her life, not just while she was finishing raising him, but long after, because if Jerome's future could be secured, he would take care of his mom one day.

# Chapter 13

I handed out the remaining amulets. Those from the Division of Magic that we had given amulets to in the initial battle, we let them keep, as they went to the hospital for treatment. Now, we had to figure out who was behind it. Uriel had found remnants of a portal within one of the evidence rooms at the Division of Magic, and the cops weren't the only ones that had been possessed. Every prisoner they had brought into their holding cells for an overnight had also been possessed, of that we were sure. We had a print out of those names and theoretical addresses. But the sun was already starting to set, and we had lots of questions to discuss.

Azrael was going to meet us at the hotel. My father decided to stay longer, we were short on exorcists and Tabitha and I were capable of jerking demons from bodies and letting my father send them back to the Stygian. Because team work made the dream work.

The Chinese had made my stomach stop growling, but that was about it. Dim Sum's wasn't going to make it on Food Network's Hidden Treasures show, not unless they did a special about food poisoning. I was fairly sure one of the crunchy things in my cashew chicken had not been a burnt carrot like I had originally thought, and I wasn't a huge fan of surprise protein sources.

Then again, I tried not to be an asshole just because, so I had not mentioned the suspected cockroach to anyone else. Especially Jerome. He was a nice kid and would have felt bad about it, even though he was in no way responsible.

Azrael had a feast laid out for us when we arrived back at the hotel. There were multiple meats, side dishes of vegetables, and we were informed of our soup choices as well as being told the salad dressing options for our practically mandatory bowls of salad. I went with the house balsamic because it was hard to screw up. Azrael had at least waited for us, though.

He had brought us two more exorcists, one a witch who was able to deaden sound, not letting it escape from our gathering. I told him about Jerome. My father made pleasantries, but obviously wanted nothing more than to go to bed. He had flexed some magic muscles he hadn't even stretched in a long time.

Hemingway mentioned the Coven of Seven, and everyone agreed it didn't make sense, covens almost always have twelve members, although thirteen is preferred. I was enjoying a Cuban sandwich when klaxons sounded, and I had this insane idea that the hotel was about to dive.

"Worse," my father pointed, and I realized I had projected the mental image of the submerging hotel to him.

If it had been Azrael pointing, I probably would have punched him. He was the youngest archangel at barely older than the Great Pyramid of Giza, and possibly my favorite uncle. Nepotism was alive and well in the Bureau of Exorcism.

Through the large windows behind me, the city looked like Mother Nature was set to wipe it from the face of the Earth. Large storm clouds had moved in and the rain was coming down so hard the drops were audible against the concrete and stone outside the windows. They were big too, every bit as big as a piece of hail. I almost thought it was hail, until the hail started. Massive chunks of ice fell straight down, despite the howling of the wind. They shattered on impact, throwing shards that looked like daggers away from the explosions. Over Lake Michigan, a funnel cloud was forming.

"Fucking really?" I muttered out loud. I could defeat zombies even when they had deer souls in them, but I didn't think I could magic my way into defeating a monster storm. Unless it wasn't just a storm, "Fucking really." I muttered again and put my head down on the table.

The klaxon got quieter as my head lay on the table, because I was covering my ears with my arms. I didn't need to hear them to know that the funnel cloud would turn into a tornado that would hit the hotel. I did need some quiet, so I could pull my thoughts together.

After a moment of that, I realized that my thoughts were together and mostly I just wanted the klaxon turned off.

"We are evacuating all guests to the bomb shelter," a waiter came to our table and told us.

"Awesome, good plan," I tried not to sound snippy and failed. "Nothing like trapping everyone in a steel waterproof container so they can suffocate when the flood comes.

"Soleil?" Azrael asked.

"Chaac," was the only answer I had. "Chaac came across the divide."

"That's impossible," Azrael told me.

"Well, yes," I agreed. "But have you ever seen hail as large as an emu egg?"

"No." Everyone answered.

"That leaves Chaac, and as the storm frightens more people, it will get worse because he will gain power from it." In my head I listed the personnel with us, three archangels, a nephilim, a witch, two vampires, two mortal US Marshals, a slew of supernatural hotel staff, "and a partridge in a pear tree." I said the last bit out loud even though I hadn't meant to.

"What does the partridge do?" Tabitha asked.

"Not much," I shrugged. "Everyone capable of doing exorcisms should come outside. Hemingway and Kemp go to your suites."

There was a tornado over Lake Michigan steadily moving closer when I got those that could exorcise, outside. Although since it was over water, I guess it was technically a water spout. However, water spouts didn't sound dangerous, and this one was currently ripping things off a cargo vessel stranded on the water.

"Who is Chaac?" Tabitha asked me.

"A major pain in the ass," Azrael told her.

"Such an understatement," I told Azrael. But at least it wasn't a prince. It took a while for my eyes to find Chaac where the water and tornado met. He was standing there, levitating slightly on wind currents produced by the tornado, and he wasn't a translucent spirit.

The witch quickly handed out pieces of chalk. I accepted it and immediately drew a pentagram. She drew an angel sigil and then blushed since Raphael was standing right next to me.

The supernatural doorman was standing with us, as was the elevator attendant. They both drew their own power symbols on the ground, one was a tree of life, the other was the eye of Horus.

I drew pentagrams because they were easy, and I was not an artist. My father's symbol was a rotund woman with no facial features and large pendulous breasts, the eternal mother. When he stepped on it, the stick figure, white chalk lines turned gold and looked alive. For the briefest flash, I could see the magic flow into him from the symbol.

Azrael had drawn a half moon shape, and like the Eternal Mother, it glowed gold as soon as Azrael stepped on it. I followed their lead. My pentagram drawing energy from the world around me and sending it into me. I felt my own magic swell with the addition of the magic funneled from the pentagram.

My father shot first, a flaming ball of magic a little larger than a pumpkin. It was undaunted by the down pour or the ice, and for the first time, I realized I wasn't getting wet. Wards kept an area beyond the canopy dry and safe from the ice missiles,"

The magic hit Chaac and he appeared to lose control of his tornado for a fraction of a second. I would have felt better if all the archangels would have been there, but Raphael was the strongest alive, so having him made me feel slightly better.

Azrael and Uriel released magic at the exact same moment. I took a breath to steady myself and released my own into the dark storm that shielded the monster. As the magic energy balls hit him, he continued to move closer. Our magic landed in quick succession but didn't do near the damage Raphael's had done. Then I remembered Focalar and my next burst of magic wasn't a flaming ball meant to singe him, but the spell of exorcism. In my head, I separated the spirit of Chaac from the monster's body.

The storm did not intensify immediately. Chaac laughed and then it intensified. Uriel turned to look at me, but he and Azrael didn't ask questions, instead I felt them begin to gather in their magic. Lisa, Brooke, our witch exorcist, the vampire Gunter Maxim, and Tabitha looked at me oddly, but they followed my lead. The magic involved in the right of exorcism feels a little weird because it isn't all that dissimilar from death magic. Lisa and Gunter focused their energies using spell words. Tabitha touched the little angel sigil amulet, using it as her focus.

I gathered magic for another go at Chaac. He was floating towards us on wind currents, I thought about calling him a show off, but one shouldn't antagonize monsters from the Stygian if it can be helped.

Cop cars were pulling up now. Their lights strobing in the storm, bouncing off the buildings and lake. No one got out and as Chaac drew closer, several threw it into reverse and backed up. The elevator attendant was strengthening the wards that protected the hotel. The doorman was pouring power into the ground that fed into our magic symbols, making us stronger. Both had to be wizards and I briefly wondered why they weren't doing something that paid more money.

A bolt of lightning struck just outside the protection of the wards, and I felt my hair stand up in response. Damn storm god. Then Chaac's feet touched solid land and the storm somehow managed to get worse. "Fan-fucking-tabulous," I thought and hit him with the magic I had been gathering. His steps faltered, and he screamed wordlessly.

Then his body danced, and the sound of automatic gunfire grew louder than the storm that raged overhead. Chaac was bleeding, which was good. As his blood hit the rain-soaked ground, it fed his magic into the pentagram at my feet.

"On three," I shouted holding up three fingers. When I pulled the last finger down, I felt the magic surge out from all of us. It slammed into Chaac and his body collapsed as his spirit was torn from it. The storm slowed. The tornado dissipated.

Chaac was absolutely not happy. His spirit floated to me, grabbing me by the throat. For something that wasn't solid, there was a lot of strength in his fingertips and tomorrow I would sport bruises from it. He said something to me in a language I didn't understand.

"I don't speak Mayan," I croaked struggling to get the words out.

"He called you a bunch of names," Azrael said helpfully. I gave the archangel the finger and then pointed at Chaac. "Send him back," Azrael told me. I considered flipping him off again. I focused my energy and forced Chaac across the Stygian Divide. He was still muttering in Mayan and I guessed he was still calling me names. I had never actually exorcized a living spirit from its body. I had always suspected I could do it, but it had been theoretical. Especially with something as powerful as Chaac.

The cops were standing around the monster's body. I wouldn't know what to do with it either. It was more than ten feet tall, solid blue, very muscled, meaning very heavy, and there were extra limbs that made it seem even more awkward to move. Chaac was what happened when a being from this plane made a deal with a Stygian demon and used his soul as a bartering tool.

Chaac had probably once been a nice enough person, he had probably wanted more corn or better looks, whatever, and he had used his soul to get it. As he aged, something from the Stygian had come and collected it and turned it into Chaac the Storm God who was actually just a monster that could control weather.

And if those responsible for the possession of the Division of Magic officers could bring Chaac onto this plane, then bringing forth a prince wasn't impossible. Or any of the other destructive monsters that lived in the Stygian.

According to my father, H. P. Lovecraft had gotten a glimpse of the Stygian and the monsters from his stories were the way he had kept his sanity. Lovecraft had become required reading when you trained to be an exorcist. Which was fine with me, because how could you not adore Lovecraftian horror. Although, after seeing Chaac, I guessed I could sort of understand why someone might not. I was positive I was going to have nightmares tonight about witches and Stygian monsters and tornadoes. Demons and monsters and witches, oh my.

"I am in over my head," I announced to no one special.

"That was actually brilliant," Uriel told me.

"Um, yeah." I shrugged. "Now, for the love of everything sacred, who the fuck brought him over and what else can they bring across the divide?"

"Language," Raphael said to me. I nodded.

"Sorry, in the name of all that is sane and holy, who the fucking hell brought him over the Stygian Divide?" I said again with more annoyance in my voice. My father hid a smile. I had been raised with parents who didn't swear, and I still couldn't in front of my mother, not really. A few here and there, but definitely no f-bombs, my mother was convinced dish soap had been invented for the mouths of daughters that swore.

"I don't know," Uriel was excited. His mouth was moving faster than his brain. "But in all my years, that is the first time I have ever seen someone use exorcism to defeat a Stygian monster. I don't know how you thought of

141

it, but it was amazing." I tried not to be offended by his comment, but it was hard not to take it personally. I tried to remind myself that my uncle was mostly a moron, even if he was very talented at teaching exorcism to all sorts of beings.

# Chapter 14

Surprise, surprise. My clock said it was three thirty in the morning when I awoke from a dream about Cthulhu the main monster from Lovecraft's short stories, and a witch trying to ride on a house in a tornado. I knew I would dream about monsters, witches, and tornadoes, but knowing it would happen and having it happen were two different things and it was annoying. I got dressed in sweats and a sports bra under my T-shirt, slipped on tennis shoes, and went down into the lobby.

"Beef jerky?" The front desk attendant asked as I got out of the elevator. There was a new elevator attendant and he hadn't had beef jerky.

"Please," I said. He handed me a bag.

"Thank you for stopping Chaac from destroying the hotel and city." He told me.

"You're welcome, except I didn't do it alone and I think I was the reason he targeted the hotel."

"The hotel is always a target," he said immediately after making a scoffing noise. "It sits over one of the original portals, one of the closed ones. So anytime something wicked blows into Chicago, the hotel is targeted. Last time, it was a giant spider."

143

"Huh," I said gnawing on a piece of jerky. "But zombies hit the other hotel I was at."

"Oh, I didn't mean to imply it wasn't at least partly because of you." He countered and sipped from a cup. "Would you like a cup of Irish coffee?" He said offering me his cup to taste test from.

"Too early for me," I responded. "Who guards your closed portal?" I asked.

"A local coven, with some very powerful witches in it." He answered.

"I don't suppose there are only seven members in this coven?"

"Nope, it's a full coven of thirteen." A closed portal is just a door with plywood over it. There were twenty worldwide and five lay in the US. The governments of places with portals demanded that they be watched carefully, because you never knew when someone was going to kick through the plywood. Their locations were kept secret for that very reason.

"I don't suppose you know any covens of seven in town?" I asked, continuing to chew on the jerky.

"No, I'm not a witch or wizard, but Bernard, our doorman, might know. He and Taylor, the elevator attendant that joined you outside earlier, run the local registry."

"Good to know. Are they home sleeping it off?"

"They live here." The front desk man said.

"That seems like you wouldn't get much of a break from work if you worked here and lived here."

"It's a service we offer to all our employees. I live here with my family."

"Crowded in a hotel room with a family," I said.

"No, we have two floors of apartments that are above ground and two floors that are below ground. I don't have to commute to work, which saves me money, I have a housekeeper which helps my wife out, and we can order food from the kitchen instead of going out to eat with the kids if we don't feel like cooking. It's how she and I can afford to send our children to private school." He told me.

"By private school, I'm assuming one of the private magic schools," I said not actually commenting on his triple irises.

"Yes, we have three kids that attend Legend School." He told me.

"Any of them want to be exorcists when they grow up, I feel like I need an apprentice." I commented dryly.

"My wife would lose her mind," he smiled at me.

"Yeah, my mother nearly did as well." The Legend School was short for the Legendary School of the Divine, the name annoyed me because angels weren't divine, and they went there to learn to deal with their powers and zealots who still couldn't wrap their tiny little brains around the fact that angels weren't divine. However, the front desk man didn't have wings, or if he did his suit was tailored so well they couldn't be seen.

"I lost my wings," he said after a moment and I felt bad it had been so obvious I was looking. "When I was in school, a bully in our class cut them off and set them on fire, trying to kill me because I refused to give him my pocket money every week."

"Must not have been smart enough to realize they had to be burned with hell fire," I tried not to sound grim.

"He wasn't. He mostly wanted to make an example of me, kill me and keep the other kids from also refusing to give up their lunch money." He seemed to drift from the present for a moment.

"Except, that would have sent him to prison, he wasn't the brightest bulb in the box, was he? If you ever decide you want them back, talk to Michael the archangel," I told him, giving him Michael's card. Michael was a recluse these days and I only saw him once every handful of years. But recluse or not, he was a fantastic healer.

"No, he wasn't, but that's often how it is with bullies, isn't it? I heard Michael had died," the front desk man said.

"Nope just reclusive even by the standards of a recluse, Michael moved to a cave when I was a kid, even I don't know exactly where it is, but he comes out to deal with special problems, like an angel without wings." I shrugged. "Thanks for the jerky. Would you leave a note for someone to ring me when Bernard or Taylor comes on duty?"

"Of course, Miss Burns." He paused for a moment. "We have made sure that we have plenty of beef jerky in stock should you desire more later."

I nodded my thanks and walked back to the elevator. This elevator attendant was human, no special irises. He took me back to the tenth floor without me having to ask. I gave him a couple of bucks for it. Hemingway was standing outside the door of my suite when I arrived.

"You're awake." He said, seemingly surprised.

"Demons and monsters and witches, oh my," I told him.

"Yeah, I don't think I should have watched from the window. I woke up because I had a dream about that thing riding a tornado."

"I imagine everyone will comment on how badly they slept come morning." I held out the bag of jerky. He looked at it for a moment and then took a piece.

146

"You have a terrible diet. Jerky at four in the morning?" He said as he took a bite of the piece he had gotten out of the bag.

"Magic is energy and exorcism magic depletes protein." I said swiping my card at the door and pushing it open. "Since I can't afford steak at every meal unless my father is paying for it, I eat cheeseburgers and beef jerky." I shrugged. "I also eat vegetables and things. It isn't like I only eat cheeseburgers."

"I had never thought of that." He said. "That explains why Walter's wife is constantly fixing barbecue when we are in town."

"She's a fairy, she doesn't know any better," I plopped down on the couch.

"Know better than what?" Hemingway asked.

"She doesn't realize humans have to do extra sit-ups to work off barbecue sauce, potato salad, and steak. Magic is what keeps supernaturals thin. I may not eat myself into a heart attack, but I could starve myself to death since I mostly use exorcism magic. However, in the case of Walter's wife, fairies are taught to feed guests and most fae are under the impression that humans are serious carnivores."

"Could you do other magic?" He asked.

"Sure, if I practiced it." I shrugged. "But I suffer from a severe lack of self-discipline. I prefer to watch movies over practicing magic. My sister has gotten much better with her magic since having kids."

"Because she's teaching them?" He asked. "Are they also nephilim?"

"Yes, and yes, but only a quarter angel. Her husband is a mortal." I told him.

"You don't like mortals?" He asked.

"I don't like him," I answered. "Dantalian has a better personality than my brother in law and is probably more faithful."

"Wow, you really don't like him."

"Nope, I used to say if my sister could live with him, I could live around him, but I've been changing my mind slowly over time they've been married."

"Do you think Grigorii was lying when he said a coven of seven brought him over?" He asked suddenly.

"No, I think a coven of seven really brought him over." I sighed and ate another piece of beef jerky. "Demons don't lie as often as everyone thinks, mainly because they can't. They can tell the truth or a half truth, but an outright lie weakens their magic."

"How so?" He asked.

"I don't know the magical mechanics of it, I just know that it does. Maybe they aren't creative enough to lie and so they have to use magic to make a lie believable." I shrugged. Besides, just because it sounded insane didn't mean it wasn't the truth.

"In your honest opinion, does this have anything to do with my fugitive or should I look for him without you?" He asked.

"Somehow, it's all related." I told Hemingway, wondering if I really believed it or if I just didn't want him to leave yet. I liked having him around. It wasn't love, but I definitely lusted after him a bit. And who knew what time might bring.

"Have you ever done a criminal investigation?" He asked.

"No, but mass demonic possession is treated like a communicable disease investigation, which is why I got the records from the Cook County Health Department." I had forgotten to call them back yesterday and put it on my mental to-do list for today. "However, I'm meeting with the registrar of covens in the Chicago area later today."

"Good plan." Hemingway didn't look at me.

"I hope so. Registration isn't required for covens, unless one of their members has a criminal record."

"Are there a lot of criminal witches?" Hemingway smirked.

"More than you'd think, criminality in supernaturals happens at nearly the same rate as in humans. One of the witches I went to school with used her powers to rob a bank. Totally ridiculous, because if she had a brain, she would have remembered that magic is traceable and realized that floating bags of money out of a bank in front of witnesses would lead right back to her doorstep like footprints in the snow." I shrugged. "But criminals aren't winning a lot of awards for brilliance, and that's true of all criminals."

"Is it possible my fugitive is responsible for these mass possession attacks?"

"Your fugitive is human, so it's unlikely." I looked at Hemingway. "You don't know much about supernaturals, do you?"

"Just what I've learned from Tabitha. I was basically raised in a barn where the paranormal didn't leak in through the cracks."

"Why?" I asked.

"My father was afraid of supernaturals. He built an end of days bunker and," Hemingway paused. "Have you ever seen the movie with Brendan Fraser where he lives in the fallout shelter his entire life with his parents?"

"Yes."

"Instead of LA picture that in Wyoming." Hemingway said. "Madness runs in my family."

"I take it that means you aren't related to the writer?" I said.

"Yes, actually, he was a cousin of my grandfather's." Hemingway told me. "So, I guess to be fair, alcoholism and madness run in the family."

"How old were you when you left the bunker?" I asked.

"I was ten. My father moved us into the bunker before I was born so that I wouldn't be turned into a vampire or anything like that, but someone reported that I wasn't in school and when the social worker showed up and uncovered the bunker door to talk to my parents about me, my father killed himself, because she was a vampire."

"I'm sorry you had to endure that." I told him.

"My father was a nut. I spent my first several years at school terrified that I was going to end up a supernatural, beings I had never met before but I was still convinced were freaks."

"That's pretty gloomy." I admitted.

"Right? When I was fifteen there was this lovely girl in one of my classes, just gorgeous with pretty brunette curls, and for the first time I was glad my father was dead, because I was sure she liked me, but she had the triple irises of a full blooded supernatural. I asked her out, she said yes, and my first date turned out to be a werewolf." Hemingway told me. "An amazing werewolf, but a werewolf none-the-less and my father would have forbidden it while my mom was just glad I was finally making friends."

"What happened to your werewolf?" I asked.

"We got engaged our senior year of high school because she got pregnant. It was stillborn, and we grew apart. We split up and both of us went to different colleges. About ten years ago, she married another lycanthrope that we had gone to high school with, he owns a car dealership in our small town and is loaded. She and I still talk from time to time when I go home to see my mom. Oddly, she talked about turning me when we got engaged, I decided we should wait until we were married, but bunker boy was nearly a werewolf, my father would have rolled over in his grave."

"Do you have any happy stories?" I asked him.

"Sure," he answered but didn't share one. "What about you?"

"My last boyfriend was eaten by a polar bear in Alaska where there honestly shouldn't have been a polar bear."

"So, you've got a knack for the cheerful too."

"I'm a nephilim, I don't have to be happy to make other people happy." I smiled.

"Then you're unhappy?"

"Most nephilim are unhappy," I said. "I think we spend so much time making other people happy that we rarely figure out what makes us happy. Thankfully, we have eternity to figure it out. Do you have much experience with criminal investigations?" I asked.

"I was a detective in robbery/homicide at the Kansas City Police Department before I became a US Marshal," he told me.

"Good, aside from the coven registry, where else do we look for a coven of witches?"

"The cemetery," he answered.

"That's an old wives' tale," I said, frowning.

"Maybe, but those zombies came from somewhere and that clothing wasn't modern, meaning they came from an old cemetery. I believe witches have to be close to their intended targets to raise the dead, hence a cemetery."

"Oh, and travel logs," I added.

"Why?"

"Because the day before I met you, I had to deal with a demonic zombie in the Three Rivers Mall."

"So?" He asked.

"Well, it just seems strange that the zombie I dealt with contained Dantalian. Then we get here, and I deal with another demonic zombie, and once again, it's Dantalian. It leads me to believe the same witch was involved both times."

"Why?"

"Because demons take turns when it's random, but witches can turn to specific demons to lend them a hand. Dantalian and Lumia were from the same bloodline, so if the witch had turned to Astaroth for demonic help, it would make sense for Dantalian to show up at both locations."

# Chapter 15

Around five in the morning, Hemingway admitted he was exhausted, but didn't want to go back to his room. He'd been dreaming about demons since he arrived in Chicago and now he got to add Chaac to the dreams. We fell asleep on the sofa in the living room of my suite.

The sun was incredibly determined to come in around the blackout curtains and rouse me from my slumber. I had a crick in my neck and my leg was all tingly from lack of blood flow, but I had been sleeping good. And daylight meant dealing with more demons. Which would turn into nightmares tonight or worse, like more naked Dantalian. I had no desire to share dream space with Dantalian, although it was better than sharing it with Freddy Krueger, but that was all I could say for the matter.

Everyone was at breakfast in the hotel restaurant when we came down. My father had this look, so I glared at him. That was the problem with mind reading fathers. Or one of the problems. Well, there were so many I couldn't have made a list if I used a five subject notebook while writing very small, but it was one of the big ones for a daughter.

I ordered bacon and three fried eggs, over medium, plus biscuits with cheese on them, because hey, I could.

And I knew the bill was going to my father. As an afterthought, I also ordered a glass of milk, a glass of orange juice, and a glass of chocolate milk, again, see above.

I cleaned my plate, because nightmares or not, I always had a good appetite and food equaled fuel for magic. I didn't want to wither away into nothingness. Besides, I didn't know what kind of magic I'd need today or how much of it, but after facing Chaac, I wasn't ruling anything out. There could be a giant three headed poisonous frog monster that came into existence over the Sears Tower before lunch got here.

Uriel had a double stack of pancakes with sausage, scrambled eggs, and two pieces of toast, meaning I wasn't the only one loading up for a day full of magical terrors and nasty beasts. The other supernaturals also appeared to be preparing for war with their food portions. Only the humans seemed to have single plates with recommended portion sizes. The rest of us looked like we were feeding tape worms. Especially since it's hard for a supernatural to get overweight. Oh, it happened, but it required dedication and effort, and pretty much no magic ever. Even lighting a freaking candle with magical flame took energy. Of course, I couldn't do that, and envied beings that could.

I finished the last couple bites of bacon and ordered a white coffee to go. My father looked pained as it was brought to the table. I smiled sweetly, took a sip, and added another bit of milk and two more sugar cubes., waiting for my father to start convulsing. Now, I was ready to rock and roll or something. Probably more something than rock and roll.

And much to my surprise, something was waiting just beyond the wards that protected the hotel. It was a protest and they were protesting me. Handing out signs and shouting at people going in and out of the hotel. I rolled my eyes looking at the terrible photo of myself that they had appropriated and drawn a circle with a line through it on their placards. Someone yelled murderer and I rolled my eyes. Which I thought showed restraint, I could have flipped them off.

Anyone that was willing to join a demon rights group either didn't know any demons personally or they did and were good with death and chaos. Azrael, ever the consummate politician stepped forward to talk about Chaac in Chicago the night before. I ignored them and returned to the hotel.

"I am so sorry, Miss Burns, I should have warned you they were there," the doorman said to me. It wasn't the one I wanted to talk to, it was someone else, but he was half supernatural. I told him it was no big deal, but I was annoyed about the ambush. I could have gone through the hotel and into the garage if I had known Beings for the Establishment of Demon Rights was out front. But, aha, I had a restraining order against the group as a whole. I turned on my heels and marched right back out front. Raphael put his hand on my shoulder and I didn't say what had popped into my head. Hemingway touched my shoulder and I turned and went back into the hotel.

"I have a restraining order, no member of BEADER, is allowed within a thousand feet of me or any location where I am," I told the doorman. He blanched and stammered. "Some of them are staying at the damn hotel, aren't they?" I asked, keeping my temper under control. The group knew about the restraining order, it wasn't the hotel's fault they were in violation and I felt bad for them.

"Yes, Miss Burns," the front desk man from the night before said. "But not for much longer."

"Did you say BEADER?" Hemingway asked.

155

"Stupid name, right?"

"Yes," he answered.

The front desk man took hold of my hand carefully and we went to the doors together. My father followed as well, and I had serious concerns about this. The doors were opened for us and the front desk man, whose name I didn't even know, yeah, I might be a snob I thought, took me onto the front steps.

"Miss Burns has just informed hotel management that she has a restraining order against your silly little organization because of chicanery just like this. Everyone staying at this hotel that supports demon rights, your things are being packed by the staff and they will be brought down to you. You will not be given a refund, and I will have you know that you nearly died last night because a storm god named Chaac decided to demolish the hotel while you slept and it was Miss Burns that saved your asses, because no matter how good our wards, they cannot withstand pummeling by a Mayan Storm God, now go away and never darken our steps again." He shouted at them. Bags began to fall from the floors above us like the hail stones last night.

Nearly every bag busted open as it hit, and I realized they were being hurled from the roof. Some of the lingerie was rather steamy, even by the standards of a woman that had stood in a sex store a few days ago talking about graffiti.

"My deepest apologies, Miss Burns, we were told they were here to protest the tearing down of the Moloch Cemetery." He bowed to me and scudded back inside.

"Moloch is a demon," I told Hemingway. "Well, he was a demon. He's dead now. But you name cemeteries after people and archangels and saints, not demons."

"That is weird." Hemingway agreed.

"It couldn't possibly be that simple," I sighed as my eyes swept the crowd.

"What?" Hemingway asked.

"We need to find that cemetery."

Inside, the front desk man, whose name was plainly displayed on his shirt, proving I was an asshole, tried to smile while also hoping I wasn't coming to yell at him. I read the name and blinked at it twice and then a third time just for good measure. "Judge, where is that cemetery?" I asked the front desk man.

"Miss Burns, my friends and family call me Jay." He said in confusion.

"Jay, my friends and family call me Asha, not Miss Burns. Do you know where the Moloch Cemetery is?"

"Of course, Asha," he gave me a look.

"Yep, no clue why it's short for Soleil," I shrugged at him. He kept his opinion on my name to himself, which was what people very good at customer service did.

"Let me get you a map, it is hard to find even with directions, and you can't GPS it." Jay said to me.

"You are amazing," I told him and really meant it, so I turned up the magic a little, so he'd feel the depth of my gratitude. He stopped looking quite as nervous as he handed a map to Hemingway.

We entered the hotel parking garage from the entryway inside the hotel and I had to smile, a lot, as the Idiots who Loved Demons were deprived of seeing our car leave the front garage entrance, by my father, Uriel, and Azrael on the steps of the hotel, giving an impromptu press conference. And then there were a dozen or so cop cars all marked Division of Magic parked about a block from their protest.

157

"I always thought they were joking when the news said there were people who lobbied for demon rights," Tabitha said from the back seat.

"They started out by sitting on the front steps of the Bureau of Exorcism. Azrael threatened to have them all possessed, so they started stalking exorcists. Last year, they filmed me killing a demon. The group tried to have me arrested on murder charges, when no one would do it, they started protesting every time they are able to figure out where I am. About six months ago, they got a little girl killed by a demon, Moloch to be exact, Azrael and Uriel killed him, because there isn't a prison on the planet that can hold a demon, and I got a restraining order. Normally, they are smart enough not to violate it."

"Why would someone want demons given rights?" Hemingway asked.

"Because, for every cause there is someone that wants to join hands and sing kumbaya, and feel like they belong." I shrugged. "Personally, I don't understand it. If they ever became possessed or had to deal with their child becoming possessed, they'd call me to come slip into their house under cover of dark and fix it."

"They were pawns," Walter said. "Someone had to tell them you were there, we've had zero news coverage, and whoever told them, did it before Chaac showed up."

"Two birds, one stone," I offered.

"Chaac was the stone," Walter said.

"Yep, pity we took the wind out of his sails," Tabitha gave a wry chuckle. "I kind of like this stuff."

"Exorcism is its own reward most of the time." I told her.

"Don't go putting in for a job transfer," Hemingway said to her.

"I won't, but it's kind of cool to be able to do minor exorcisms," Tabitha told him.

"Uriel can teach you more, and it would be an asset to a team like this," I told her. "For that matter, Uriel could teach all of you stuff. Humans can do exorcisms, too."

"Don't forget to navigate." Hemingway said to Tabitha.

"Hemingway is old fashioned and prefers to shoot the bad guys," Tabitha was still smiling, and it had nothing to do with me.

Unfortunately, we didn't need the map, not for the last half mile. There were protestors on both sides of the street, which meant if Moloch Cemetery was where the zombies had come from, all the evidence would be trampled. Most of the protestors were not there regarding demon rights. They were there because, according to their signs, Moloch Cemetery had been the first criminal graveyard in Chicago. And the mayor was in front of the cemetery with a couple of guys wearing hard hats who didn't look like construction workers. I wasn't sure saving a graveyard full of the bones of old criminals was worth the fuss and muss, but I wasn't a history buff. It was hard to stay interested in it when you grew up with your father telling you what the books and teachers kept getting wrong and he knew because he was there.

Hemingway got out and he and his companions hid their badges from the TV cameras. I guessed it was possible Don Rabblings was watching the news about this event. Or would see the highlights at some point.

As we walked with the crowd someone shouted my name. I didn't turn around to look at them, instead I looked down and kept walking. Knowing my luck, it was someone with BDR and I would be asked to leave, since they were here first.

Moloch Cemetery was everything an old cemetery should be. Large iron gate. Tall stone walls covered in ivy, some of it the itchy kind. Big old weeping willow trees, meaning it had a wasp infestation problem, with a cobblestone street and sidewalk leading up to it.

My name was called again, and I finally turned. Jerome and his mom were walking towards me. I gave them a smile and small wave, as I slowed down. Lisa gave me a look and I smiled at her too. Talk about a witch in for a surprise.

"Hiya, Jerome," I said as they caught up to us. "This here is Lisa, and she works with me; she's a witch and an exorcist."

"Cool," Jerome said.

"You here to protest the closing of the cemetery?" I asked.

"No," his mom said. "This thing is an eyesore. We're here to talk to the public about the fact that the not so nice kind of witches hang out here. My husband told us never to come here, even during the day." Valerie told me.

"Is this close to your house?" I asked.

"Three blocks," Jerome pointed. I nodded but wanted to explode. We were three blocks from Jerome's apartment building, which was only a couple of blocks from the Division of Magic.

"Soleil," Lisa said. I turned, and her face was white. Walking towards the mayor and other men near the cemetery gate were a half dozen people in hooded robes. If there had only been seven, I would have gotten excited.

"Did you make any more amulets after I left last night Jerome?"

"Sure did, there was no power. I couldn't play video games, so we went to the craft store after you left, and I bought more pendants. Mom said I didn't have to do my homework last night because I was changing schools, and we talked about moving and where I would want to live if we did." He told me. "They aren't the pretty angel sigils, but your dad said anything would work." Awesome dad. I thought and nodded my head. Jerome looked every bit of thirteen, chattering away, not fully understanding what was going on, just knowing it had a lot to do with him and those nifty amulets, and maybe his mom had won the lottery. He didn't understand his mom had won the lottery the day he was born and that the only reason she was even considering moving was because of him, which is why she had asked his thoughts. I scolded myself, no she probably asked for his opinion on where he wanted to live because I got the impression Valerie was a very good mom.

"Cool, do you have any with you? My friend Lisa needs one." I told him. "And so does your mom." I dug out money from my wallet and handed it to Jerome. Jerome gave me a lovely silver and red crystal rose, that I bet cost more than ten dollars just for the single pendant and bail. I gave it to Lisa who slipped it over her head and let out a small surprised gasp. "I know, right," I said to her and Hemingway held up the pendant with Gabriel's sigil on it. Valerie pulled a necklace from beneath the collar of her shirt that had a big J on it.

"I managed to make seventeen last night because mom couldn't go to work with the thing over the lake, so she cut and tied all the cords for me."

"That is excellent." I told Jerome checking to make sure he was also wearing one. He was. Somehow, I needed the Mayor of Chicago to get one from Jerome. "I know you can draw a power symbol, but can you do protective circles?" I asked remembering him drawing a pentagram for me.

"Of course," he said.

161

"Good, get ready to draw one for you and your mom," I told him, and Hemingway helped move Jerome and Valerie into an empty spot near a doorway.

"Oh boy," Jerome said.

"Yes," I agreed while I said a string of curse words in my head that Jerome at thirteen didn't need to hear.

"Are we in danger?" Valerie asked.

"I doubt it," I told her. "Stay very close to your son though."

And then Lisa had to point out I was wrong, she said my name, as a magic ball went whizzing past us. It collided with an older man. Jerome took a step towards him, but I grabbed the teen.

"You have lots of magic, enough to protect you and your mom. We will help the others." I looked at him, leaning down so we were eye level. "Here's the deal, Jerome, I feel like if those guys in robes find out how powerful you are, they are going to come after you. So, keep your magic mostly hidden." I kept eye contact and he nodded gently. "And can I get the rest of the amulets?" Jerome handed them to me as his mom pulled out an ink pen. He shook his head at her and pulled out his tagger's spray can. He drew a circle on the ground around his mom and himself. I felt the magic lock into place. Walter was checking on the man that had been hit by the magic spell.

"Lisa, stay with them, until my dad or uncles show up." I told the witch.

"What about you?" She asked.

"What about me?" I countered and looked at Jerome. "He does that spell in bulk on the pendants and the cords. He must stay safe." Lisa looked profoundly impressed. I really wanted to call my father and have him fly here. But Raphael probably sensed that I needed him, and he couldn't fly and talk on the phone, no matter how much I wanted his reassurances that he was on his way.

Another magic spell whizzed past me and hit Hemingway. I started to go to him, but he waved me on and the amulet he wore burned with a cold blue light that told me it was working. No demons in him, not yet. I didn't know how much hammering the sigils could take, but they felt powerful enough to take a lot.

Another slammed into him and he ducked behind a car, sigil still acting like a flashlight. One raced towards me. Holy hell, this was the penalty for lusting after coworkers, you got hit by possession hexes. My sigil burned, as did the hell fire in my arm and then the hell fire began emitting sparks as the hex tried to open my body to a stowaway. Angels could not be possessed, although nephilim could if the demon was strong enough. The information was public knowledge, but it didn't stop people from trying to hex nephilim and angels into demonic hosts.

The hood from one of the people trying to grab the mayor fell, and it was the head Idiot for Demon Rights. Fucking really! I shouted into the air above the crowd because I wanted to walk up there and throttle her. I hadn't liked her when I woke up this morning, her being here in a robe trying to possess people didn't make me like her more.

I stomped past the mayor's security goons who were busy with the oh-great-robed ones and handed him the amulet. He almost dropped it but didn't and let it hang from his fingertips.

"Put it on so the Beings for Demons, can't force you into possession and make you sign wacky demons should have rights legislation for the city of Chicago," I told him.

"Who are you?" He asked.

"Soleil Burns, exorcist with the Bureau of Exorcism, and his daughter," I said hooking a thumb over my shoulder at my father who was landing behind me somewhere.

"You're an archangel?" He asked.

"No, I'm nephilim, my father is the archangel Raphael." I told him, as he began to put the amulet on. I started handing him the others. "Give these to your people." He blinked at me, like a man confused. His tiger pendant was glowing. Oh fan-fucking-tabulous...

The mayor of Chicago tried to pull the pendant off, but it was stuck and burned his hand." The demon rights people were late to the party, and he had not given any indication of possession. That was impossible.

"Soleil, move!" My father's voice shouted at me and I jerked back from the mayor.

Energy just missed me, hitting the mayor in the chest. The mayor laughed, and the sound was like broken glass in a grinder. I forced myself to not cover my ears as I gathered magic. Someone screamed. The Head Idiot was looking like someone just peed on her. And maybe someone had. She was turning tail and running towards me.

"We didn't do that, Soleil." She stammered.

"Blech," I responded.

"Soleil, we only infect with incubi or succubae," she pleaded. That was definitely not the sound either of those demons would make.

"You should definitely run like hell, unless you also know how to do exorcisms, and then you should perform a few on the people your group infected with demons, as you flee from this one." I told her.

"I do know, let me help," she said.

164

"I told you how to help," I told her. "If you stay here, you are liable to get yourself killed," I didn't add that would piss me off even more than what she had just tried to do, because I would feel guilty if they died.

"Soleil, we're outnumbered," Uriel shouted.

"No, we aren't," I told him, throwing him the five amulets I had left. I did not look at Jerome, but I wanted to. Oh, good lord, this was going to get messy. My magic had gathered around me thick enough I could see it. And I was sure it wasn't enough. I dropped to one knee and drew a pentagram. The demonic mayor laughed at me, which was sort of what demons did before they got ready to try and kick your butt. I did not return the laugh. This demon was stronger than me if he could hide that he was even there. I had never seen a demon do that, never.

A net flew over my head, a magic net, not unlike a fishing net. Normally, it would have immobilized a demonic host. This demon tore it to pieces before it could even land on him. I did not cast the spell of exorcism, instead I let the magic swirl around me. Because the magic net meant that the Division of Magic was on scene.

"Soleil," I heard Jerome yell my name and I wished I had the ability to make him invisible. The mayor's eyes flicked to him, but they didn't comprehend what they saw. I needed a fairy. Lisa must have seen the look on my face, because suddenly Jerome and his mom disappeared, but there was a pentagram about a foot from his protective circle and there were a couple of witches, including the Idiot from Demon Rights, opening cuts on their hands. Blood magic is almost as powerful as death magic. I dashed backwards towards the pentagram that was already glowing red with the magic from the blood. Raphael, Uriel, Azrael, Lisa, and a few others were drawing their own power symbols on the ground.

And now, even mortals were cutting their hands and pressing their palms to the ground, letting the greedy earth drink of their blood, and my power swelled until I felt I would explode. Uriel cast a spell, it hit the demonic host in the chest and the demon inside didn't even shudder at it. We were in trouble.

I beckoned him forward. Dantalian was a braggart and narcissist, as were most demons. This demon might take the bait. He didn't step towards me. Or not, shit. I readied for a distance attack and then the demon's eyes swung past me, into the protective circle Jerome had drawn and I knew he was seeing past the fairy glamour that kept Jerome and his mom hidden from my view.

"You, come here," he said to Jerome and the jig was up. I didn't even know his freaking name and he had just spotted the most powerful wizard I had ever met in my life. The sigil hanging around his host's neck exploded in a shower of molten silver. Yep, this was going to suck.

Jerome didn't move, so the demon did, taking three steps towards the boy, closing the gap to less than ten feet. I'd give him another step and then I would bring the furies of the universe down on him to keep him from harming Jerome. I looked at my father. Who only responded by firming up his footing.

The demon took another step and I reached out and grabbed him with my hands. Belgaphor's name flashed in my brain. I didn't hesitate. I didn't let myself question. There could be no doubt in my abilities. I squeezed my hands into fists around his suit jacket and pushed my magic forward, into the body of the mayor, while picturing Belgaphor coming out of him.

And the mayor crumbled at my feet. Lisa and Hemingway jumped forward, grabbing the confused man and dragging him towards theoretical safety. I held

Belgaphor the Creator with my hands and magic. Turning slightly on my pentagram. My father reached out his arms and then Uriel cut his arm deeply, letting the blood splash down onto the concrete. My father's magic touched my own, flaring a little, and he took Belgaphor from me.

Azrael began to move his hands and a swirling red portal started to shimmer into being between he and my father. My father stepped forward. Belgaphor screamed, but not like most demons, and then Raphael shoved him into the portal and the red swirl disappeared.

I fell to the ground. My legs felt wobbly. The excess magic drained back into the earth and I let it.

"Soleil are you okay?" Jerome asked.

"Yes," I answered. "It was just more than I expected."

"Soleil, you grabbed a prince," Lisa's voice sounded small and scared.

"Dinner on my dad," I told her and dropped my head into my hands. "Tacos." I sighed.

"Well, that's better than your normal string of swears," Lisa still sounded far away.

"No, I want tacos," I told her. My hands were shaking and if I stood up, I was going to pass out, so I stayed seated on the road, hoping to get runover by a taco truck.

I had grabbed a prince. There had been plenty of help, though, I hadn't done it alone. Everyone had made little blood sacrifices so that I could grab him, life is all about team work. In a fair fight, he would have slaughtered me.

"Soleil," Jerome touched me. "You don't look good."

"I'm sure I don't," I answered Jerome. "But you helped more than you can imagine." I told him. Then I noticed his hands weren't shaking. He wasn't scared. Everyone else was. Even me. So why wasn't Jerome?

"Jerome, did you summon a prince?" I asked.

"No," he said, and I believed him.

"Why aren't you scared?" I asked.

"Because if you are afraid of them, they have more power over you. Plus, he was facing you and some angels and other good folks, evil never triumphs over good."

"You should put that on a fortune cookie," I told him.

"Nah, I told you I wasn't a thief," he answered, and I frowned at him. "It was on the fortune cookie yesterday."

"Fortune cookie prophesy, how interesting." I said.

"All of Dim Sum's fortune cookies are prophetic," Jerome told me. Which was good because their food was awful. "He writes them a few days before and he just knows who gets what cookie when they order."

"Well that's awesome," I tried to sound like I meant it, because I did, but I was too tired. "What was your fortune?"

"About a week before you arrived, I bought dinner for mom and me with my earnings from the market, and I don't know why I felt I needed Chinese that night, but I did. My cookie told me I would meet an angel who would save me."

"I'm only half angel." I told him. "I guess Dim Sum needs to work on his fortune telling skills."

"Full angel in my opinion," Valerie said. "When that thing turned to look at my son, I just knew this was going to be it, and then I saw your face and I knew, if I died defending Jerome, you would finish raising him as your own." Valerie told me. I nodded at her. And then Valerie collapsed. Jerome panicked, as did I. Suddenly my legs worked. I shouted for an ambulance, but with the crowd, it would never get here in time.

"Dad!" I shouted, my voice high and terse. My father raced over, picked Valerie up, expanding his wings and took to the sky. Jerome was silent and his face ashen. I touched his arm.

"Her cookie that night said your burdens will soon be lifted," Jerome told me. "She wouldn't let me see, but I peeked at it, after she went to sleep. I thought it meant yesterday, though. She told me your dad was going to hire her to work for him and we were going to have enough money to move out of this place, and I was going to go to school with others like me." A single tear slid down Jerome's face.

# Chapter 16

Hemingway packed Jerome and I into a cop car with lights and sirens and drove like the devil was chasing him to Cook County Hospital, which is where I was sure my father had taken Valerie. We beat the ambulances from the demonic street fight. More importantly, so had Valerie.

Jerome and I asked around and finally got a nurse to tell us that Valerie was being looked at in the ER. We went and sat down, Jerome looking like a thirteen-year-old with the burdens of the world on his shoulders.

He had already lost his father and while I realized life wasn't fair, I was going to be really mad if Jerome lost his mom. She was a good person, her energy proved it. As was Jerome. He didn't see living in the ghetto as a bad thing, he saw it as a necessity of his situation. Rent was cheaper. His mom was working two jobs just to put food on the table. So, what if their apartment was small, the neighborhood sketchy. He was grateful for it all. And now, he might lose it.

Hemingway went to find us snacks from a cafeteria or vending machine and came back with tacos and a bacon cheeseburger. Jerome picked at one of the tacos, I ate like I hadn't eaten in years, demolishing the cheeseburger in five bites. and washing it down with the tacos.

It took an hour before my father and a doctor came out of the ER to talk to Jerome. He looked grim.

"Miss Burns?" He asked.

"Yes," I answered.

"You must be Jerome," the doctor said.

"Yes, sir," Jerome answered.

"Your mom is very sick and needs special treatments. I have stabilized her for now, but we need to keep her for a few days." The doctor said. "Miss Burns, she wishes to speak with you privately, before I let Jerome in to see her." Jerome looked like he was going to protest, but my father walked over and wrapped Jerome up in a hug and covered the boy with his wings. I followed the doctor back to her room. There was a woman with a clipboard there that I instantly hated.

"Miss Burns, I need a favor, please, as a dying request." Valerie said to me.

"Except you aren't dying, you just don't realize it yet." I told her.

"Semantics to be discussed later. I have a sister, but she doesn't like Jerome very much because he's special. I can't give her custody of him as a result, would you take him?"

"Of course." I tried to fight tears, but they fell anyway.

"I found out a year ago that I have cancer. I have done some treatments, but my insurance wouldn't cover most of them because it was caught very late. They call it end stage breast cancer. I am going to die, sooner rather than later," Valerie told me. "But I need to know Jerome is going to have a good home when I'm gone. Raphael told me you have a big heart and no kids of your own."

"I can do you one better, Valerie." I said to her. "When you get out of here, you and Jerome both come to

171

St. Louis. Washington University is doing amazing things with cancer treatment. You can both live with me while you get the care you deserve. Jerome can go to St. John's School of Magic, it is nearly as good as the School of Witchcraft."

Valerie stared at me, blinking repeatedly and rapidly.

"You just met us, why do all this for us?" She asked.

"I can see energy, all angels can. Your energy says you are a good person, one of those great people who do more good than bad. You probably help turtles cross the highway in rush hour. Jerome is the same. I didn't meet his father, but I have to think he got his heart from you. And even though you are talking about dying, you are worried about Jerome, not what will happen to you. A mother's love is a beautiful thing. Jerome has already lost his father. I can't do anything about that. But maybe, just maybe, I can do something to keep him from losing his mother, and when the day comes that I can't, then I promise to love Jerome and remind him of your love for as long as he and I both live." I told her. It was her turn to shed a tear. The woman with the clipboard pushed it forward and I snatched it out of her hand. It was freaking paperwork for who was going to pay the bill. I shoved it back at the woman.

"Seriously, the woman is worried she won't live long enough to find a guardian for her son and you want to know how she's going to pay for this visit? Worse than demons." I snipped at her. "Go out and find the really tall guy with the huge fucking wings and hand him your damn clipboard."

"I am just doing my job," the woman said.

172

"Well, you should tell your bosses that your job sucks." I told her.

"I have," I heard her whisper and then I felt bad for snapping at her. But she left to go have an angel pay for this visit.

"I'll get Jerome." I told Valerie.

"I can get him," the doctor said, and Valerie grabbed my hand. "Can he stay with you or your father tonight?"

"Of course," I said and told her what hotel we were at and gave her my phone number. Jerome walked into the room, quietly, his face pensive and sad. My heart wept for him.

"Jerome, I have to stay for a few nights, all the excitement wore me out. However, Miss Burns, agreed to let you stay at the hotel with her and her father."

"Soleil," I interrupted. "Please don't call me Miss Burns, Soleil or Asha is preferred."

"And when I get out, we are going to go to St. Louis and stay with Soleil while I get better."

"This is why your energy changed some, isn't it?" Jerome asked.

"Yes, I have cancer Jerome. I've been fighting it, but I need help."

"I can help," Jerome said.

"I know, and you have been, but you also need to be a thirteen-year old and learn magic. You can't do that if you are taking care of me all the time."

"Soleil and Raphael want to help me get better and they want to help you learn all the stuff a teen who can beat demons should learn. Would it be alright if we let them help both of us?"

"There's no Dim Sum's in St. Louis." Jerome said slowly.

"Nope, but there's a restaurant called Thai Magic with fabulous Thai food and magic bubbles in their take-out boxes of spring rolls that explode into sweet and sour or plum sauce depending on what the person likes. And I have a feeling if you told Miss Karncharna-chai about Dim Sum's fortune cookies, she could come up with something similar for you, and possibly, you alone. Karncharna-chi likes to tailor dining experiences to the diner."

"But would she be good at prophesy?" Jerome asked.

"I don't know, I've never asked her for a prophesy, although in hindsight, I should have, often."

"It'd be okay, mom," Jerome said. "Whatever you need to make you better." I don't know if my heart broke even more at those words or if I was just being abused by my emotions because I had been able to pull out a prince from the mayor.

"You know, the Mayor of Chicago owes you a favor," I told Jerome. "Tomorrow, we'll go see him."

"Mrs. Dussain, we need to move you to a room. Your family can come back in a few hours." The doctor interrupted us. I glared at him and hoped he felt my anger. Not that it would mean much since I was also making him feel happy.

The waiting room was standing room only. Most of the beings were waiting to be triaged. The archangels were still visible, though, standing taller than everyone else, because archangels are just freakishly tall.

"How's Valerie?" Hemingway ran up to us and asked as soon as he saw Jerome and me.

"She's resting," I said, trying to avoid an actual conversation about it.

"For tonight, Jerome will stay with me, I called the hotel and arranged for a gaming console and the hottest

174

games to be brought to it." Raphael told me. "I figured you might be needed to handle the demon problem and since I can't pull them from their hosts like you can, you are more important than me." If I hadn't known better, I would have said my father was glowing with pride as he said it.

"I need clothes," Jerome said.

"No problem," my father answered him, holding out his hand. Hemingway and I walked out as my father, wrapped Jerome tightly in his arms and took off with the boy.

"How bad was she hurt?"

"She wasn't hurt, she has terminal cancer and the excitement exhausted her."

"Oh man," Hemingway said. "I hate to hear that. What happens to Jerome?"

"She and Jerome are moving to St. Louis so she can get the best treatments available there, and not have to worry about anything, including working, and Jerome can focus on school and learning magic."

"You going to find them an apartment?"

"Nope, they are coming to live with me. If everything fails, Jerome becomes my ward."

"There is never a dull moment around you, Soleil."

I frowned and wished I could fly. But I couldn't, so I got back in the SUV with Hemingway. He was right, there was never a dull moment. Well, maybe a few, but not many. It was two in the afternoon and I had faced protestors. I'd pulled a prince out of the mayor. I had agreed to be the guardian for a child I had met just 35 hours earlier. And the best part was that there were ten more hours left in this day for more shit to happen.

However, Hemingway got me tacos from a fast food place on the way back to the cemetery crime scene. He complained that buying tacos in Chicago was just

175

sacrilege and I could have at least gotten a Nathan's Hot Dog. I had made sure he knew how blissful my tacos were.

# Chapter 17

Lisa and Gunter looked exhausted when we got back. So exhausted I felt bad for what I was about to ask Lisa to do. However, Lisa didn't complain, and we went into the cemetery.

There were open graves, but there shouldn't have been and that was a problem. When a zombie digs out of a grave, it collapses the dirt around the coffin into the hole, leaving an open grave. However, these weren't collapsed so much as unburied. The coffins lay on the ground next to the holes, as did a slew of shovels. I was willing to bet the shovels had been bespelled to dig the graves themselves, so that the witches involved hadn't needed to do manual labor.

Lisa was trying to find their magic signature. And she was having trouble. I handed her one of my remaining tacos and she ate it like she had never eaten before. She handed me back the paper wrapper and sighed heavily. Then she sighed again. When she sighed for the third time, I realized the scene was too trampled. I read the names on the graves and none of them had lived past 1852. One was marked as a vampire, which didn't surprise me all that much, since I had seen the fangs.

"What are you looking for?" A young woman asked.

"Magical signatures," Lisa answered.

"This place has been trampled on by more people than the entrance to the Louvre." She told us. She wore a nice suit and looked familiar.

"I saw you yesterday," I said, recognizing her finally.

"Thanks for that. If it never happens again, it will be too soon." She told me. Her eyes were triple irised, but her body language screamed cop.

"I don't suppose you know how it happened?" I asked, not getting my hopes up.

"Nope, everything seemed normal enough, one of the neighborhood ladies brought us cookies, then next thing I know, I'm struggling with the urge to smother my husband with a pillow while he slept, every night." She shuddered. "Then you showed up and it hurt. Not yesterday, but the day before, it hurt to have you in the building. I really had to fight not to kill my husband while he slept after thatand then you showed up yesterday, after which I felt kind of normal, and then I felt like I had gotten over a really bad illness and was waking up from delirium."

"Who brought the cookies?" I asked.

"Mrs. Woodlawn, the wife of the guy who owns the Chicken Shack. She always brings us cookies on Wednesdays, says we need the extra sugar to fight the bad guys and the mid-week blues." She told us.

"Ever heard of the Coven of Seven?" I asked.

"Yeah, real bad news." She answered. "We can't figure out who they are, but I'd bet these open graves are their work. They raise zombies once a month and let them loose on the El Train, the problem isn't the zombies, it's that they don't put the right human soul in them, if they even bother with a human soul." She told me. "The last bunch, they put wolf spirits into. They ate five people before we stopped them."

Well that was fun and exciting.

"You can't trace the magic back to them?" Lisa asked.

"Nope, believe me, we've tried." She said. "Rumor in the neighborhood is they are looking for something inside this cemetery, they raise zombies to eliminate those graves from further investigation for them. But no one knows what they are looking for."

But there was something, beyond the strange magic I was feeling all the time in Chicago, it felt like my father or one of my uncles was standing very close to me. I expected to turn around and find an archangel at my back. I did and saw nothing, though. Good grief.

Just nine more hours and this strange day would go away. I looked at the graves and decided I needed a fortune cookie. Dim Sum's was packed, and I guessed most people were here for the fortune cookies. I ordered strawberry chicken and was told I was wrong, I wanted garlic vegetables and crab rangoon. I definitely did want crab rangoon. Lisa ordered Mongolian beef and vegetable egg rolls, no one argued with her.

My garlic vegetables and crab rangoon were delivered by a man in his sixties who told me the answers I sought were not in the cookies and that the second cookie was for Jerome and Jerome only. I ate the crab rangoon and took my garlic vegetables to go. I opened my fortune cookie and shoved Jerome's in my pocket.

*Your sun will be shortened today.* Well, he was right, the answer I sought was not in the cookie. And there was eight hours until midnight and only three hours until dark. And all I'd accomplished was to get some Chinese food I wouldn't eat.

Hemingway took my garlic vegetables and handed it to a homeless guy outside the cemetery then he told him to find a shelter for the night that wasn't near here. Chicago police had cordoned off the streets near the cemetery and were posting guards. I was glad I wasn't one of the guards.

Lisa tapped my shoulder and showed me her fortune. It read, "When the Sun Goes Away Stay Indoors." The answer I sought wasn't in Lisa's fortune cookie either. Disappearing sun, how did you make the sun disappear, now that was the real question. I tapped my foot on the ground. Hemingway pointed towards the SUV and we all climbed in. Azrael and Uriel said they would catch up. We could add disappearing suns and hexed cookies to my what the fuck list of the day.

Normally, exorcisms are boring. You go there. You talk to the person. The demon's name becomes visible in your brain. You say the magic words, you push magic, and the demon goes away. Or you yanked the demon from the host, pushed magic, and it winked out of existence, returning to the Stygian, if you were me.

I tried to remember if Tabitha had yanked a demon from its host and couldn't. It had become chaotic and jumbled by sheer volume of demons. Most mass infestations were like three demons in a household, not a whole division of police officers.

I didn't buy that Mrs. Woodlawn had hexed the cookies herself, there was no reason for it. Plus, someone would remember who brought the cookies, that would be a stupid thing to do. The who and how still eluded me, then. Maybe someone else had hexed the cookies Mrs. Woodlawn had brought to them. Maybe we needed to talk to Mrs. Woodlawn.

The sun hung too low as we went back to the hotel. I checked my watch twice and it shouldn't have been sunset yet, but it was going down. I wanted to recharge my batteries and start fresh tomorrow. And the sun was disappearing, good lord, what now.

"Soleil?" Hemingway asked. His eyes were looking at something in the sky. It was red and fiery and hovering over our hotel. It was a dragon. My hell fire brand and my sigil necklace both began to emit light as we got closer.

"Into the parking garage." I told him. Lisa looked a little freaked out. Tabitha was calm, though. I didn't know how a being went about slaying a demonic dragon, but I was going to give it a good old-fashioned try with magical might, even if I still didn't have the know-how. I doubted it would respond to the spell of exorcism like Chaac had. Damn, I needed wings.

"I'm going to my room," Lisa said as she jumped from the car before Hemingway had fully parked.

"She seems a little unstable." He commented.

"She has a comfort zone and anything outside it freaks her out, so she hides."

"Dragons are out of her comfort zone?" Hemingway asked.

"I think dragons are out of everyone's comfort zone." I told him. Tabitha agreed from the backseat.

Uriel and Azrael met us in the parking garage.

"Did you see the dragon?" Uriel asked.

"Kind of hard to miss," Hemingway told him.

"Why did the sun set at five in the afternoon?" That seemed more important than the dragon.

"Power imbalance," Azrael said. "Some very powerful people are trying to bring the Stygian here, no more divide."

"Well that's just nuts," I told them.

"Wait, here?" Tabitha asked slowly. "Can they do that?"

"Probably not, it was created by Lucifer, and he created it by sacrificing his true form," Uriel told her. "But that doesn't stop people from trying."

"Is that a 50/50 probably not?" Tabitha asked.

"More like 30 percent not," Azrael told her.

"You may go inside if you want," I told the vampire.

"That would make a great story for my kids, while my new friend Soleil battled a dragon and tried to stop the world from ending, mommy was in her hotel suite eating peanuts and drinking rum drinks."

"I was just pointing out options," I told her. "And if you can get umbrellas for the rum drinks, I'll eat peanuts with you and leave the dragon to a knight, oh shit."

"It isn't a dragon," Azrael said. "It's a monster." I nodded despite not wanting to.

"I have to give Jerome his fortune cookie," I told them.

"Yeah, because that's way more important than a dragon circling the only portal in Chicago." Uriel said through clenched teeth and I nodded, mostly to annoy him. Uriel was a little stronger when he was irked.

We all marched inside. The bloody klaxon was going off again and there were a lot of supernaturals in the hotel lobby. A few were complaining about the klaxon and I agreed with their complaints, it sounded like a warning on a submarine. And my father and Jerome were among those in the lobby. Jerome was eating beef jerky and holding onto a bunch of amulets that were looped on his arm. Supply and demand made the world go around, oh and beef jerky, definitely beef jerky.

Jerome looked at the cookie when I handed it to him.

"I didn't want Cinese," he told me.

"You didn't get Chinese, an older guy that looked like a serial killer brought it out with my meal and told me I couldn't get what I needed from a fortune cookie and told me I had to give that one to you and only you." I told the kid.

"Best fortune cookie ever," Jerome said.

"How so?" I asked.

"I didn't have to struggle to get down his nasty food with it," Jerome said, and I burst out laughing despite the dragon outside and the setting sun. Jerome broke open the cookie and looked at it confused. After a moment he handed it to me. The slip of paper was full of text and I was surprised it all fit in a fortune cookie. Jerome ate the cookie as I read *"the tiny sun will take care of you as she takes care of all of us, your sadness need not darken the world, let her guide you, you must tell her about your father."*

"Tiny sun?" Jerome asked after I read it.

"Me," I said. "Soleil means sun. Raphael and my mom, Sophia, thought it would be funny to name me Sun Burns." Jerome smiled at that, a big goofy grin that brightened his entire face. I could tell he was trying not to laugh. Children weren't the only ones that thought it was funny my parents had named me sun burn.

"You're the tiny sun," Jerome said after a moment.

"Yes, and according to that, your sadness is why the sun is setting early today." I told the kid. He struggled putting his hands palm up at shoulder's width.

"I don't know how I did it."

183

"Me either, but one problem at a time," I told him. I carefully sat down on the floor, cross legged. Jerome sat with me.

"I was beginning to think the Dim Sum cookies were crazy, even if they were almost always right," Jerome told me once we were both sitting. "I have been getting cookies that talk about tiny suns for as long as I can remember."

"Damn, he's good," I said and covered my mouth. I was going to have to work on my swearing since Jerome and Valerie were coming to live with me.

"I hear worse on TV," Jerome said to me.

"And video games," my father stretched his wings over us. No magical spell needed, no one would hear our voices through the thick feathers.

"Jerome, tell me about your dad," I encouraged him by looking up at mine.

"He was a wizard." Jerome answered, and I could see he hadn't talked about him in a long time. "He was powerful. When he was alive, we lived in a nice house outside the city. I don't remember it, of course, but he told me about it. And mom doesn't know I know, but he has come to me in dreams to tell me he loves me and tell me he didn't want to leave us." I nodded.

"Dad was killed by his coven, because they wanted him to do something he didn't want to do. There were twelve of them. Dad has shown me their faces, but I don't know their names. They don't like this world. They want to unite all the planes." I nodded again, encouraging him to continue.

"Dad and four other coven members were killed because they wouldn't go along with it. But the coven was being paid to commit crimes, to make supernaturals look bad, so humans would hate us. Paid by a person my father

184

met once. I know what they look like. And what they feel like. Dad showed me all of that."

"Jerome, how did they kill your father?" I asked feeling it was important.

"They cut out his heart." Jerome told me, and I hoped on everything holy the kid hadn't been shown that.

"Okay, so there were twelve right, but they killed five, meaning you know the faces of the seven left in the coven?" I asked. "Hot diggity damn," I jumped from a seated position to my feet and took Jerome with me. I pulled him into me and hugged the boy. He needed a hug and definitely deserved a few of them, even if it was from me.

I felt him break down and start to sob against me and I stroked his back. He didn't fight the tears, he let them come and after a moment or two, I realized I was crying with him. My father took both of us into his massive arms and I felt his wings encircle us, they glowed lightly with a pure white light.

"Jerome, I promise, you will never be alone in this world," I told him.

"You are my sunshine," he gave a wry laugh through his tears. I nodded.

"I am going to do everything I can for your mom, and for you."

"I know," Jerome told me. "Last year I got a fortune cookie that told me the tiny sun would move the heavens for me because she was pure of heart and made of love. And you are, when I saw you come out of the police station yesterday, your energy was the brightest I have ever seen and a deep crimson color, the color of love. I told my mom I had never seen a being that had so much love in them as you did. I feel like I have always known you." I nodded, my tears falling a little faster, a little harder.

"The sun is rising again!" Someone outside our little hug group shouted and I realized that Jerome was very sad, but he didn't have to be. We would get through this and while I didn't know the first thing about raising kids, not really, I knew that we would figure it out and that Jerome and Valerie would be patient with me.

I felt like I had known Jerome his entire life too. I didn't lie to him and tell him it would all be okay, I didn't know the first thing about cancer treatments or Valerie's condition, not really. I just knew she was a fighter and would continue to fight for her son and now she wouldn't be alone, I'd be there to help her fight. Together, we might do great things.

I sent someone to get colored pens or pencils and drawing paper. Jerome knew what the Coven of Seven looked like. I had just been asking the wrong flipping people. I should have asked Jerome.

Hemingway came back with crayons from the restaurant and I gave them to Jerome and asked him to draw the faces of the coven members that had killed his dad. He looked at the crayons.

"Dude, it was the best I could do." Hemingway said.

"Well, hopefully, they don't look like Looney Tunes when I'm done." He said, and the crayons began to move out of the box as Jerome waved his hand over the paper.

"Soleil," my father said. I looked up and saw a ghost. He was a tall, handsome man with chiseled cheek bones that could probably cut glass. His head was shaven, but it looked good on him. Around his neck he wore an amulet of the sun.

"Thank you," his voice was soft, barely above a whisper, like most ghostly voices, and I understood why he had visited his son in dreams, where he was defined.

"I didn't do anything," I told him looking at Jerome. "Your son did it all."

"Miss Soleil, before Jerome grows up, you will have done more than you know." He told me and then he faded.

"That was my dad." Jerome told me.

"I know." I answered him.

"That was an awesome necklace, I want some of those for my next demon prohibition amulets."

"We can do that," I told him. Even though Jerome was standing and talking to me, the crayons flew over the page. The magic was working on instinct. Training Jerome in magic was going to be easy or as easy as it ever was to train a teen in magic. Sometimes they became difficult and rebellious. I took my father's hand, remembering my own teen years when I had wanted to be anything on the planet except a nephilim.

# Chapter 18

And now I had a damn demonic dragon to deal with. I looked at Jerome. He made me happy. Maybe I needed a couple of kids. The problem was, I had seen my sister give birth and... just wow. I was shocked we weren't living on a dead planet. Best birth control ever. There had been screaming, bleeding, sweating, and then she had said things that had made me wonder if she was possessed.

I didn't want any of that. Kids would be great, but I was sure my female bits would not survive the not quite miracle of birth. Of course, I'd need to talk to Valerie and Jerome about it. I didn't want them to feel put out if I decided to adopt a kid or take in foster children.

First, the dragon circling the damn hotel. I wasn't sure how to defeat dragons, it felt lame to do the spell of exorcism on him, like I'd done on Chaac. It made it seem like I was a one trick pony, but then, I pretty much was. So maybe shaking it up wasn't such a great idea.

"Suggestions?" I said looking down at him. He was more than a foot shorter than me, but judging by his father, that would change.

"Nope," he shrugged. "Be yourself."

"Be yourself?" I asked.

"You were named after the sun," Jerome said, and I got his meaning. I was named after the sun. The first sketch tore itself from the drawing pad. And it did look a little bit like Daffy Duck. Crayons were not good for drawing detailed faces. I'd get him some colored pencils after I defeated the dragon. The sun was shining again, I could do this.

Lisa looked at me and I nodded. Her cookie hadn't mentioned she needed to stop hiding just because the sun came back up. She could stay. Hemingway pulled his side arm and walked out the front doors with me.

The dragon continued lazy circles over the hotel. My father came out, too, and I stared at him.

"The marshals are protecting Jerome, and Tabitha said she'd rip the throat out of anything that tried to touch him."

The pentagram was still where I had drawn it. Usually magic power symbols disappeared after the person using them stopped taking magic from them. Otherwise, there'd be magical symbols all over the place. The all-knowing pentagram, how interesting. My father began to draw his eternal mother symbol again. I watched as the lines began to glow and I moved my foot onto the pentagram. It shocked me, sending a jolt through my entire body. I could tell someone else had used the pentagram for something not so awesome.

We needed to get security video of everyone out that was out front while we were gone. I knelt and drew a new symbol, not a pentagram this time, but the sun. My foot found it and the magic was amazing. Belgaphor the Creator had nothing on me. Of course, I wasn't dealing with Belgaphor, I was dealing with a dragon, but from now on, I would draw a sun not a pentacle. Part of me told me I was an idiot for not thinking of it before now and needing a kid to point it out to me.

The dragon took notice of us, standing out in the sunshine, with about an hour to go before it set for real, like it should. And if the dragon wasn't gone before dark, it would be harder to get rid of. There were news vans pulling up to the hotel. Just what we needed, a bunch of yahoos with no clue that the dragon was more dangerous than they realized.

"Lisa is handing out the new amulets that Jerome made," Raphael said.

"Maybe she ought to give one to the idiots out here," I told him. He snorted, because not all angels can be perfect all the time, not even the archangels.

"You are going to ask Michael to help Valerie, aren't you?" Raphael said.

"Yes."

"If he refuses?" Raphael said.

"Then he refuses, and I get her into experimental treatment programs with Barnes Jewish and Wash U." I told him. "And I pray, a lot, that if she dies, I don't fuck up her kid."

The dragon made his circles look effortless, but I knew better. Dragons are not aerodynamic. If they were, airplanes would have more creative designs.

"I'll follow your lead, Soleil." Raphael told me.

"Great, I'm clueless," I admitted. "I can try to separate the demon from his true form, but I need to know his name and I don't."

"You did it with Chaac," Hemingway said.

"Yeah, but Chaac is named monster, I don't think Dragon is the dragon's name. It isn't like there are a lot of extra limbed blue monsters that can control tornadoes running around, even in the Stygian."

190

"Do you want me to fly you up there, so you can ask him?" Raphael asked.

"Nope, I am not good in flight," I told him. "Let's bring him to..." Damn, the dragon dove and landed on the news van behind us. And while technically I wanted him on the ground, I didn't want him eating reporters. Or cameramen, I thought as he snapped one up in his jaws and chewed noisily.

"Are you telling me there is more than one monster that looks like a dragon and eats people?"

"Probably," I shrugged and pushed magic towards the dragon, gentle prodding magic, meant to get his attention more than anything else. The dragon jumped off the news van and he was bigger, not just because he was on the ground, but because all the news people were incredibly terrified by him eating the camera man.

"Oh shit," Hemingway said as the dragon stalked towards us.

"Yep," I agreed, pushing more gentle exploratory magic. The dragon got closer still, but stopped at the base of the stairs, where the hotel wards started. And then he lashed out at them with his tail, banging it against the invisible wall that sounded like a bell from where I stood within the wards. Hemingway's hands went to his ears, they were bleeding. He covered them, and then my father took over, wrapping Hemingway up in his wings. My father's ears were bleeding too, which meant mine probably were as well and we all had ruptured ear drums. Someone grabbed my arm and I turned to see Azrael tugging at me. His lips moved, but I didn't hear the words. He stuck a wadded-up feather in my ear and it felt like liquid ice. The dragon swung its massive tail again, and I didn't hear it slam against the wards.

I hopped off the sun symbol and skipped down the stairs of the hotel. I stuck my arm through the wards and felt just the tiniest buzz that made my hair stand up. My hand found dragon scales. They were rough and cold under my finger tips and the dragon laid down.

He swung his massive head to look at me. He wasn't a demon, he was one of Belgaphor's creations. He had sad yellow eyes that filled my soul with sadness. I felt myself start to cry again, ridiculous angel genes.

My brain screamed a second too late. I felt magic hit the wards and the wards shivered under it. A witch stood on the other side of the dragon. Her face was contorted with rage. I kept my hand on the dragon's scales. Magic slowly filling him. She fired again at the wards and I felt them shiver again. She was trying to brute force her way through them, if she brought down the wards, the hotel, its guests, and maybe its portal would be unprotected. I kept my hand on the dragon, slowly letting my magic fill him. If I could fill him with enough of my magic, I might be able to get his help. I took another step down, half my body protected by wards.

She mirrored me and took a step, this time towards the hotel. The magic forming in her hands was a massive sphere of black energy. I had never seen magic like it before and when she fired it, it should have broken the sound barrier. The wards shivered harder and I felt their electric buzz drop, my hair no longer stood on end. She was going to bring them down. I screamed at her, filling the air with my magic. The wards snapped into place, the electric feeling intensifying, bisecting me. I either had to get the hell out of them entirely or go back behind them. I stepped out. The wards made a clanging sound as they reached their full capacity. For a moment, I thought all the magic being shoved into them was going to break them, bring them down simply because they had never had so much magic in them.

It was her turn to scream, she continued gathering magic, the blackness getting even larger and the world seemed to die in that darkness. Death magic. I kept a hand on the dragon, willing him to understand me. I opened my thoughts to him. I was an exorcist, I could do death magic too. The dragon coughed, and the cameraman reappeared on the ground, covered in slime and other nastiness. The dragon stood up, his head turning to me again. Then his jaws suddenly snapped down on the witch with the black magic at her fingertips. He snorted, coughed, and gagged. I kept a hand on him, trying to help ease the magic that she had taken with her into the belly of the beast.

Yep, Soleil Burns, exorcist, nephilim, and dragon master. That was me. Oh, and adoptive mother if things worked out like I planned. Of course, they wouldn't, because they never did. The dragon shuddered, and I saw his belly begin to glow. The bitch was trying to magic her way out of him. I kept my hands on him, forcing more magic into him. The magic of the sun. Magic filled with love, warmth, and kindness, even when it was being destructive. I wondered if my parents had known I would become this. My parents weren't capable of seeing the future, but that didn't mean one of the other archangels couldn't.

A slit began to appear in the dragon's side, blood oozed from it. "I don't know what you did to become a dragon, I whispered to the beast, putting my face on his scaly haunch at his rear hip, "but I promise to help you escape this fate."

The bitch appeared a black sword in her hands, she peeled the slit in the dragon's side open as she stepped out and I grabbed her, forcing my magic into her. She screamed, her head thrown back, black energy escaping her lips with the scream. She fought to pull away, her sword flailing behind my back. Swords are not meant for close quarter combat. I hugged her tighter, pulling her as close to me as physics would allow. Her screaming got louder, until I thought it would crumble the skyscrapers around us.

I leaned over, putting her and I against the dragon, and continued to force my magic into her. The dragon moved gently, curling up, I felt its head slide against my calves and I felt safe with him there. The witch collapsed, her hair turned white. She stared at me, hate in her eyes and her lips moving. The spell fizzled out and the blackened energy fell harmlessly to the ground. I touched her again and she shrank away, trying to scoot backwards, she moved closer to the dragon. Who still leaked small amounts of dragon blood onto the earth. A sun symbol was under my feet. For a moment, I wasn't sure where it had come from, but it was drawn in bright yellow crayon. I sat down on the ground, on the sun symbol, slowly being covered in dragon's blood. The dragon huffed, and a slight wisp of smoke came from its nostrils. Streaks of orange and red filled the sky and the sun setting to the west of Lake Michigan reflected off the waters and made the colors look even more beautiful. A tear slipped from my eye, a tear full of amazement, as I took in the stunning sunset on the lake. And then it hit me. I leaned back against the dragon.

"What's your name?" I asked it.

"Chloe," the dragon spoke. "My father promised me to Belgaphor so he could win a war."

"Chloe, that's a beautiful name, did your father win his war?" I asked.

"Yes," she answered.

194

"And so you kept his side of the agreement and went to Belgaphor." I continued to look at the sunset. "Do you know in what year you entered the Stygian?"

"The year of our lord, thirteen hundred and sixty-two."

"That is a long time to be trapped as a dragon," I told her and felt her sigh. "Do you want to be a dragon?"

"I do not remember being anything else anymore." Her large bulk shuddered.

"Then you are free to be released from this beast's body, if you so choose, your obligation has been met," a new voice said. It wasn't an unfamiliar voice, just unexpected and I tore my eyes from the sunset to look up at the dark angel that cast his shadow over us. The archangel Gabriel is in fact dark. He has black feather wings, black hair, deep brown eyes the color of fertile mud, and skin a shade or two darker than my own.

"Will I die?" Chloe the dragon asked.

"Most likely, is that so terrible though? While I condemn your father's bargain, I am sure you had siblings and a mother that you missed very much while in the Stygian."

"Yes, I did," she told Gabriel.

"Then take my hand and I shall release you from this form," Gabriel told her. Chloe's body shuddered once more and she moved.

"Thank you," she said, I think to me. I nodded as she stood up, shifting her weight awkwardly onto her dragon legs. She put one large taloned paw on Gabriel's hand. Light began to shine from within her skin. The scales fell to the ground. I picked one up, marveling at the beauty as the light from Chloe's body intensified, making the scales appear as a rainbow. And as all of us watched, the dragon disappeared and a beautiful red-haired young

195

lady took its place. Her hair was plaited and hung to her waist. She was nude, but not naked, and she was breathtaking as she shimmered in the nimbus of the light that shone out her skin. Gabriel was glowing as well. Light emitting from beneath his skin, making him look even more alive somehow. His wings emitted a dark light that was more blue than natural light ever could be.

And then Chloe was gone. Her spirit and body both delivered to a place with more grace than the earth would ever have. Angels might not be divine, but it didn't mean they couldn't do some divine things.

"Niece," Gabriel held out his hand to me and I took it. I hugged Gabriel and he stroked my hair. "You're handiwork?" He asked. I pulled away and followed his eyes to the witch that still sat on the ground, too weak to get up.

"I think so," I told him.

"Soleil the Sun Angel," he inclined his head to me, not really a nod. "You have found love," he told me.

"I have?" I asked, confused.

"Yes," he answered. And that was how archangels gave information, annoyingly incomplete and mysterious. I thought about it. I was lusting after Hemingway, but I was sure it wasn't love. "Whatever you are thinking of, isn't it," Gabriel told me.

"Awesome," I snipped.

"I know you find it infuriating, but you will find all your answers internally Soleil. Why then should we just hand you the answers when you are so strong?"

"Yep, totally infuriating." I shrugged. He laughed, and it felt good. Gabriel was the messenger. He knew much and told very little. Each archangel had a special skill and Gabriel's was probably the most annoying to me. I did prefer to just have answers given to me. He picked up the white-haired witch and I felt the wards not want to admit her. Jerome had filled them with magic, made sure they didn't break and expose everyone to the dangers outside of them.

"That, that is your answer," Gabriel told me. I didn't kick him, but I wanted to. Instead, I gave him the finger. "Such language." He laughed again. And the answer was there, it wasn't romantic love that I had found, it was purer, not tinged with lust, it was the love a mother felt for a child. Even if Valerie lived to be a million years old, I would still love Jerome as if he had come from my own body. Yep, Gabriel was annoying.

The wards finally let us pass, with the help of Gabriel. We dragged the witch up the steps. The sun had set and while it wasn't full dark yet, it was close. "Gabe," my father hugged his brother. Gabriel, Raphael, and Azrael got along the best.

"Sophia called me and said she was concerned about you and Soleil."

"We're here," Uriel said.

"And so, you are," Gabriel answered. Azrael cracked a smile. Azrael was the youngest and often provoked the infighting among the brothers, but today he held his tongue, as did I. Because Gabriel was right, I preferred him and my dad helping me out to Uriel, but beggars can't be choosy and all that.

"A few more and we could put together our own coven," I added and then reminded myself that I was supposed to be neutral and quiet. Mostly quiet. Jerome looked then came to stand by me. And Gabriel nodded to me and smiled at Jerome. Damn. He was a know it all, literally.

Raphael touched the witch and drew back from her, a strange look on his face that I couldn't read. He didn't touch her again. Instead, he put silver handcuffs on her and put an amulet over her neck. Not one like Jerome made, but one that my father had made. My father could read minds because his special divine skill was that he saw intent. The amulet was to weaken the witch, make her basically mortal, remove all but the magic that everyone could do. In other words, she could draw a circle to protect herself from magic and she could find lost keys, maybe.

Gabriel handed the witch over to a cop. He looked at my father for a moment. Raphael shook his head in response to the inquiring look. We all trekked back into the hotel, or rather the hotel restaurant. Gabriel ordered several bottles of wine and Uriel refused a glass when they were poured. Gabriel shot him a sour look.

"This is your family?" Jerome asked me.

"Some of it," I told the teen.

"They have issues with each other," he told me.

"Don't I know it," I answered. "But they can work together for the greater good when necessary."

"There are more," Raphael told Jerome, handing the kid a glass of orange juice. "I have lots of brothers, no sisters though. And sometimes we get along really great, and sometimes just being in the same room together is annoying."

"Like my mom and my aunt," Jerome said. "They do nothing but argue when they are together since my grandma passed away."

"Yep, exactly like that," Raphael said. "However, we each have our own little families and then we belong to this one big family, and sometimes it's easier to deal with the little families than the big one."

And that was the best explanation of family I had ever heard. My father was different around his brothers. The more of them were together, the odder they all acted.

It was a fact of life that we mostly ignored. We ate, drank, and tried to be merry. However, for all the laughter, we all knew that tomorrow was going to suck. No amount of laughter would change that. Tomorrow we had to go after the other six members of the murderous coven. A coven strong enough to pull monsters and the spirit form of princes from the Stygian. I had gone up against a lot of bad guys, but none like this.

However, tonight, I wanted to laugh. I wanted to enjoy the warmth of family, both new and old, and friends both new and old. Tabitha refilled my wine glass and handed me a fried pickle. She had told me that she had escorted a very determined Jerome outside to strengthen the wards along with the elevator attendant I had been hoping to talk to earlier in the day, about the coven of seven.

It had worked. The hotel staff had told me the wards had never been stronger and asked if I would be willing to let Jerome boost them once a year, or sooner if needed. I told them I would ask his mother and they had looked at me surprised. I think they had assumed I was his full-time legal guardian and he had somehow met up with me outside the hotel, possibly brought to me on the wings of an angel. Which wasn't completely impossible I guessed.

I ate until I thought I would explode. Judging by the look on Jerome's face. He had too, as he should, since he had done a lot of magic today too. Jerome and I played rock, paper, scissors, while the dishes were cleaned up and then a huge cheesecake was brought out, with an assortment of toppings and I reached down and unbuttoned the button on my jeans... Because you know, cheesecake.

I took a slice and Jerome asked if we could split it because it was roughly the size of the Great Pyramid. I did, giving him the slightly bigger half since he was a growing

199

boy doing tons more magic than he was used to. He covered his slice in fresh strawberries and then dribbled chocolate sauce over it. I put strawberries on the upper half of my partial slice and then added cherries to the bottom part. Then I added a healthy dose of chocolate sauce to the part with cherries. Jerome snatched a bite of the cherries and smiled. I agreed with him, it was delicious.

He asked if he could take a piece back to the room, in case he got hungry later. I told him of course, and the waiter brought us a to go box. Jerome added cherries and chocolate to the cheesecake and closed the box, setting it protectively in front of him.

A few moments later, we all had pieces of cheesecake boxed up, topped with our favorite toppings. Because even though I was so full I felt like the blueberry girl from Willy Wonka, I had been waking at 3 in the morning to find food for a couple of nights now. The waiter told us they were keeping a skeleton crew in the kitchen all night in case we wanted cheeseburgers at 3 in the morning and I thanked him and silently hoped the cheesecake was enough if I woke up in the wee hours of the morning again.

While we had eaten, the front desk had sent a concierge out to get colored pencils, a new sketch pad, some silver sun pendants, and some silver chain for the pendants to hang from. I had nieces, I knew how to make jewelry and we had everything we needed for them.

Hemingway walked Jerome and I to our suite, our new one. My father had moved us into a two-bedroom suite on the twelfth floor. There was a gaming system in the living room. As well as a list of all the movies the hotel had to offer. Jerome was too full to be sad. But I expected that he might have a little trouble sleeping in the hotel, while his mom was at the hospital. However, she called him almost immediately upon us entering the room and I could hear him telling her about the magic wards he'd helped protect at the hotel and about dinner and that he had gotten her a piece of cheesecake with cherries on it that he would bring her in the morning.

Raphael had the room on one side of us and Gabriel was on the other side. I felt safe nestled between my family. No matter how old or powerful I got, I always felt safer when my dad was around. The thought made me sad. Jerome didn't have his dad to make him feel safe. And for tonight, he wouldn't have his mom either. I didn't curse the divine and Jerome wasn't the only kid on the planet to be fatherless and have a sick mother that he was in danger of losing, but it did make me unhappy.

There was a knock on the door and I opened it to see Gabriel in the hallway. He looked at me for a long time, not saying anything. Then he opened his arms. My family was big on the power of hugs. I let Gabriel hug me.

"The walls might be sound proofed, but I can still feel your sadness through them," he told me. "I know you feel things very deeply, Soleil, you always have, but is your sadness justified at the moment?"

"Yes." I told him.

# Chapter 19

Jerome came back into the main living area of the suite and I stiffened, pulling away from Gabriel.

"Soleil, is everything okay?" Jerome asked.

"Yes," I told him. "I am just exhausted, I can't seem to get my emotions into check."

"Because of me?" He asked too wise for his years.

"No," Gabriel answered for me. "Because sometimes Soleil forgets she's allowed to be happy, even when others aren't. It is something I am hoping you can help her with."

"Oh, okay. May I play a video game?" Jerome asked.

"Sure, but only for an hour and it can't be Grand Theft Auto." I told him.

"Man, that game is lame." Jerome answered.

"See, prayer answered." Gabriel smiled and squeezed my hand and went back to his room. I plopped down next to Jerome on the couch and watched him begin to play a game that had zombies in it. What's this?" I asked after a moment.

"Days Gone," he told me. I nodded having no clue what the game was about. I liked to play video games, but they were puzzle games, I still had a copy of Myst on my computer at home that I could play. I was really enjoying the simplicity of spending time with him, watching him play his game, then damn klaxon sounded.

"If that's because of zombies, we'll have to talk about your gaming," I teased him.

"Let me guess, you want me to stay here, lock the door, and not let anyone in." He said.

"No, actually," I stood up. "I will go nuts if I can't see you, especially since I don't know who or what is the cause of the alarm. So, you are going to stay with me, like superglued to me."

"I can do that," Jerome hit a button on the controller and a pause symbol popped up on the screen. we exited into the hallway. The archangels were already there. As was the elevator attendant. He was staring down the hallway and I guessed we were waiting on other residents to come out.

"What's going on?" Raphael asked.

"Someone gave our gargoyles life." He told him. Well, that's fun. I thought. Nothing like a bunch of massive stone gargoyles moving around the hotel and then I heard a window shatter. The gargoyles were within the wards, meaning the magic to give them life had come from inside the hotel, and now the gargoyles were probably going to rip the place apart piece by piece.

The door to my suite was yanked off its hinges and pulled into the room. So, it had been one of our windows that was broken for the gargoyles to climb through. Fan-fucking-tabulous. I moved Jerome in front of me, protecting him from the yawning blackness that had once been our door. I pushed the boy forward a step and then I took one with him. And hot breath moved my hair a little. I pushed Jerome forward a few more steps.

"Down, we should go down," I told the attendant.

"I was told to wait for everyone," he answered.

"There won't be anybody if we don't go, now," I told him, pushing Jerome into the elevator.

"Think the elevator is safe?" Someone asked me, and I ignored them as I pushed the button for the lobby. It stopped on the tenth floor and Tabitha, Walter, and Hemingway got in the elevator.

"I just saw a stone lion thing climb past my window," Hemingway told us. "I brought a shotgun." I nodded and pushed the lobby button again, harder, and the elevator began to move. It stopped on the eighth floor as well and I rolled my eyes as a short witch pushed her way onto the crowded elevator. She looked like she was in her sixties, which meant she was probably a couple thousand years old. I didn't yell at elevator doors, but I furiously poked the Lobby button again.

"I don't think pressing it hard makes it work better," Hemingway said, and I stabbed at the button again with my thumb. The doors finally closed.

And we stopped on the fifth floor. The doors opened and a woman in her twenties, who wasn't a supernatural, got on the elevator. I stared at the doors and hit the lobby button again. The doors didn't close. "Wait for me!" Someone shouted from down the hall.

"Are you fucking kidding me!" I shouted at the doors as they slid closed and then opened back up. The owner of the voice pushed his way onto the elevator. I hit the lobby button again.

"Where's the elevator attendant?" The guy asked.

"Busy," I hit the button again and he suddenly realized Hemingway was holding a shot gun and stepped back out, forcing the doors to open all the way again. "Oh dear lord in the name of everything holy, I could have gotten there faster using the escalator." I sneered at the doors as they started to close again.

"There isn't an escalator," Jerome told me. And I nodded. Then we stopped on the fourth floor. I got out and Jerome followed me. As did the marshals. I stomped over to the stairs and opened the door to the stairwell. It was very breezy, and I could hear traffic. I looked up and saw nothing. Looked down and saw nothing. However, I was certain that the stairs shouldn't have had their own breeze and traffic noise.

I stomped back to the elevators and hit the button for an elevator. It opened with the small witch and the two mortals still in it. I felt like I had entered the Twilight Zone.

"Going down?" The witch asked.

"I'll catch the next one," I told her. And the doors closed again. There was a ding and the other elevator bay opened. My uncles and the elevator attendant stood inside. The five of us squeezed in with them.

"Why aren't you in the lobby?" Raphael asked when we got on.

"Long story and if this elevator attempts to stop at any floor other than the lobby, I will probably start screaming and never stop again." The attendant hit a switch and all the lights on the panel went out except the light for the lobby. "There is wind and traffic in your stairwell." I told the attendant.

"Yeah, they took out the top floor of the stairs, and their first attack was to knock a huge hole in the wall on the second floor. That's why I came to get everyone in the elevator."

"Awesome." I sneered at the doors. They dinged and opened into a very crowded lobby. We got out, the elevator doors closed behind us, then I heard it begin to go

205

up. The man at the front desk was wearing a name tag that said Ernesto and he was baring fangs at the short witch who was complaining to him about the crazy people in the hotel. I was sure she was talking about me, but I didn't care. I took hold of Jerome's hand to ensure we wouldn't be separated. A man in a doorman's uniform was trying to get everyone's attention. His name tag said his name was Julian. Julian had wings. They were carefully hidden under his suit jacket, but they still poked out a little as he raised his arms and shouted for everyone to quiet down.

He tried five or six times and then looked at the floor. Azrael stepped up next to Julian and suddenly everyone was quiet and paying attention. I guess it wasn't every day an archangel told them to shut up.

A handful of things happened simultaneously, dividing my focus in too many directions. Julian began shouting instructions about the emergency, Jerome said something about his mom's boss being in the room, a gargoyle came through the front door like a Mack truck, and Hemingway shoved one of the crayon sketches Jerome had drawn into my hands. Then Jerome was gone. My eyes searched the crowd and landed on him as he screamed my name. Mathilda Wellesley was dragging him outside by his wrists.

My eyes flicked to the sketch, and Christine Lindsey's face looked back at me. Even in crayon it was so life like, I kept expecting her to blink. The nervousness, the outburst from Mathilda at the discovery of Christina over her husband, all of it staged. I missed it thinking they were just two unrelated victims, even though I had thought it myself, Mathilda would have known nearly all the cops that worked at the Division of Magic and with her husband in charge, she could have come and gone as she pleased. Oh, holy shit.

206

I grabbed Hemingway and dragged him through the crowd, into the restaurant, away from the gargoyle. We exited into the parking garage. I called the hospital and Valerie confirmed that she worked for Mrs. Mathilda Wellesley and had for the last fifteen years as a housekeeper with a maid service.

So, Mathilda knew all about Jerome and Jerome's powers, and that's what Jerome's father had been fighting against when his coven killed him. They wanted Jerome. And they had killed his dad, made it look like someone else had done it to Valerie, and they had kept tabs on Jerome all this time. Valerie also told me that until yesterday, Mathilda and her husband, a cop that oversaw the Division of Magic were listed as guardians for Jerome if something happened to her. But after meeting me, she had changed her mind and called Mathilda to let her know about it.

Which was why they had come after me with Chaac. The oppressive magic I kept feeling had been attached to me somehow at the airport, a tracking spell ensuring they always knew where I was. I was betting the zombies the first night had been sent because we had been to the Division of Magic. Sometimes, I couldn't see the trees for the forest. But Christine hadn't felt all that powerful. However, covens amplified a witch's magic, which is why they existed. And even the weakest member could gain lots of power through the strength of the coven.

"We need all the information we can get about Mathilda Wellesley." I told Hemingway as he sped out of the parking garage, tires squealing against the concrete. "Like where would she take Jerome."

"To wherever the coven meets is my guess," Hemingway said.

"Mathilda Wellesley is about as magical as a piece of chalk, so she isn't a member of the coven, I don't think she'd take him there." She wasn't magical, she was just the one putting up the money for this chaos, for whatever reason, she had a vested interest. Belgaphor was not the most powerful prince, he wasn't even in the top nine. However, the big guns required human sacrifices or bargains like Chloe's father had made. Human sacrifice was dodgy ground. Sometimes the stain it left on a soul was so dark that it leaked into the physical form of the person. Which explained the deer soul in Wellesley, he had let them take his soul, but since they had still needed to control the Division of Magic, they had reanimated his corpse with the deer soul. Possibly as a volunteer.

"Let's pretend you commanded an insane posse of marshals who wanted to get into human sacrifice, where would you do it?"

"A cemetery named after a demon," Hemingway turned the wheel sharply and we raced towards Moloch Cemetery. Hemingway was good, because I hadn't thought of that as the location. I had literally been talking out loud. But it explained why they had possessed the mayor, so it wouldn't get torn down or, at least, it made it look better when they showed up to protest it being torn down. No doubt at the last minute, there would have been someone persuasive enough to stop the mayor from wrecking the cemetery, but the loons from the demon rights group had started to upstage them, so they had needed to improvise, and it still stopped the cemetery from being torn down, right? Mission accomplished. Fan-fucking-tabulous.

# Chapter 20

The streets were deserted and looked like a war had taken place. The guards the police had posted were all still standing guard, but their energy was back to a sickly yellow. Yep, exactly. I bet they were just as tired of being possessed as I was of exorcizing them.

Hemingway stopped the SUV about half way down the block. There was a rustling noise and my father and uncles joined us. One of the cops drew and fired his gun, hitting Gabriel in the shoulder. Petty differences between the brothers weren't going to matter for long. Gabriel swore, and another shot was fired.

"Are you fucking insane?" Gabriel shouted at them. I was willing to bet the demons inside them probably actually were close to being insane. They fired another shot. Hemingway lined up his own shot and fired. The cop fell to the ground.

I looked past the sentries. There was a lot of light in the graveyard. Considering it was night, I didn't think light should be coming from within the walls. But hey, maybe the city of Chicago had installed street lights or something in there. It didn't dance and flicker like torches.

Azrael was helping Gabriel. Raphael jumped off the car and joined me and Hemingway. He was probably not getting his deposit back on the rental fee. Not after four archangels had stood on his roof. I was also betting the rental insurance would try to weasel out of paying the repairs. Of course, Hemingway wouldn't make the archangels pay for it, but he totally should.

The second cop fainted as we got close. I reached down and pulled the demonic soul out of her and it was the young lady that had told me if she never became possessed again, it would be too soon. I hoped all this didn't make her change careers. She was going to be a great cop.

The cop Hemingway had shot was still breathing. I gave my father the demon spirit from the lady cop and he exorcized it as I pulled the other spirit out of the bleeding cop. It kicked and shouted and spat at me. Demon spirits can be pesky. My father touched him, and the wiggling stopped.

He turned to enter the cemetery and stopped. I looked at him as his hands pushed against an invisible barrier that worked just as well as a wall. I worried our plan wasn't going to work. If Dad couldn't cross it, I worried my half angel bloodline would keep me out too. Raphael stepped back, and I put my hand against the air where he had been. There was a small tingle, like a minor electric shock, but then my hand passed through the wards and I was within the confines of the graveyard. There were several people with handheld lanterns standing around. Probably waiting for some star alignment or something. I could see Jerome. He was shackled to a tombstone. And in my head, I saw his father shackled to the same one before a Stygian monster showed up and ripped his heart out. Now all my questions about his father's death were answered.

No one was paying attention to me or Hemingway and I guessed the spell that kept my father out, also kept sound out. Although, if there'd been a fairy to throw some glamour on me and make me invisible, I wouldn't have turned it down.

Mathilda Wellesley's back was to us and the others were chanting. I hung my head. Not because they were chanting but because they were chanting to focus their energy and have Beelzebub appear to them. For the record, if Beelzebub appeared in his true form in the middle of Chicago, there were going to be a lot of people that never slept again. And with that thought, my mouth overrode my brain.

"You should definitely set your sights lower and aim for Mammon or Astaroth or maybe Belgaphor again, however, if you couldn't get Beelzebub to show up last time you sacrificed a powerful wizard, he isn't going to show up for your lot now." I suddenly blurted loud enough for them to hear. Their chanting faltered.

"I thought you said angels couldn't get in," Mathilda practically screeched at them.

"Ah, the nonmagical, how sad." I said to her. "That part worked, there are four archangels stuck on the other side."

"But you got in," she screamed at me.

"Not an angel," I pointed out to her. Jerome visibly relaxed a little. I winked at him. We'd get out of this just fine as long as no one lost their head. "So, as I was saying, nothing you lot can do is going to get you Beelzebub. I don't normally shatter the hopes and dreams of wizards and witches, but you just aren't powerful enough. Perhaps if you sacrificed Christine and Mrs. Wellesley, replenished your coven to twelve or thirteen, and had a really strict entrance policy on magical abilities, then you might pull it off, but how are you going to manage all that tonight?" I said. Hemingway had stopped walking and he fired a shot, hitting Christine in the head, understanding why I picked

211

her out for him. Bullets hurt, even when they don't kill. Christine flopped like a fish as her body tried to heal the injury. Her blood spilled upon the ground from the small wound and the Earth drank deeply of her magic.

"And the Lord said, let there be light, and there was, and he saw that it was good," I said and the light from the lanterns grew brighter for a moment before the bulbs shattered. A sun symbol appeared at my feet. However, his silver shackles remained, because silver might as well be kryptonite, it was why everything was made out of it, including the pendants Jerome charmed.

"How'd you do that?" Someone asked.

"A magician never reveals their secrets," I answered. Of course, my secret was Jerome, but even if it hadn't been, I wouldn't have told them. Hemingway was moving now, moving towards Jerome. Everyone let the marshal pass, unsure what to do. No doubt they were still trying to figure out how the heck I had gotten past their magic and entered a demon's graveyard. It worked for me, because it kept them busy.

Hemingway fired a couple of shots and the shackles loosened.

"Blood in, blood out," I said to Jerome and the coven turned to look at me. My sun symbol was already glowing with a lovely golden light. Jerome touched the ground and I felt the spells around the cemetery shatter and my sun symbol suddenly burned as hot as lava, melting the earth into glass in the pattern. When this was over, I intended to dig up the vitrified sun and take it home with me. It would be cool as decor for my house, in front of one of the windows.

And the dead beneath our feet began to wake. I could feel them trying to breathe. This hadn't been exactly what I meant, but he was mostly untrained and working on instinct. Hemingway picked Jerome up and he ran, even carrying the boy, towards me. There was a loud scream and one of the coven members had finally worked out that the ground was moving under their feet.

I watched in detached horror and fascination. Hemingway didn't put Jerome down, he headed towards the exit. Which was good. The first hand to shoot up from the ground had talons, not fingers, and despite being quite rotted, it was bright red. I was willing to bet a dollar or a donut that it was not human and had never been human. Mathilda Wellesley tried to run for the exit and I stopped her with a look.

"You wanted demons, you're getting them," I said to her. "You should sit back and enjoy the show." I felt Gabriel come up behind me. He was panting heavily from pain. He stood close to me.

"See you don't need the answers given to you and we can go, if you want."

"No, I told Jerome to do it, so I'm going to force myself to watch. And then I will force them all back."

"Soleil," Gabriel said.

"Oh, I am aware that his true form is here." I told my uncle. "Dad can help me with him, if I need it."

"She is as crazy as you," Gabriel said, and I knew he was talking to my father. In the very center of the graveyard a large stone slab cracked open and a hand the size of a Prius shot through it. There was much screaming and crying amongst those still in the graveyard.

The coven of seven had been reduced to six and I was going to let them be reduced to zero and not feel bad about it or even cry about it. Tomorrow, they'd figure out that Mathilda Wellesley had interrupted a ritual and the ritual had backfired and killed the coven and her. They would probably all get medals of honor from the mayor, unless he was able to recall someone putting Belgaphor into him.

The Earth shook like it ached as the large hand pulled its body free of the ground. The thing that came forth was large, red, and not happy. He glared at me and then at the archangels, but he didn't move towards us. Instead he spread his large, impressive wings that dripped fire from the feathers.

Before us stood the archangel no one spoke of. The most powerful of the brothers. The one not meant for this Earth. The mastermind of the Stygian Plane.

"You, little one?" His voice felt like I was being smothered by air.

"Not exactly, Lucifer," I told the uncle I had never met, the one that had not walked on Earth in his true form for as long as anyone could remember.

"You helped someone, though. What do you wish of me?" He asked.

"Only that you do your part to keep the Stygian Divide in place. This meddlesome coven has been sacrificing witches and wizards to bring forth your legions and your monsters."

"What if I am tired of ruling the Stygian?" He asked.

"Are you truly tired of such a thing, Uncle?" I asked.

"No." He answered.

"I thought not, and I know you normally do not meddle in the affairs of man or the domains of your brothers, but this coven found a loophole. They have been using archangel blood to feed their spells and bring forth princes."

"These puny beings?" He asked, pointing at them, maybe. His hands were so large, it was hard to tell if it was at a single one of them or at all of them. "Whose blood did they get?"

"Zadkiel's," I told Lucifer.

"You desecrated the grave of my brother Zadkiel?" Lucifer asked them. They didn't answer, but they didn't have to. Lucifer's eyes saw all and the vial of blood glowed under the robe of one of them.

"Yes, Lucifer, when they called forth Moloch all those years ago, they did so to get him to desecrate Zadkiel's grave."

"If I remember right, it was my brothers that killed Moloch."

"Yes, brother, it was Azrael and Uriel," Raphael said to Lucifer.

"It is good to see you, brother." Lucifer said. "And Gabriel."

"Lucifer, if you wish to join us on this plane, you may, I can break you of your bargain with the Stygian."

"While I miss the sun and my family, I do not regret the bargain I made with the divine. The Stygian is where I belong, helping keep order on Earth, for all of you."

"I can help with the sun, sir," Jerome said. I didn't shush him. Jerome pulled a small silver necklace from his pocket that had one of the sun pendants hanging from it. The boy bravely stepped forward and held the necklace out to Lucifer.

"It is warm, boy," he said.

"It is hers," he said, pointing to me. "I captured some of her magic and put into the pendant, so I would always have the sun with me."

"She is yours Raphael?"

"Yes, Lucifer," Raphael answered. "She is my youngest, Soleil."

215

"Her magic is like the sun, warm, life giving, and bright," Raphael said. "We named her for it." I didn't point out my sister was also named for the sun.

"Thank you, young wizard." Lucifer said, placing the insanely small necklace near his neck. After a moment, his skin absorbed the pendant and a sun appeared near his heart.

"Do I need to take all these fiends with me?" Lucifer spread his arms and I got the impression he meant the zombies.

"No, Uncle, I am strong enough to put them back to rest, after the coven and its patronage done for," I told him.

"Who knows, brothers, one day, if you keep producing offspring as strong as this to deal with the Stygian, maybe I can give up my place there." Lucifer looked at me. "You realize you are now going to have to do something different with my true form, correct?"

"Yes, Uncle," I told Lucifer and he lay back down onto the ground of shattered tombstones. The coven members looked terrified as lesser demons in their true form sprang forth from the Earth along with the zombies and began to attack the coven and their patron.

We all stood. I covered Jerome's eyes, there was no need for him to watch such horrible things happen, even to bad people.

Raphael went a step further, wrapping his wings around the boy and keeping the screams from reaching his ears, just as it kept the sight from reaching his eyes. And I was grateful.

"We are going to have to talk about how you knew," Gabriel said to me.

"I felt him," I told my uncle. "And when I stepped past the magic, but dad couldn't, I knew it wasn't designed to keep archangels out so much as it was designed to keep one in. Everyone but Lucifer was accounted for and since Zadkiel is in St. Louis, I figured Lucifer was close by, and Chicago isn't that far based on how an angel flies. Plus, people just don't name graveyards after the demon of child sacrifice without a good reason."

"Well, we got the bad guy," Hemingway said to me.

"Not yet, we didn't. There's still a possessed fugitive running around that we need to catch. However, it's going to have to wait until there's sunlight and I have slept." I told him.

"And had at least one bacon cheeseburger," Hemingway smiled at me.

"And that," I agreed.

"I'm pretty hungry too," Jerome told me and we all walked out of the graveyard, which was no place to be after dark anyway.

# Chapter 21

Hemingway started the SUV and I opened the door, jumping out of the SUV and into the road. I had told Lucifer that I would put the demon zombies back into the ground. And had nearly forgotten, which would have meant a half dozen true form demon zombies with no direction because we hadn't put any souls into the animated corpses, which would have led to them eating the poor, unfortunate citizens of Chicago. Carelessness like this was why everyone thought zombies were evil, well that and no one likes for their dead relatives to show up on their doorstep in the middle of the night because someone didn't bother to put a soul into them.

And just to show me that if I hadn't remembered, they would have reminded me, the true form of Moloch broke the iron gate on the cemetery and tossed it into the road. I had never put a zombie back into the ground, but I had a knack with all things demonic, surely, true forms, even if they didn't have the spirits in them, were no different. Of course, sometimes I was wrong about shit. This could be one of them. I walked towards Moloch.

I had been told the demon's spirit had been scary, his true form was worse. Giant white body that looked a lot like decaying whale blubber that someone had shoved into a sausage tube and very red lips, like Red Delicious Apples, stood out like wet blood on his white face. He was all bumpy and scaly, because nothing is sexier than a man with skin that had that just so amazing lizard mated with a frog feel. The eyes were just black sockets and I didn't know if that was because his eyes had rotted away or if he just hadn't had them to begin with. He had a giant set of white horns to go with his pale flesh. And the horns had small hairs all over them.

Being dead might have improved Moloch's overall appearance, at least now he had an excuse for looking this way. He could blame it on decay. I pushed a little magic at him, just to see what happened, and then he exploded, everywhere, not unlike a whale carcass filled with dynamite. I gagged.

Being dead had definitely not improved his smell and being exploded was just ensuring that everything could smell him. In my seventeen years as a certified exorcist, I had seen and smelled some nasty things, but this one made them all seem pleasant, almost heavenly.

Moloch bits were turning black and shriveling up into nothingness. Which was good, because I didn't think the city of Chicago had enough money in its coffers to pay anyone to clean him up. This entire area would have ended up condemned.

There were a handful of other true form zombies running around and I was surprised by the variety. Beings really only come in being colors, black, tan, white, but demons came in a wide variety, there was a veritable rainbow represented by the true forms running around. And not all of them looked like whale blubber in a sausage tube. Most looked hominoid to some degree, even if they were a bedazzling ruby red hominoid.

I almost wanted to find little girls with My Little Pony shirts and have them start gluing jewel tone plastic crystals to true form skin to give them some pizzazz, but they were zombies and they would probably eat the little girls, which would be bad. I resisted the urge and pushed magic towards them again. The true form zombies continued to amble around the cemetery, instead of going back into their graves, which was a problem, but it beat exploding zombies.

I pushed a little more magic and they all exploded. Not exactly what I had intended, but the pieces of demon were starting to shrivel and disappear already. I stood there watching the human zombies for several minutes. I gave another push of magic and the zombies climbed back into their graves.

I felt pretty good about myself. I had put zombies to rest and exploded the true forms. And then my brain started to work, and I frowned at the zombie free cemetery. The door alert still buzzed from inside the SUV and I could hear my uncles and father grumbling about the tight fit with their wings. And leaning on the center console, half in the front seat, was the real magic behind the zombie's going back into their graves.

And he was just as hungry as I was, despite the massive feast at dinner. I gave him a thumb's up and walked back to the SUV.

"Took you long enough," Jerome said as I got in the car.

"Whatever," I gently pushed on his head, moving him back into the second row of seating between Raphael and Gabriel. "I almost got Moloch guck on me."

"It is a good thing you didn't get Moloch on you or you would have had to call Uber to get back to the hotel," Hemingway told me.

"Hey, you exploded Moloch, I put the others back in the ground, so you wouldn't explode all of them," Jerome told me. I didn't know whether I believed him or not. For tonight, I was willing to share credit on the Moloch incident.

"Dude, sir, what's your name?" Jerome asked from the back seat. "She only calls you Hemingway. I know Tabitha and Walter's names, but I don't know yours."

"I'm totally thinking it is officially, Dude, sir," I teased Hemingway.

"Duke," Hemingway said.

"Dude, sir, is better," Raphael chirped from the back seat.

"Dude, sir, is taken by my twin brother," Hemingway smiled in the dark as we drove towards our hotel, where the gargoyles should have been resting, peacefully, after their source of magic was mostly eaten by true form demon zombies. I was fairly sure Duke Hemingway was not going to write that into a report or anything, and if he did, I'd deny it to my dying day.

The hotel was cleaning up a freak stone incident when we arrived. It didn't appear the stone had damaged anything, though. The front entrance was perfect. No one would have guessed that an hour ago a large gargoyle had smashed into it trying to get inside. There was another news van. Hemingway skirted around it and into the hotel's parking garage.

The archangels got out and stretched their wings while sniping at each other. Car rides make archangels bitchy, who would have thought it. To our delight, there was a small amount of kitchen staff still on the premises. Jerome and I each ordered a bacon cheeseburger and onion rings. And as the waiter went through the list of stuff he could have put on it, he asked if he could add mushrooms, jalapenos, and grilled red peppers. I said yes to all three of these things and added them to my own burger as well. Then I added extra cheese to both as well.

"You're going to give this kid high cholesterol by the time he's a senior in high school," Hemingway told me.

"Possibly, if he could get high cholesterol, ever, then it would be a problem, but he can't. So add extra bacon to both burgers as well." I told the waiter.

"You are incorrigible." Hemingway told me.

"And Mr. Crankypants is on a diet because he's getting old, so just a Metamucil shake for him." I smiled.

"Oh no, I want the same thing they are having," Hemingway told the waiter.

"Me too," Gabriel sat down at the table with us.

"Jerome, Raphael was just telling me about your mom being sick," Gabriel said to the kid and I considered kicking his angelic ass out the door. "I'm going to go talk to my brother, Michael, and have him come see your mom. I don't know if he'll be able to help her or not, but if we all keep them both in our prayers, maybe," Gabriel said. "However, I have been told that you and your mom are joining our family and I am really happy about that."

"Uh, thanks, I think." Jerome looked skeptical.

"Exactly, Gabriel, did you decide to get people skill tips from Uriel?" I poked fun at both uncles.

"Well, uh yes, actually," Gabriel did an impression of Christopher Walken that cracked Jerome up. It made me grin too.

"You're too young to have seen that movie," Hemingway told him.

"My mom really likes The Prophesy," Jerome told him.

"Me too," Gabriel said. "And Christopher Walken might be more attractive than me, but really, that just made

222

him even better as me. Kevin Durand did an okay job, but I feel like I have more personality than Gabriel did in *Legion*. Meaning the problem wasn't Durand's acting, but the source material on that one, and most of the time, Gabriel just doesn't exist. Everyone writes about Michael or Lucifer. Depending on which way they want the film to go. *The Prophesy* is one of my favorites, because at least they were original in making Gabriel the psycho who should have fallen instead of Lucifer."

"Yeah, what's with that?" Jerome asked.

"There is a collective memory of Lucifer being unhappy on Earth, so everyone just makes him evil, when let's be real, you saw him tonight, in his true form, he just couldn't blend in with mortals like me or Raphael. It was mostly bad luck. But then demons started to appear on Earth and Lucifer realized he could build a home for himself, away from the judgmental eyes of man, and have it provide some good. He designed the Stygian Plane, we all did our parts to help, and then he moved there, permanently," Gabriel said. "But he couldn't take his true form across. Ironically, it was too big for the Stygian Divide. At the time, we were hanging out here, with the Native Americans, so he asked us to bury it and we did."

"Still one of the hardest things I have ever had to do," Raphael said quietly, joining us at the table. "Letting Lucifer make that crossing, I mean. And knowing that my brother wouldn't be joining us for any holidays or stopping by to have a beer when we got married."

"It was tough," Azrael said and ordered a beer. "And every night since Zadkiel was murdered, I have thought about digging him up."

"Me too," Gabriel said. "But come, let's talk of happier things, except I can't think of any."

"We probably solved two or three dozen crimes tonight," Jerome offered. "Including the death of my father, who was written off as an accidental death."

"He accidentally ripped out his own heart?" I asked Jerome.

"That was the coroner's determination." Jerome said.

"Is the coroner an idiot?" I asked.

"No, he was one of the men in the graveyard tonight."

"That would be a yes on the idiot part then," Gabriel said. "The thing covens like that don't realize is that demons aren't exactly good for anybody."

"You should go tell BEADER that." I told Gabriel. "And remind them that there is no termination date on my restraining order."

"Are those nuts still hassling you?"

"Yes," Jerome answered for me. "Next time, though, I'll just let them get themselves possessed, and then they can try it for themselves."

"That's the problem, they have been possessed, most of them are people who had their sexually interesting demons exorcized."

"People are freaks," Jerome stated and we all nodded in agreement. Our food was delivered a few moments later and conversation stopped while we all ate.

"Soleil, I'm nervous about going to magic school, what if I don't make friends."

"Who are you kidding? The new kid with all sorts of power, and you can probably play a bit of sports, you'll have friends in no time. Plus, you live with a nephilim, the chicks will dig that." Raphael told him.

"You just assume I can play sports?" Jerome took a tone with my father, but I could see the smile under it.

"No, because I saw the trophies in your room."
Raphael answered. "And Soleil likes baseball, which works out for both of you, judging by what your trophies were in."

"A baseball playing wizard, and you are worried about not making friends?" I asked. "I think our witchcraft school has a decent baseball team if I remember right."

"I won't wear Cardinals gear," he told me.

"Maybe not this year, but after living in St. Louis for a year or so, you'll see why the Cards are better than the Cubs." I smiled at him.

"Baseball is happier, I should have thought of that." Gabriel said after a moment.

"Come on, kiddo, let's get some sleep so you don't look like a zombie when I take you to see your mom tomorrow."

Jerome smiled, and it lit up the room.

# Chapter 22

We got to sleep until 9 in the morning, it was blissful. Once up, we all met for breakfast in the hotel restaurant and made a plan for the day. My father and I were taking Jerome to see his mother first, while Hemingway and the rest of the marshals gathered information on Mathilda Wellesley and Christina. Gabriel, Uriel, and Azrael were going to drop a tip by the Division of Magic via pay phone on their way out of town about the cemetery events the night before. Hemingway listened to that and said nothing, which I found impressive. And they were going to check on the tips about Don Rabblings to see if they could get a fix on his location within Chicago.

Raphael, Jerome, and I headed to Cook County Hospital via limo, because sometimes vanity my name is Raphael. I had to admit there was more room for his wings in a limousine, but it had always felt ostentatious to arrive anywhere in one.

Valerie Dussain looked like warmed over death, and I wasn't even sure even Michael, God's healer could save her, but I was going to try to convince him to at least make the attempt, if it was the last thing I ever did.

But not today. Today was about Valarie and Jerome spending time together, even if it was at a hospital.

My father had the hired car take me to meet up with Hemingway and the marshals at the Division of Magic station house.

It was like nothing had happened, physically. The building was fine, no residual energy sickness from all the demons running through the building, which was good. The detectives inside it were not firing on all cylinders. Most of them looked pale and sickly. The worst of them were still in the hospital having their wounds cleaned and dressed, fighting the infections demons brought, and talking to psychiatrists that worked with those that had been possessed. Possession was an ordeal, mentally and physically, and unless it had happened to you, it was hard to relate to.

I got a standing ovation when I walked into the squad room full of cubicles after the desk sergeant buzzed me in. I blushed. I accepted the thank you's and told them how amazing they all were and that most of them had been easy to exorcize because they had fought the possession for so long. I might have been a natural born exorcist, but I was still just one person and exorcism required more than just me, the host had to want for it to work without fracturing the psyche completely.

The marshals were set up in a conference room, and the female detective that I had exorcized twice was leaning on a cane, pointing to a whiteboard in the room. She was going to be physically battling her demon induced wounds for a long time. I walked up and hugged her as I entered the room. She awkwardly sort of hugged me back. I got it, not everyone was a hugger. But I grew up around angels and angels believed in the healing power of hugs. She didn't hit me with her cane or direct any violence at me, so even though it had been awkward for her to be hugged, especially at work, by another woman, she had accepted it.

I looked at the map near the whiteboard. And the addresses on the whiteboard. Don Rabbling had picked the worse neighborhood in Chicago to hide in. Riverdale was a rough area with low rates of employment and high crime rates. It was basically a bunch of apartment buildings stacked on top of each other with houses here and there, but the houses were owned by gang leaders, black magic practitioners who used magic to kill and advance their social standing, and drug dealers.

There was a shooting every night. The cops were not welcome, and there was pretty much a standing order to kill them on sight. Hemingway was coordinating getting witch support. Tabitha was good, but she was a vampire, not capable of casting spells on the fly. He also wanted a member of the fae who had strong glamour. I agreed with both of those, and for good measure, I suggested an ogre if they had one. Contrary to myths, ogres are not stupid, but they are big and capable of taking a lot of damage, both physically and magically. They could even absorb death magic if it hit them square on, something no one else in our group could do. Besides, ogres looked scary as hell and made people think twice about their actions. If we could have had a legion of ogres, I would have been happy. Sadly, Chicago PD had two, and one was at the hospital being treated for possession sickness.

The detective left and came back with our reinforcements. She was going to be our witch. It was a good fit. Rabbling had been seen with a girlfriend in one of the apartment complexes in Riverdale. We didn't have an exact address, but that wasn't surprising. There was a chance that if he was possessed I'd be able to see and follow the magical signature of the demon. Of course, there was also the chance that multiple beings in Riverdale were possessed.

The marshals suited up in kevlar vests, which was fine. It even helped with some magic. I did not take a vest. Anything that shot me was going to figure out damn quick that the difference between angels and demons weren't as great as most people thought. The Division of Magic had their own SWAT vehicle, and I admit, I was excited to ride in it.

The inside was every bit as cool as I had hoped. There were cameras that watched the outside, a few silver cages built into it for transporting bad guys, and a gun cage that held cool things like assault rifles and a grenade launcher. There was also room for magic wands, magic staffs, and any other magical support items the occupants used. All the handcuffs were silver except ten pair which were iron for arresting things like fairies, leprechauns, and ogres. The steel cuffs and shackles hung on one side, the silver directly across from them. There was room for ten. We had seven because broken bones had happened in the crowd crush at the hotel with the zombie invasion and the other two marshals were still down.

We slowed down for a traffic light and bullets thunked off the steel and silver sides of the armored vehicle. We had treads so we didn't have to worry about the bullets piercing the tires. No dents appeared in the wall from the bullets and even though I should have been terrified, I was instead excited. I enjoyed helping the police and people like Hemingway do good. It made me feel like I was making a difference since most people fought their demons, and I basically just came along and cleaned house.

There were exceptions, of course, I referred to them as demon groupies and it was a paraphilia, but one that made scratch my head. I would just never understand why someone wanted to hang out with a parasitic demon.

The vehicle cornered like a tank and we swiped a parked cop car. At least it belonged to the city, though. It made paying for damages a little easier and no one was going to go on TV to complain about it.

I was sitting where I could partially see out the front window. We were approaching a group of row houses that had seen better days, like before they were built. Most of the windows were covered with plywood or black paint and I saw a half dozen demon signatures moving around the houses and street in different directions. Good lord. I was going to try to isolate a single signature in this mess and I didn't even know who the demon was or what its signature looked like. Good thing I liked a challenge.

The armored vehicle turned into the parking lot of an apartment complex, there were probably five buildings, but in this neighborhood, most residents didn't have cars because having a car meant it could be borrowed by a stranger without permission. It was easier to take the bus or El train, and probably less expensive as well. I couldn't imagine how much car insurance was for parking a car in this neighborhood. The monthly rate was probably more than my car insurance premium for an entire year. But I drove a piece of shit, because possessed people kept tearing it up.

The armored car pulled up into the grass in front of one of the outdoor stairwells that went to the complex we suspected Don Rabbling was in. Don was a bald guy with lifeless brown eyes and sallow skin. Being possessed might liven him up. He had killed his wife and three kids because he didn't want to be married anymore and divorce is expensive. Especially for someone that had leprechaun bloodlines.

As far as power went, leprechauns weren't up there. Most of their magic involved filling their own piggy banks with money. I had never met one that could do anything more than plan my investment portfolio. Most mortals could do more magic than leprechauns.

Which meant we might have a possessed leprechaun. Technically, leprechauns were members of the fae, protected fairy folk. However, fairy folk took killing people very serious, and if he hadn't been wanted by regular authorities, Don would have faced fae justice already, which would have resulted in his lifeless body being dumped on the steps of a police station.

However, members of the fae were willing to enforce the laws of the mortals upon their own kind. And Don had been convicted and was on death row in Joliet Federal Penitentiary, meaning fae justice had been done, by mortal courts. The difference was time. The fae were swift at dealing out death penalty punishments and mortals moved slower, odd considering the difference in life spans.

Hemingway's fingers brushed the back of my hand as everyone got ready to exit the vehicle. We all stepped out and onto the concrete sidewalk and frogs began to fall from the sky. Stupid leprechaun. There was a demon trail on the ground, but I didn't know if it was the demon in Don. However, the signature was very clear, meaning it was a powerful demon, so I lead the group the way the trail went.

Don had already seen us anyway, judging by the frogs. If it wasn't him, it was someone else and he'd know soon enough. The trail led up the stairs and to the third floor. Billy Grunde was right behind me, and I could feel his fae magic keeping the damn frogs from landing on me. I really did love ogres. We walked around the balcony that lead to the apartment doors and were pelted with rocks by people on the ground. Seriously? I didn't shout at them, but I thought it at them really hard.

231

The building shuddered. The demon knew we were here, awesome. The door to apartment 399 was glowing, never a good sign. Billy stepped in front of me and we moved to stand in front of the door, well off to the side.

"Bureau of Exorcism, I have an order to remove the demon from its host," I shouted at the door and the door exploded outwards, showering tiny plywood shards down onto the concrete walkway and over the railing onto the people below, who suddenly seemed to have something else to do.

I peeked my head around the ogre. Don Rabbling was short, even by leprechaun standards, at maybe five feet tall. And he was absolutely possessed. He glowed and glared at me. It was hard to look intimidating when you were glowing, but the demon inside Don managed.

"Demon, this is Soleil Burns, I command you to come to me," I shouted at Don, or rather the thing in Don. Most of the time, this works and the demon comes to me so I can learn its name. Not today. An assortment of knives went sailing past my head. Billy made a motion with his hands and I nodded. Billy stepped forward and entered the apartment with me walking practically on his heels.

Magic was wildly flung at us and Billy took the brunt of it, letting the magic soak into his ogre skin. Billy got taller and more muscular and then someone shot me in the back.

"Are you fucking kidding me?" I turned and saw a woman in the corner of the room, a crib behind her, and large hand gun in her hands. Her hands were shaking as I stalked towards her. I grabbed the gun by the barrel and she fired again, point blank range. It caught me in the abdomen. I jerked the gun from her hands and tossed it out the window, which was closed, but it went through the glass just fine. "This is the example you want to set for

232

your kid? Shoot angels and take up with demonic leprechauns?" I asked her, my voice hard and steady.

"Demons?" She frowned. I grabbed her by the shoulders and pulled her away from the crib. Then I picked up the sleeping infant and handed it to the woman. I then shoved both of them towards the door. Billy was beating on Don. His giant fists clubbing the leprechaun over and over, magic bursting from each as they landed on the smaller man. Billy's magic was a beautiful shade of blue, like ocean water.

The demon punched back, and Billy slumped to the floor. His eyes searched the room. Hemingway grabbed the woman and pulled her and the infant to safety. I felt protection spells snapping into place.

Don tried to pick Billy up, but the smaller man, even with the demon in him, struggled at the mechanics of it, and I realized whatever demon was in Don had a true form much bigger than Don's.

"Bring back my food, bitch," the demon buzzed at me.

"Go fuck a gorgon," I told the demon and then took a step forward. I already knew the sire, just by the sound of its voice. Only Beelzebub's offspring could sound like a million bees, it was part of the reason for his name, it was the sound he made.

I grabbed Don. I was in trouble. Beelzebub wasn't the sire, it was the prince himself. And he made Belgaphor feel like a lesser demon. Beelzebub's magic hit me square in the chest, taking my breath away and causing blood to pour from my gunshot wound in the gut. My necklace with Raphael's sigil glowed with the intensity of a small sun. Beelzebub turned his face from it. I took another step forward, closing the gap between us. I wrapped my arms around Don and pulled the leprechaun in for a hug.

Beelzebub screamed and the sound of bees was so intense I could hear nothing else.

My body felt like it was on fire as Beelzebub's magic covered me in bee stings and his voice droned in my head like I was standing in a giant pissed off hive. But I didn't let go. I drew blood from Don Rabbling, opening a gash in his forehead that Beelzebub had to tend to, try to heal. Scalp wounds are messy, though, and Don's blood flowed freely, dripping like tears onto the nasty, dirty carpet.

"Soleil," Hemingway shouted as a sun began to appear at my feet. I pulled Don closer to me and slipped one foot onto the sun symbol. It was now being supercharged by leprechaun blood and I could feel the magic fill me until I thought it would explode my eyeballs from their sockets. In my mind, I grabbed the spirit form of Beelzebub and jerked him from Don.

I heard Don curse and the spirit of Beelzebub began to solidify immediately in the air in front of me. Don had made a deal with Beelzebub. And Don had wanted to be possessed. I felt Billy stir and he touched my sun, smearing a faint line of his blood on it.

Beelzebub laughed at me. I pulled his solidifying demon form into me, wrapping an arm around it. The laugh turned into a scream that made my brain feel as though it were bleeding. A spell raced into the room from the shattered window. It slammed into Beelzebub and he shimmered just so, translucency returning to parts of him.

I desperately tried to focus on Beelzebub crossing the Stygian Divide. My brain fought against me. I held the prince, but just barely. I stared at Beelzebub and felt doubt. He stopped screaming and laughed again. I was going to lose. I had never lost control of a demon I was trying to exorcize before, not unintentionally that is. I had tossed a few to get away from their magic and to toy with them, but that had been on purpose. Beelzebub was stronger than me and I knew it. It was not the demon's magic working on my mind that made me think it.

I stepped back from the sun and watched the color fade from it. I was not stronger than Beelzebub, but I was not alone. I closed my eyes and let the feel of the bees continue in my head. I stopped fighting his magic.

"You are beaten nephilim," Beelzebub said to me and I submitted to the sensation of the bees. I let them sting. I let them drown out all other sound in my brain until they were all I could think of and all I could feel.

"Yes, I am only half angel, but I am the daughter of Raphael and the niece of your captor, I am the sun," I told Beelzebub. "I am warmth and life and love. I am everything you fear, demon." My mind cleared. Billy had left his hand on my sun symbol. The witch detective was creeping into the room and she held a knife that dripped of her blood. Tabitha also came in and Beelzebub's eyes shot to the empty door frame. I was not alone. I stepped back onto the sun and felt the magic surge. It was warm and beautiful, and for a moment, I saw the sun set over Lake Michigan in my memory and it was louder than the sound of the bees.

I pictured the massive frame of Beelzebub crossing the Stygian Divide, with the darkness sucking at him, trying to claim him. And I felt him grow fainter on my fingertips. Go back demon. I whispered. There was a loud bang, like a gunshot. Part of the wall fell down in the apartment, turning the two tiny apartments into one.

The walls were blackened, and the sun symbol had burned itself into the carpet. Don Rabbling was hairless. Blisters on Don's skin were already healing. Billy sat up. Blood drying on his shirt and mouth.

"Now that's how you use magic," he smiled at me and then lay back down. For a moment, I worried he had died and his spirit had spoken to me one last time. The crib was in flames as was the ratty worn out couch. Don held out his hands and nearly begged for the handcuffs. Hemingway clapped the steel around Don's wrists and I felt the pull of Beelzebub's magic.

"Don has a deal with Beelzebub," I told Hemingway.

"Okay, I'm not an interdimensional lawyer," Hemingway said.

"Gabriel," I told him. I heard Tabitha talking behind me.

"One interdimensional lawyer at your service," I heard Gabriel say.

Gabriel touched Don who shrank away. Gabriel swore. I wasn't sure if he was swearing at Don, swearing in general, or swearing at Beelzebub. Or all the above. Gabriel swore more than most angels.

The second time, Gabriel was forceful, grabbing Don by the hair roughly. He looked at the leprechaun and swore again. That time it was definitely at Don.

"His deal keeps any fae from killing him," Gabriel looked at Billy. I wanted to swear but didn't. It had been a smart bargain.

"What did the demon get in return?" I asked. Gabriel looked out the door.

"Oh," I said in response while releasing lots of creative swear words in my head.

The infant was brought into the room, but it was already too late. Its tiny soul had been unable to battle against the demon that had taken up residence. I couldn't exorcize the demon without killing the child. And, I would not kill a child. It just wasn't happening. The child had the double iris of so many half human, half supernaturals. It was going to grow up with a demon in residence.

"Bring me the child," Gabriel said. I handed him over reluctantly. Gabriel lifted the infant and blew gently on its arm. Gabriel's sigil appeared, much like my hell fire brand. It had its own internal light that shown through the skin. "As long as I live, and the child is on Earth, I will know where it is." Gabriel told me and that was the best we were going to get of the situation.

"You did well," Gabriel said after a few moments of silence.

"Thanks," I told him as he handed the infant back to me. Despite the sigil, the energy hadn't changed. In my head, the demon laughed and I felt his power. Fan-fucking-tabulous.

# Chapter 23

I woke up in my hotel suite. Jerome on the couch playing Days Gone. Hemingway sitting with him, a controller in his hand as well. My dad sat at the dining room table working with Jerome's sketch pad. The colored pencils flew over the paper and I had no clue what he was drawing, but I was sure it was nifty, because it was my dad.

"You're awake," Jerome said, never turning to look at me. His eyes still on the TV.

"Yes." I answered.

"I'll order food," Raphael said. "Gabriel told me what you did."

"Good, maybe you can explain it to me," I told him. "But not right now, my head still feels like my brain was stung by bees."

"It was." Raphael said.

"Nearly everyone had to go to the hospital to get checked out." Hemingway said.

"I don't remember that."

"You didn't go." Hemingway said. "Gabriel insisted on bringing you here instead."

"Okay," I said.

"Don't worry, Asha, it will be fine." My father said and that kind of freaked me out.

"If you are trying to comfort me, you are doing a terrible job, Dad."

"Sleep for now, Asha," he responded, and I did. I dreamed of playing with dolls with Helia. We were both very little and the yard was full of dry grass that was starting to turn brown from lack of rain. No, it wasn't Helia. Helia was in the tree house watching me play with someone. Another little girl with golden hair tied up in pigtails. Her face cold. I felt like she didn't want to play with me but was being forced to. She reached out and grabbed my doll, my favorite doll, she had red hair made of yarn and her eyes looked like scarecrow eyes.

"I'm warning you, give it back to Soleil," I heard Helia yell from the treehouse. "Give it back now!" Helia stomped her foot and the tree froze. The boards under her feet broke and Helia fell to the ground. I shouted for my sister. She stood and walked towards us, blood flowing from a cut on her leg. "Give it back, Katrina, or else," I said. Katrina laughed at me. I touched the ground and felt it absorb the blood my sister had lost to it upon impact, and I pulled on it.

The magic raced through me, and I felt like I would die. It was so hot. Then flames erupted from my hands and the grass caught fire. I grabbed Katrina and screamed into her face and felt her flesh begin to bubble under my hands. It scared me so much. And then I ripped Katrina's soul from her body and flung it into the flaming grass. Gabriel came running out to see why we were screaming. He said my name, carefully, slowly.

"Soleil, put Katrina's soul back," he nearly whispered the words to me.

"I hope she burns," I told Gabriel. "No, child, you do not hope that at all."

239

"She is always mean to me," I told my uncle. "And to Helia. Last time she was here, she told Helia that if she didn't get to be princess of our treehouse, our treehouse, not hers, she would rip off Helia's head and burn it."

"Just because Katrina is mean does not mean you should be as well." Gabriel told me. I felt my hands begin to shake and the fire that burned through them calmed, quieted. "Love, Soleil, magic should be about love, not hate. Love makes it more powerful. Love made you turn the land to ashes, to help your sister because you love her. Katrina does not love, and therefore, she is weaker than you. You should never use your magic to pick on those weaker than you. Hate froze the tree that you have loved so dearly. Channel your magic into freeing the tree. Warm it up, and watch it heal."

Little me focused on the tree and I saw it begin to drip water. And as ice dripped from the tree, a tear dripped from me. I will never use magic because of hate again," I told Gabriel. "My sister, the ash maker," Helia said, but she was smiling.

"You froze our favorite tree, Helia, your magic was cold." I told her. "It felt of death."

"What do you know of death?" Katrina's spirit yelled at me. I felt another tear fall.

"Katrina, forgive me," I begged of her. Then I touched her spirit and pictured it entering her body once more.

Once her soul and body were reunited, Katrina threw magic out at me and Helia. I grabbed Helia, jerking her out of the way and felt my own magic flow into me again. I looked up at Gabriel. He touched my head.

"That is enough, Ash Maker." He said softly. "I will deal with Katrina." He grabbed my cousin by the wings and dragged her kicking into my house. She hurled curses and magic at us as she went, but she didn't dare turn the magic on Gabriel. I sat outside in the burnt grass. Helia touched my hand.

"It is okay, Asha." She whispered and hugged me. And I felt her magic mingle with my own. And the grass healed, everything I had turned to ash turned green and fertile with Helia's magic to dampen my fire. But I sat in her arms for a long time, willing her to be healed,

Then my dream faded as a voice pierced it. It did not feel like bees, thankfully, but it held no life in it. It was tired from a life of pain. Michael took me by the hands, and I felt the bee stings recede.

"No, Uncle, I need you to heal another." I told him, pulling away. "I will heal with time; Beelzebub's magic is not eternal."

"Soleil, it will heal slowly, and until then, you will constantly feel his touch." Michael told me.

"But I am strong and every demon I touch leaves a mark on me, I feel them all for a time, some can invade my dreams, I have touched them so often we have a link that crosses the Stygian. But I am an exorcist. I have been all my life. The string of demonic pain is too much for most. Possibly even you, for you have seen and felt much cruelty in this world. It is your burden and your gift. I would not have you take my demonic pain to go with the earthly pain you endure. I have centuries to heal. The person I need you to heal has but one lifetime, and it will be cut short if you cannot use your gift on her. I have never asked you to heal anyone for me, Michael, because I know that you take their pain into you. And I would not now, if I did not feel with all of my being that it was necessary. Not just to save her life, but to save my own. Because my fate lies with her."

"Are you in love with her?" Michael asked.

"No, uncle, but I love her. She may not be of our blood, but I feel no different about her than I do Helia."

"Your willingness to suffer Beelzebub's torments in her place convinces me that she is worth healing, and I will do what I can for her. When you are better, rested, and have eaten, and gained some of your strength back, you shall take me to her, so I can see for myself that she is no different than Helia." And then Michael disappeared because he's annoying that way.

"I heard him, but I did not see him," Hemingway said.

"Michael can only be seen by his bloodline, it is to keep everyone from forcing him to heal them," Raphael said. "It is a powerful gift, but powerful gifts are also great burdens." I nodded in agreement with Raphael. Then a sandwich showed up at the door with mixed vegetables, no liquid smoke on them, and french fries, lots of french fries, enough for everyone in the room and then some. I ate sitting on the little cot that my father had delivered for me to recover my senses on.

"Will Michael heal my mom?" Jerome asked as I ate the last bite of the delicious sandwich.

"If he can," I told Jerome. "Michael must take on the injury or illness to heal. And sadly, he cannot save everyone." I set the fries down, having lost my appetite. I noticed my necklace was glowing softly. I touched it, it wasn't warm. I was not in the presence of a demon, I was in the presence of demon magic. It would take a while for Beelzebub's magic to go away. Until then, the necklace would probably glow all the time.

I went to my room and awoke sometime later. The word Helia filled my thoughts, and I called my sister randomly to say hello to her. Something I never did. She was stand-offish at first. We did not discuss her work. We did not discuss my work. We did not discuss her marriage to Ted the Cheat. We discussed burned grass on a hot July day with our cousin Katrina acting like she owned our stuff because both her parents were angels and we were just nephilim who deserved nothing. We discussed the fact that Katrina had never moved out of Uriel's house because she couldn't hold down a job, any job, not even one where making people feel good was the only requirement, and it was an innate talent for her. Helia laughed. A sound I had not heard in a long time.

Gabriel had, of course, been right. My love for my sister had given me the power to rip Katrina's soul from her body, even though we were just kids. In the end, love conquered all, which was ridiculous but sadly true. And then we discussed her marriage and whether she loved Ted the Cheat or just loved the life they had together. She admitted she stayed for the children and the life, because she was married and that carried more weight than being divorced.

Helia and I agreed the world needed more love in it and more hugs. Everything was better with a hug. We hung up and the smile stayed on my face as I walked into the living room, where Walter, Tabitha, Hemingway, and even my father were playing a game with Jerome. The world definitely needed more love and more hugs.

A few hours later, I stood at the foot of Valerie's hospital bed, my hand touching my uncle, keeping Michael visible for her, so he would not have to waste energy doing it. Michael had been standing there about five minutes, doing nothing that was visible to me or to Valerie. We were getting attention from hospital staff, because there was an angel at the foot of a bed in ICU, and not just any angel, but the archangel of death.

243

"I can heal her, but it will come at a steep price," Michael suddenly said. "Her cancer is not because her body began to reproduce cells incorrectly." Michael looked at me, not meeting my eyes or Valerie's.

"It's a death curse," Valerie said after a moment.

"Yes," Michael answered and his voice broke. "It is a powerful death curse, I cannot imagine why someone wanted you dead so badly that they would do this to you. I see your life when I look at you, and you were good to everyone."

"Jerome," I breathed.

"The young wizard didn't do this," Michael told me.

"No, Uncle, someone did this because they wanted Jerome orphaned."

"Soleil, you must choose, I can save her, I can remove the magic that fuels the death curse, but if I do, I will probably die, I am old and weak. But I have lived a long life and would gladly go home. You have never asked your family for anything, always trying to forge ahead alone. For you, I will do this."

I could not choose Valerie over Michael, no matter how much I wanted her to live. I opened my mouth.

"No!" Valerie shouted at the angel. "If I die, I see my husband, my mom and dad, and Soleil takes care of Jerome for me. I will not let you risk your life for me, no matter how much I want to live."

"That is why I am willing to do it, good lady." Michael said to her.

"I'm not," Valerie said. "If you died, this life would not be worth living, my happiness would die as well." I took a deep breath steadying myself. Michael leaned over me and kissed my forehead.

"I'm sorry my news was not better, Soleil, now let me heal Beelzebub's magic from you," Michael said.

"Thank you, Uncle, but no." I let go and could see by Valerie's face when he disappeared to her. Michael left a moment later, no doubt returning to his cave. Michael had separated himself from the world because of these sorts of requests, and I felt guilty that I had even asked him.

"You have an amazing family," Valerie said.

"They can do awesome things," I agreed.

"No," Valerie smiled. "You have an awesome family that loves and supports you and wants to help you."

"I know." I told her. "And they will love you and Jerome as well."

"I don't care about me, I care about Jerome."

"A mother's love is selfless," Raphael said walking into the room. "I saw Michael leave."

"Yes, it wouldn't work," I told my father.

"Then we shall make her as comfortable as possible until we find something that will," Raphael said. I nodded. "Hemingway would very much like to see you before he leaves. They caught their bad guy and return today."

"Okay," I waved to Valerie and Jerome came into the room. He ran over and hugged his mom and I wiped a tear away.

# Chapter 24

I stood outside of the Hotel Diablo, thinking the irony of the name was probably intentional. Hemingway, Tabitha, and Walter stood on the steps with me, soaking up a few final rays of sunshine. The two injured marshals were in the car at the bottom of the steps.

"Keep in touch, you have the gift," I hugged Tabitha. "Uriel is a jackass like ninety-nine point nine percent of the time, but he is good at training exorcists of all sorts. Plus, I want to see that beautiful baby when it arrives." Tabitha narrowed her eyes at me.

"What baby?" She asked. I touched her shoulder and looked at her belly. "Three weeks, maybe," I told her. "I can tell you the gender if you want."

"I didn't think you could use your magic like that." She said after a moment.

"I can't," I told her. "But Gabriel is a different story, he isn't called the messenger for no reason. He told me I had to take extra good care of you, because babies don't get souls until they are born and so they are empty vessels for the right a-s-dot."

"I have never heard that term." Tabitha said.

"It's a computer programming term and an inside joke between Helia and I. Even though we are bigger than our mother physically, she will still wash our mouths out with soap for dropping f-bombs, or any swear word, in front of my sister's kids." I smiled.

"You going to get home okay?" Tabitha asked.

"Have you seen the freaking cars my dad keeps ordering?" I smiled wider. "He has decided that he is going to rent a jet to fly Jerome, me, and Valerie back to St. Louis, a jet with medical services onboard."

"I am going to miss you most," Walter said. "Until I met you, I had never met a nephilim or an angel or an archangel, and now I've met all of you, I just don't think my world will be the same."

"You pulled that crap with your wife too, didn't you," I teased.

"Yes, but it was as true then about her as it is about you." I hugged Walter. "Mr. Kemp, you and your family are welcome to come visit me and mine in St. Louis any time you want. I would love to meet the fairy that manages to put up with you. And fairy children are so adorable."

"Until they break stuff," Walter said.

"That's true of nephilim children too, my nieces are adorable until they break things, but that's just kids in general." I told him.

"Too true, we will definitely take you up on the offer."

"Good, I am always looking for reasons to go to the zoo or art museum or science center or any of the other family-oriented things."

"Soleil, I have learned a lot from you this past handful of days," Hemingway said. He reached out and hugged me but kept me from moving into him to hug him back. I felt resistance in him but wasn't sure why. "We are now no longer colleagues, and I have asked Azrael to never send you to work with my team again."

"Well, that was mean," I told him.

"Perhaps," Hemingway moved closer, folding his arms around my back and kissed me, deep, gentle, and full of need. "But I can't do that to a coworker, and I can't ask one out to dinner, it is against the rules, and I am a stickler for rules. So, it helps if we don't work together anymore. Because I have wanted to do that from the moment I met you."

"You know, there's only a four-hour drive from St. Louis to Kansas City."

"Or a twenty-minute flight. Would you go out to dinner with me?"

"Yes," I told him.

"Just us, no archangels, no marshals, and hopefully, no demons."

"I can't make any promises about any of those things, Duke. But I am willing to try," I told him and kissed him softly on the lips.

"That is all I can ask for." Hemingway said.

"Go, get home. It will be a while before we leave, but I'll call you once I'm there."

"For the record, I like zoos too," Hemingway told me and I couldn't help but smile. "And kids, even teenagers."

"Good," I nodded once. "Go before I change my mind and have to figure out an excuse on why you missed your flight."

"That would be bad," Hemingway said.

"I'll call you, or you can call me," I told him. He pulled away.

"Is the kissing part done?" I heard Jerome say from behind me. He and Raphael were coming up the steps of the hotel.

"In a year or two, you'll be sad when the kissing part ends." I teased him.

"Yeah, but I'll be sad when the kissing part ends for me, not you." He said. "Old people kiss weird."

"Thanks," Hemingway said. I let him go and watched them all leave.

Gabriel had told me that love conquered all when I was a child. He had often reminded me of it as I grew up. I had always doubted him. Today, for the first time, I did not doubt him. Even as Beelzebub's magic pricked at my brain and soul. I understood that love made us stronger.

And Jerome handed me a necklace, a beautiful silver chain, a gorgeous silver sun gemstone with a black diamond set in the center. I felt the magic in the necklace the moment I touched it, and it was warm magic. A mix of Jerome's and mine.

"It's breathtaking," I told Jerome.

"Your dad paid for it," Jerome looked at his feet.

"You picked it out, didn't you?" I asked him.

"Yes." He said. "I thought it was too much, but Raphael disagreed. Then I filled it with your magic and some of my own."

"I can feel the magic, and it is stunning," I put it on.

"Do you really like it?" He asked.

"I love it, Jerome," I hugged the kid and he felt small in my arms despite his strength.

"We got one for my mom too. I'm going to cut your dad's lawn to pay him back for it."

Raphael pulled out a second jewelry box from a small little bag and handed it to Jerome. It was another sun, this one with a moon hanging from it and where the sun and moon met, there was a beautiful emerald.

"It's her birthstone," Jerome told me. "I don't think she's ever had a real emerald necklace before." I could feel the magic in it.

"She will love it," I told him. "Just as I love mine."

"I wasn't sure about the black diamond, but your dad said you'd like it."

"I do," I told him. "Did you know naturally made black diamonds are among the rarest gems in the world, which is cool, but they can also hold a large amount of magic?" I asked him.

"I'm going to be mowing your dad's grass until I'm forty." He told me.

"Nah, you'll go to school, get a job afterwards, and then you'll be making enough money you won't have to mow his yard to pay him back for the necklaces."

"I wanted something extra special for both of you." Jerome said. "Something I could put a lot of magic into. I didn't know gemstones could hold magic." As I examined my sun, I saw a tiny thread of gold snaking through the outer edges. If Jerome really had picked it out, the kid had great taste, like champagne taste.

"Jerome, I love the necklace, and it is amazing that you were able to hold some of my magic to put in it, but never sell yourself short. I am positive your mom feels the same way, you gave both of us something special, kiddo," I told him. And he hugged me. I laughed a little.

"Want to help me put this on?" I asked, handing him my necklace back and kneeling. I felt the cold silver touch my skin. And as the sun settled just below my neck, warmth flooded the necklace and it hung warm and alive around my neck. I was sure that no matter how beautiful any of my jewelry was, I had nothing as amazing as this piece. And it would have been just as beautiful without the black diamond as it was with.

# Chapter 25

We lived in Hotel Diablo for six days after
Hemingway and the marshals left. Every day we went to
the hospital and spent time with Valerie. She had sobbed
uncontrollably when Jerome had given her the necklace he
had gotten for her. She had sobbed even harder once he
had put it on her. And both the sun and moon on the
pendant had glowed faintly. Jerome and I had gone to the
cafeteria to get food while my father stayed and talked to
Valerie.

Now, I was home. My small cottage was just the
right size for the three of us. I didn't have guest rooms
anymore, but I could live with that. Or rather, my guest
rooms were occupied. Valerie was stronger. Now that
Michael had touched the death curse, I could feel it in her
too, fighting to exhaust her.

Jerome demanded he start cutting my father's grass
immediately. He owed him a debt and he was determined
to make good on it. So two days after they moved in, I
took Jerome to my parents' house and introduced him to
my mother, who hugged him three or four times before
letting him go outside and cut the grass.

Valerie and my mom worked with an attorney and
drew up papers giving me temporary guardianship of

Jerome, giving me the ability to enroll him in school. It was June, but school was only a few months away and Jerome was a little behind the other kids that had been training since they were five. Valerie's sister came to visit once in the month of June. She was a train wreck of a woman with more problems than any one person needed in one lifetime, but as I heard her complain about them, I realized they were problems of her own making. She liked bad boys and the father of her two children was a bad boy who had run out on them and refused to hold a job, because he didn't want to pay child support.

I could see why Valerie had not wanted her sister to take custody of Jerome. She could barely figure out how to put shoes on her own children, she would have resented having Jerome too. As a matter of fact, the entire day visit she didn't even look at her nephew.

The first week of July, Jerome blew the administrator of the school away with his entrance exam to the school of magic. And at the end of the meeting, Jerome handed him an angel sigil to keep demons away. The test giver accepted it, shocked by the magic in it.

By the end of July, we had fallen into a rhythm at my house. On Saturdays, Jerome went and mowed my parents' lawn. And then helped me with chores around my house. Sundays we went to Ballpark Village and had dinner, and if the Cardinals were in town, we went to the baseball game.

I had a handful of dates with Hemingway, and by the end of the fifth, lust was beginning to turn into love. I returned to work August first. Jerome started school. Valerie saw a faith healer every Wednesday who attempted to isolate her death curse and put it into a crystal.

I was the happiest I had ever been in my whole life, and exorcisms had become easier, because Gabriel was freaking right, love conquered all, damn it.

Printed in Great Britain
by Amazon

84360773R00150